ZUZU'S PETALS

SUE HEPWORTH

snowbooks

Proudly Published by Snowbooks in 2008

Snowbooks Ltd.
120 Pentonville Road
London
N1 9JN
Tel: 0207 837 6482
Fax: 0207 837 6348
email: info@snowbooks.com
www.snowbooks.com

British Library Cataloguing in Publication Data
A catalogue record for this book is available from the British Library.

ISBN Hardback: 978-1905005-871
ISBN Paperback: 978-1905005-833

Printed and bound by J. H. Haynes & Co. Ltd., Sparkford

ZUZU'S PETALS

SUE HEPWORTH

To my mother and father,

with all my love

Life is short and we have never too much time for gladdening the hearts of those who are travelling the dark journey with us. Oh be swift to love, make haste to be kind.

Henri Frederic Amiel

CHAPTER 1

Sometimes it's the smallest things that tip us into the biggest moves.

I'd been in my house in Ranmoor Hilltop Road for seven years – four with Mark and three since he left – and I woke up one September morning and knew the time without looking at the clock, just from the sun's position on the wall, and I realised it was time to move on.

And the same September day, a postcard arrived from my father.

Darling Corinne,

I bought this in the Heaton Cooper gallery in Grasmere this morning. Doesn't he capture the colours well?- the granite, the rusty dried-up bracken, the faint purple haze of the leafless winter birches, all set against that platinum sky. It's a shame you don't find time to do anything creative these days.

We've just had a super dinner of lamb chops, raspberry trifle, and a rather fine Stilton for afters. I'm sitting in the hotel lounge

with my leg up, and Ma has gone out for a walk round the garden
and down to the lake.
     Loads of love,
     Pa. xxx

He was right. Why wasn't I doing something more creative?

I'd been talking about it for long enough, telling Viv and Elspeth how I planned to make and sell greetings cards – those individually hand crafted ones, and also ones with arty photographs. I wanted to develop a proper business and sell cards in bulk, not just a shoe box-full at a craft fair twice a year. And I'd been learning how to make stained glass, and maybe in time I'd be sufficiently skilled to do that for money as well.

So that was the day I decided to give up painting and decorating for old people. I would sell the house and move somewhere smaller and cheaper, so I'd have some capital to live on while I got established.

By the end of the month I'd put my house on the market, and I was buzzing with excitement and nerves. And then, just as I found a buyer, the Duke's Estates put a row of terraced houses up for sale behind the school in Nether Green, only half a mile away. I'd always liked those houses. It was as if it was meant.

CHAPTER 2

On the evening of my moving day, Viv and I were due to go to Elspeth's house for a meal. But when the removal van had driven away, I felt completely drained, and every bit of me ached, and I couldn't face the thought of hauling myself up off the sofa again and going out. I was just reaching for the phone to ring Elspeth and tell her I was too tired to drag myself round to her house, and would she mind if I cried off, when my sister Megan rang me.

"I'm cooking dinner," said Megan, "but I'm worrying about you. How did it go? Are you OK?" I could picture her standing in front of her Aga, stirring something, with her head on one side and the phone tucked under her chin. Megan can talk on the phone while she makes a bechamel sauce, flicks through the Radio Times to see what time Judge John Deed is on, and peeks outside her back door to see if it's raining on her washing.

"You do think I've done the right thing, don't you?" I said. Every now and then a bubble of worry rose up and disturbed my confidence.

"Of course you have. You've thought it through, and made a proper plan and...stop worrying, Corinne. You're just tired. What kind of a day have you had?"

"It was OK. It was the packing I hated. But maybe it's the time of year. February's always grey and cold. You look out of the window feeling desperate for fresh air, and then you look up at the leaden sky and change your mind. It's much better when it snows. You get that fantastic brightness reflected into the house."

"You and your light," she laughed. "Look, I'm really sorry I couldn't get time off work and come to stay, and help. And I can't come next weekend either because I promised Ma I'd go up there. Pa's not been well, and she sounds really tired."

"Is he still not right? I thought it was just a bug."

"She says he's had no energy since Christmas. Then he got that bug. Now his symptoms have gone, but he's still feeling lousy. No energy and not sleeping well. And she said he's been getting up in the night with stomach ache and sitting on the loo for ages and then getting chilled. And some days he's a bit confused. Anyway, better go. We've got people coming and I'm not nearly ready. Bye."

I sank back into the sofa cushions. Why hadn't I realised that Pa wasn't well when I spoke to Ma on the phone? Why hadn't she told me? Maybe she thought I had enough on my plate with the move.

I suddenly felt so lonely that I changed my mind about going to Elspeth's. I found my coat and drove to her house.

As soon as I'd rung the doorbell and walked into her hallway, I was hit by the aroma of a delicious meaty stew, and I realised how hungry I was. Usually when you walk into Elspeth's house you smell fusty books, and the next thing to happen is you trip on a baby buggy or a tricycle. Today her grandchildren's toys were tidied away.

"Hello," I shouted, and Elspeth shouted back from the kitchen, "Viv's here, so can you let the sneck down on the door?"

Viv was sitting sideways on a chair in Elspeth's breakfast room, holding a mug of something and rubbing the back of her neck, like she does when she's tired.

Elspeth, wearing an apron and holding an oven glove, with a tea towel round her neck all tangled up in the chain of her reading glasses, was standing in the archway that led to her kitchen. Her hair was even frizzier than usual, probably on account of steam from the cooking. I could tell she'd been into the university that day because she was wearing her teaching costume: a tweed skirt and a fawn twin set. Last time Viv and I were discussing clothes, Elspeth said "I have never felt the need to propitiate the goddess of fashion."

They turned when I came in the room and said "Hi," in a cheery way, and then carried on talking.

"So there we were in Saltaire," said Viv, "and two of my eight year olds raced down to the other end of the gallery and I chased after them, thinking omigod, what now? But they stopped in front of a painting of a swimming pool, and I just got there in time to hear Wayne say *Ey up, Darren, I didn't know 'ockney had a blue period.*"

Elspeth roared with laughter as she poured me a mug of tea from the pot on the table, and then she said to Viv "But what about your headteachers' meeting tonight?"

I love the way we are together. It's as if we're sisters. There's something that's deep down comfortable about the way they kept on talking, not feeling that they should break off and ask me how I was, or go through all the social niceties, explaining what they were talking about and drawing me into the discussion.

I put my coat on the back of the chair next to Viv and sat down at the family-size table. Elspeth has the table pushed against the wall since her three children have grown and gone. A large fruit bowl full of oranges habitually sits there, and a vase of dusty dried flowers. In front of those was a litter of books and letters, a crumpled *Guardian*, and some patterned knitting in ivory, crushed strawberry and lilac (knitting that I guessed was for one of Elspeth's grandchildren).

"My meeting?" said Viv. "What a load of old cobblers. *All kids count!*" She said it in a sing song voice, while making air quotation marks with her fingers.

"Is that something to do with numeracy?" I asked.

"No. It's the latest codswallop from the bloody government. Why do they think that stringing three words together and calling it an initiative will make up for the treadmill of continual testing?" This launched her into one of her usual rants about the prevailing zeitgeist in education. She paused for a swig of tea, and then she said, "And tomorrow I've got to do my bloody SEF."

"Your what?" called Elspeth. She was in the kitchen now, looking at something in the oven.

"Oh, it's a God-awful form for the school inspection. They're murder. I'd rather dig dead dogs out of drains, having first sucked the water up through my teeth. Anyway," Viv said to me, "How was the move? How are *you?*"

"OK. Not bad."

"Really?" she said. She leaned forwards and put her hand on my cheek and turned my face towards hers and examined it like a teenager looking for blackheads.

"My God, you look pale. All the colour's bled out of your face. Your lips are beige! You look as though a mortician's just about to start work on you."

I laughed. "It's exhaustion."

"Are you sure?"

"Absolutely. Don't worry." I sat back in my chair and took a sip of my tea. "It's what they call a significant life event, isn't it? Moving house? As well as all the physical stuff."

"Sure," she said. She was thinking something that she wasn't coming out with, which is rare for Viv. Then she said, "So what were the removal men like? I got a glimpse of the foreman. He looked a bit of all right."

Viv had called round early that morning on her way to school to wish me well and give me an encouraging hug. She gave me a tin of luxury chocolate biscuits, "To keep you and the removal men sweet." She was habitually smart and stylish, with make-up carefully applied, but tonight she looked ragged and drawn – like me.

"The removal men were very obliging," I said. "They were broad Sheffield, and whenever I asked them to do something they said *Right, love,* or *OK, me ducks.* But the foreman spent most of the morning sitting on the dining room windowsill, playing with his mobile phone. Did you notice his shirt? That rich acid green, but mellow, like the green of a Rowntrees Fruit Gum, no, more like wet moss? Anyway…I was surprised he was so useless when he had the gumption to choose such a fabulous shirt."

"What is this?" said Elspeth as she came in and plonked a handful of cutlery on the table. "A meditation on the semiotics of workmen's attire?"

"Just Corinne's usual hang-up on aesthetics," said Viv. She picked up the cutlery and I piled up Elspeth's rammel at the back of the table and got the table mats out of the drawer while Viv set the table. Elspeth returned with an earthenware dish.

"There. Steak and kidney pie. The vegetables are almost ready."

"And then," I said, "when we got to Ferndean Row, they couldn't get my dining table in either of the doors, and they had to take it to pieces on the street. The fuss he made! You'd think they'd never had to dismantle a piece of furniture before."

"But why do you want such a massive table in a terraced house?" said Viv.

"Come on, you two. You are worse than the children. Stop talking and help yourself," said Elspeth. "There. Vegetables."

"Talking of veg," said Viv. "I've got a favour to ask you, Corinne. You know my deputy head – Juliet – who retired last year? She's asked me to look after her allotment and-"

"Oh no, no, no, no. I know nothing about gardening."

"Will you just listen?"

"Sorry." I mimed locking up my lips and throwing away the key. Then I broke off a bit of the pastry from the pie and popped it in my mouth. "I'm ravenous, and this is amazing. Did you make it yourself, Elspeth?"

"Corinne!" Viv said impatiently. "Will you listen? Juliet's totally obsessed with her allotment, says she never wants to do anything else for the rest of her life but garden."

I snaffled another bit of crust. Crunchy and buttery – delicious. "So why does she-?"

"Her daughter, who lives in Texas, has just had triplets and is suffering from post-natal depression and Juliet wants to go over and help, and she asked if I would look after her allotment."

"Why doesn't she just give it up and get another one when she comes back?"

"Do start, you two," called Elspeth who was back in the kitchen again. "I just want to wash up these pans."

"The waiting list on these allotments is five years long," said Viv. She helped herself to some steak and kidney. "Imagine someone being that keen on bloody gardening! She says the weeds would go wild if she left it fallow, and the allotment committee would have her thrown off. So she wants a sort of caretaker. Someone who won't be tempted to do anything radical."

"But I don't know anything about gardening." My garden at the old house had been a kind of anti-garden - that ridiculous front with the vertiginous rockery, and the flat yard at the back with a rock face behind. I never once did any gardening, just got in a gardener to weed it and cut it back every couple of years. "I know absolutely nothing, Viv."

"Neither do I. But she just wants someone to keep it tidy and keep the allotment police off her back. I thought we could share it. It's only ten minutes walk from your new place. And I owe Juliet so much. She was a cracking deputy. She's asked everyone else."

"Oh, all *right*."

"Fantastic. I'm meeting Juliet up there tomorrow, so I'll pop round and see you, after." She took a sip of water and then said, "Hey, did you see that story on the local news last night? About the milkman whose wife died in her sleep and he didn't tell anybody? It was really weird. He was so broken hearted he kept her body in bed and slept with it and by the time they found out, the body had mummified."

"What I don't get," I said, "is why it didn't get maggots in it. Why it didn't go bad."

"It must have been in the winter. The central heating must have dried it out."

"But what happens to all the internal squishy bits?"

"They just dry up."

"What, like a kipper?"

"Yes, only much bigger."

✳ ✳ ✳

The next day was Saturday, and I was painting my new back bedroom at Ferndean Row. Every few brushstrokes I'd look round at the other walls I'd already finished. I didn't like the yellow, now it was on the walls. I'd wanted a rich, bright yellow – a cadmium yellow – the kind of yellow that blasts you with happiness. In this light and in this room this yellow wasn't right. I should have been patient and done it properly and tried tester pots on all the walls and looked at them at different times of day, but I'd rushed it because I wanted to get the furniture arranged and to get on with what I'd moved for – my cards and my glass.

I laid the brush carefully on the edge of the tin and stood upright, rubbing my back through my paint-stained dungarees. I needed the stepladder and went up to the attic bedroom to fetch it, but once I was up there I got sidetracked by the view from the skylight.

From my old house there were extensive views. I'd been able to see the park with its putting green clutching the side of the hill, the school where I used to teach in a former life, and an expanse of Victorian houses and the bare-branched tops of stately trees. From here, down in the valley half a mile away, all I could see was a corner of the park between rows of roofs, the back gardens of the four houses in the terrace, and the copse of silver birches that they backed onto.

When you tell a stranger from another part of the country that you live in Sheffield, they always look pitying, because they think they know it from a passing view from the railway track or from the M1 – both of which are routed through the old industrial wasteland on the east of the city. But if you look at the aerial views on the internet, Sheffield looks really green, especially on the west side, which is where I live. There are lots of trees and parks, with footpaths that lead out into the Mayfield Valley (which is as pretty as it sounds) and then there's the Peak District.

I carried the stepladder down to the back room and then went into the front bedroom to get a tissue. The new Kingfisher Turquoise on the walls gave me a hit again. It did that every time I walked into the room. At least I'd got that colour right.

I'd just picked up my paintbrush again when someone came clomping down the passageway between the houses and banged on my back door. I went down and opened it, trying not to get paint on the doorknob from my sticky fingers.

"Viv!"

"I've come to tell you about the allotment."

"Do you mind talking to me while I paint? I don't want to stop just now, and I've just wasted half an hour, messing about. My back's killing me, but I want to get this last little bit finished."

She followed me back up the stairs. "God, these are steep," she said. "Perfect for throwing yourself down when you've had enough." She stood on the landing and talked to me through the doorway. "Didn't you have a yellow bedroom at Ranmoor Hilltop?"

I picked up my paintbrush and tin again and climbed up the stepladder to do a bit by the picture rail that I'd missed.

She was right. At Ranmoor Hilltop it was the room I'd picked out for the nursery that I'd painted yellow.

"I always like to have one yellow room," I said. "It reminds me of my bedroom on the farm, when I was little." And just like that I was back there. I could see a shaft of morning sunshine lighting up the yellow wall by my bedside table, the one that Ma made me from an orange-box. I could feel the weight of the heavy blankets as I snuggled in bed, I could smell the bacon frying downstairs, and Pa was bellowing up from the hall, "Come on, you lazy chundies, let's be having you."

I dipped my brush in the tin of paint. It was lemony and insipid. It had no heart.

Viv lounged against the banister and said, "When I was little I had to share with Auntie Jessie. It was brown brocade. And she snored. Ugh! Anyway, this doesn't get the baby washed. I've got a guy coming round in half an hour to give me a quote for a hot tub. So. Clip your ears back." She gave me all the gen on the allotment and we agreed a time and a day to meet up there. Then she said, "I've been wondering about putting a personal ad in the *Guardian* – you know – for a man. I thought if we both did it, it would be fun. We could-"

"You do it. I want to concentrate on my cards, my crafts, my glass."

"Are you telling me you're giving up men?"

"I'll go out with any if I come across them, but-"

"Think about it, babe."

And she'd gone before I remembered to ask her to help me move the chest of drawers in my bedroom. It was struggling with the chest that had tweaked my back.

I hadn't even closed the back door behind her when someone else went pattering down the passageway between the houses. Maybe it was my elusive next door neighbour. He might help. After all, he'd only just moved in himself. All four houses in the terrace had been sold at auction at the same time.

I opened the kitchen door and rushed out to try to catch him. He was wheeling his bike over the cobbled bit in front of the houses and onto the smoothest part of the lane that led to the main road.

He cocked his lean, Lycra-clad leg over the crossbar and sat down. He was a bit too scrawny for my liking. I don't go for muscle men, but neither could I fancy someone who is all sinew. Clutched in his teeth was one corner of a large brown envelope. He was wearing a short sleeved turquoise jersey and black arm warmers. His cycling jersey was one of those with a pocket below the waist at the back. It bulged.

"Hello!" I shouted

He flinched, but he didn't turn to look in my direction, so maybe he hadn't heard me. He just glanced down at his feet and flicked a pedal over, slotting his shoe into the pedal clip. Cleat - that's what it's called – a cleat. Mark and I had sometimes watched the Tour de France on telly, and twice we'd seen it for real, when we were on holiday. I can remember standing sweltering together at the roadside, our fingers linked because the heat made any more intimate body contact unthinkable. Before the peleton arrived we could hear the racket of support cars and police, and cameramen riding pillion on motorbikes, and then the pianissimo whoosh of colour and shimmering spokes would rush past like a swoop of dragonflies. We'd had good times in the beginning.

I bent down to adjust my slipper and looked up towards the road again, but the guy on the bike had disappeared, so I ran out of the dim passageway and onto the cobbles just in time to see him reach the corner where our lane joined Fulwood Road.

"Excuse me!" I shouted, but he launched off and was gone. Was he deaf? I'd shouted loud enough. Had he been pretending not to hear?

I traipsed back down the passage and into my back door, defeated. I'd have to wait for Viv to come another time… or…I could listen out for him coming back.

I went back upstairs to finish the painting. It was a chore to be got through. After the six months of limbo since I made the decision to move and do something different, I was itching to actually get on with my new "career." Decorating just felt like more delay.

It was different when I'd moved into the Ranmoor Hilltop house with Mark. Then I'd thought of the decorating and furnishing as a joy to be indulged in: I'd felt as if I was designing a stage set – for our life together as a family.

It didn't turn out like that. For one thing, it soon became clear how different our tastes were. We tried to compromise, in the beginning, which meant we ended up with colours and styles that neither of us liked. Then we divided up the rooms between us so that, for example, I decorated the dining room and Mark picked the colours and furniture for the sitting room.

I hated what he'd chosen. I loathed the bare dark floor boards, the walls with cracked plaster with three tones of dull emulsion, sand, grey, beige, each colour merging messily into the next as if there were a damp problem with white salt marks. It looked as if a recalcitrant decorator had started to strip off ancient paintwork and given up half way through the job. The colours were so dull, and it looked so unloved and so uncared for. Yes, it might be super trendy, but I detested the heavy dark oil paintings he hung on the walls, with their six inch thick gold frames, all chipped, all battered. He didn't care what the paintings were, it was the size of them and the frames that he was buying, to fit in with the look he had chosen.

He bought an old leather suite at an auction. It had split seams with the stuffing hanging out and I wanted to give it some TLC, to mend the seams, to treat the leather. At least it would look better, even if it was as uncomfortable to sit on as a heap of boulders. But he wanted to leave it as it was. And he had chosen faded curtains with ripped linings that draped on the floor. Even if they'd been new, I would have hated the curtains in that revoltingly lavish pattern of shiny rust on a hospital green background.

I have nothing against old things: I collect them myself. But I like them repaired, or polished, or refashioned into something else. If they are worth saving, they are worth cherishing.

I wanted the things in my house to be colourful and cared for. Back then I'd chosen border tiles in the bathroom covered in bright spring flowers, imagining my future toddlers sitting in the bath, with me pointing to the daffodils and tulips and those little vivid blue ones I don't know the name of, trying to teach them their colours. And I'd imagined them sitting painting at the big kitchen table, and at Christmas time I had seen them standing on stools helping me make mince pies, with one of them – a girl – sitting on the table swinging her legs, telling me what she wanted Father Christmas to bring.

I'd finished painting the new back room and was downstairs rinsing the brushes in white spirit in a jam jar, when I heard light footsteps in the passageway again.

I put down the jar and burst out of the doorway and

through the little picket gate and nearly collided with a bicycle wheel held at the height of my face.

"For goodness sake, are you trying to knock me out?" I shrieked, and instantly regretted it: I was out there to ask him a favour.

"Knock you out? Do you think I'd risk damaging my wheel? I've only just had an aerodynamic rim fitted." He spoke in a broad West Riding accent – just like my Gran's.

"Is that why you've got it in mid air?" I said. "Because it's aerodynamic? Isn't it usual to keep the wheels on the ground, or am I really, really stupid?"

"What?"

He had very short dark brown hair, greying at the temples, and he was wearing a black towelling sweatband. He had pronounced cheek bones and a black smudge on his mouth. Had he been sucking a stick of liquorice?

I tried to lighten the mood. "Are the aerodynamics because you have a thing about ET – that bit when he flies off on his chopper into the sunset?"

"What?" he said, distracted, as if he wasn't listening. He was examining one of his pedals, then flicking something off it. It began to spin.

"Never mind," I said.

"I always wheel it up the passageway like this," he said in a calmer tone. "It's easier to get it through my gate." His cheek muscles twitched.

I knew he was trying to be conciliatory, but I was in one of those moods and I said "You bloody nearly brained me."

"That's not my fault." He sounded sniffy again. "You came tazzing out without checking if anyone was coming in the opposite direction."

"Oh, I heard you coming."

"What?"

We stood there, me with my arms folded, him still holding his bike with the wheel in the air, staring at me through the spokes.

"I tried to catch you earlier, when you were going out. I saw you leaving and I called to you – you were setting off on your bike - but you ignored me."

"Ignored you? I don't think I can have heard you."

I noticed the "don't think" in his sentence. The hint at ambiguity. He'd heard me all right.

"Look," he said, again in a pleasant tone. "It'd be a shame to get off to a bad start. Let's try again." He lowered his front wheel to the ground and held out his hand. "I'm Rob Walker."

"Corinne Metcalfe." I smiled and shook his hand. I felt fabric and flesh. Weird. He withdrew his hand and I saw that his gloves were fingerless, with leather on the palm and crocheted cotton on the back.

"Right," he said. "Well, now that's sorted out, I've got to go. Got to get some work in. Really tight deadline. Got to rush."

"Maybe you'd like to come round for a coffee some time?"

But he'd raised the front wheel again, nipped through his gate and moved out of sight.

I followed him. He was standing outside his back door. His bike was leaning against his hip and he was hoisting a bunch of keys out of his bulging back pocket.

"Would you like to come round for coffee some time when you're not so busy?"

He thrust his key into the lock, opened the door, and turning his head a fraction, said "That'd be champion," then he turned away and with deft and infinite care he wheeled his bike over the step and into his kitchen, as if it were spun of fragile glass and the slightest knock would shatter it. He kicked his kitchen door shut behind him without looking round, and I was left standing outside, like piffy on a rock bun.

CHAPTER 3

The couple who had moved into number 1 Ferndean Row (Rob Walker was in number 2, I was in number 3, and I hadn't met the owners of number 4) had organised us all into sharing a skip. It was a massive one, and I was amazed that the skip lorry managed to get it down our little lane.

Everyone was much quicker off the mark than me and it was already half full when I started to clear out my wash house. The first thing I threw out was a rusty old bike. I hauled it down the alleyway, over the cobbles, and leaned it against the skip while I peeped inside it to see what was already in there.

There were the usual ripped out kitchen cabinets and bits of plaster and broken bricks. There were mildewed books with brown-edged yellow pages, fading black and white photographs in cheap brown bakelite frames, the pictures laced with white salts, crystallised from damp. There was a dark varnished chair with a gash in the rattan seat, and mirrors with dark spotting where the mercury has worn off the back. Right at the bottom there was a pile of fabric –

curtains, bedspreads, cushions, tablecloths - which looked fifty years old at least. One particular piece caught my eye: it was sage green and covered with cream cabbage roses - delicious. But it wasn't just that piece I wanted, I wanted every last scrap of fabric for craftwork - rag rugs, patchwork, or mini-collage greetings cards.

I reached over the edge of the skip, but no matter how much I strained, I couldn't reach any of it. I was damned if I was going to let all that lovely stuff end up in a landfill. And I needed to rescue it quickly before someone threw more rubbish on the top.

I took some old bricks from the skip and built a little tower, which wobbled because of the cobbled lane, but even standing on that, I still couldn't reach what I wanted, no matter how much I stretched over the lip of the skip. I hauled myself up by resting my elbows on the skip edge, then onto my stomach, and stretched some more. Still no joy.

There I was, wedged on the edge of the skip with my bum in the air, saying "Sod it, sod it," to myself, when a voice behind me said, "Some folk," and I froze.

"Common as muck," said the voice. "And this is Nether Green, not Manor Top. I'd expected better from the locals."

I felt like a worm.

Even before I turned round I could tell it was Rob Walker, because of the accent.

He was standing there with his arms folded, grinning. He had a black smudge on his mouth again. Did he never wash his face?

"Mad as owt," he said. "Are you all right?"

"Yes thanks." I tried to sound demure and composed. I wriggled out backwards and jumped down. Ouch! I twisted my ankle on the uneven surface of the cobbles.

"A bit desperate, isn't it?" he said with a smirk. In this light I could see his face better than I had the other day. He had laugh lines radiating from the corners of his eyes, but his eyes looked as though he had a tragic, art house movie playing inside his head.

"Do you have self esteem issues?" he said.

"Pardon?" I said. I bent down and rubbed my sore ankle.

"Throwing yourself in a skip?"

"Oh, very droll. I was trying to get something out of it, not throwing myself in."

"'Course." He was dressed in his cycling gear again. His legs were smooth and shapely but very thin. Too thin.

"So what did you throw away and change your mind about?" he said.

"Nothing. I didn't," I said, dusting myself off. Thank God I was wearing my oldest dungarees. "It's all that material. I can't believe anyone would throw it out. It's vintage stuff. Who would put it in a skip? Why didn't they take it to a jumble sale or a charity shop?"

"There's too much old fashioned junk clogging up the world. Clean breaks are best. Anyway, no-one who had any taste could want that."

"I just said *I* liked the look of it." Hadn't he been listening?

"You wouldn't want it when you got a closer look. Trust me. I found it in the wash house and it was beyond taste. Wouldn't know taste, if taste came and bit it on the bum. What I want to know is – who's left that Raleigh there? How could they chuck *that* out?"

"I put it there."

"It's yours?"

"I found it in *my* wash house."

"That's sacrilege."

"You're *joking*. You must be. Look at it. The tyres aren't just flat, they're worn through to the threads, the handlebars are pitted with rust and half the spokes are broken. And it's impossible to move the brake levers even a millimetre – go on, have a go."

He walked over to the bike and squatted down while he appraised it. He stroked the frame, and then patted it and said "Grand," and stood up and turned round.

"The chain's a bit stiff, the brake cables need fettling, but the lugs are sweet. All the rest is minimal. Can I have it, then?"

Fettling, grand. And earlier he'd used the word "champion." I love Yorkshire words. They take me back to holidays spent with my Gran in Barnsley.

"I don't know if you can have it," I said. "Would you mind helping me get all that fabric out of the skip?"

"What?" He sounded incredulous, and he made a face - mouth pulled straight and tight, wide eyes, raised eyebrows. His expression was so exaggerated, it could have been used in a manual to teach autistic children to recognise facial expressions – in this case, disbelief. "You really want me to help you get that manky gear out again?"

I stood there with my arms folded.

"How about the bike?" he said. "You've already chucked it out."

"Did I actually say I didn't want it?" I said, with a smile. "I could have just been leaning it there temporarily."

"*Do* you want it?"

"Will you help me get out the fabric?"

"Go on, then," he said, his voice soft and smiling. "You're a bloody tyrant, you are."

"Great, but have you got time to do it now? I can see you were about to go out on your bike."

"No, I'm not. 'S fine."

He wheeled the old Raleigh away and when he came back he pulled himself up and into the skip in one graceful movement. Then without a word he started to rearrange the contents so he could get to the fabric. He hauled it all out – silently placing each item in a pile at the edge of the skip so that I could reach it.

I was bending down engrossed in sorting the fabric and folding the stuff I wanted, making a pile of it on the road, when he jumped down and said "That's it. Can't see any more."

I said "OK, thanks," unable to tear my eyes away from the purple quilted loo seat cover I'd just picked up. A monstrosity. He was right. Some of this stuff was as far beyond taste as a corner shop greetings card, the kind with embossed gold letters and a verse inside. And it all smelled so musty. When I looked up again, Rob Walker was disappearing down the alley between our houses calling over his shoulder, "Mind you don't catch fleas."

"Thanks ever so much," I called out.

He raised his hand in acknowledgement, but he didn't look round.

I carried all the fabric upstairs to the attic and dumped it in a corner for sorting later. As I turned to go downstairs, a scrap of paper wafted off the top of a box of papers that I hadn't sorted out since the move. I picked it up and straightened it out on the window sill. It was a till receipt dated March 1st 1996, a receipt for the dress Mark bought me in Glasgow, that time we went to see his sister and I dragged him to see the Scottish Colourists exhibition. I can remember standing in front of Cadell's *The Red Chair*, completely entranced, and Mark whispering "How long are you going to be?" The only pictures Mark liked were pen and ink drawings in black and white.

That was ten years ago. I still had the dress…deep red, shot silk, tiny cap sleeves, slim skirt, narrow black patent belt. Vintage fifties. Very Audrey Hepburn.

I sighed.

But then I reminded myself – this wasn't about moving on from Mark and finding another man, but about being more creative. Yes, I'd go out with people, and oh, yes, I'd have sex when I got the chance, but I wasn't expecting to find someone I could be happy with on a permanent live-in basis. Anyway, I'd found that I liked the personal freedom of living alone, and I had my friends for company.

The next morning I drove up to my parents' house in the Yorkshire Dales. I couldn't wait until I had an empty few days to see them. I was so busy sorting out the house that free time was in short supply. I was worried about them – Pa because he was still not well, and Ma because she was as old as him – 84 – and yet she was looking after him all on her own.

As soon as I turned down their lane and saw Hollycroft, their 200 year old squat, stone cottage, I felt a sense of peace. I thought of it as home, though I didn't live there as a child. They'd been there for twenty years, since Pa retired and since Steve, my brother, took over the family farm, a few miles down the dale.

I parked on the road and walked through the wrought iron gates, across the stone flags, and as soon as I got to the porch, the door opened and Ma was there saying "Here you are! How lovely! What a long way for you to come."

I hugged her close.

Each time I saw her she seemed to have shrunk some more. I kept my arm around her shoulders and my head bent down next to her soft warm cheek, and we walked through the front door, into the low-ceilinged dining room.

Pa was sitting in his reclining chair next to the window. He'd had deep vein thrombosis in his right leg for years, and he liked to have it raised when he was sitting down. *The Telegraph* was on his knee and on the windowsill was a mug of what smelled like Bovril. I gave him a hug, and he said what he always said when I first arrived: "I had a shave especially, so I could give you a kiss."

The only thing about Hollycroft that changed between my visits was the arrangement of pictures on the walls. This time, hanging opposite Pa's chair was a large coloured etching from the 1700s, of a cowman with his beast. In the window recess, close to his chair, the picture never changed: it was a painting of a Victorian farmhouse kitchen with a fire in the range, and a woman suckling her baby. It's a Heaton Cooper print.

"Did you come via Leeds or Leeming?" he said.

"Leeds is impossible these days, Pa."

"What did you say?"

I repeated myself, but louder this time.

"Sit down then and tell us about your house," he said.

"Let her get her breath first, Ralph," said Ma. Then to me she said, "Shall I make you some coffee?"

"What did you say?" said Pa.

Ma said loudly "Turn up your hearing aid."

He did as she said, and she went out to put the kettle on.

"Still reading this old Tory rag, Pa?"

"What?"

I pointed to the paper on his knee. "Why don't you get a decent paper?"

"This is best for the racing. What do you want me to get? The *Guardian*? The thing's unreadable!"

In the afternoon I drove to Leyburn, their local market town, to get Ma a load of shopping. Their village didn't have a shop any more and Ma didn't drive, and she worried about Pa driving when he was so off colour. When I'd put all the shopping away, brought in the washing from the line, and made them some afternoon tea, I sat with them in the sitting room by the fire.

Pa dozed, and Ma and I talked.

"He's had a good day, today," she whispered. "Having you come has perked him up a bit. But he's not right. I need to speak to the doctor again."

When Pa woke up he seemed vacant and distant, in a world of his own. He didn't join in the conversation. He had the telly on to watch the racing with the sound turned off, but every time I looked at him his eyelids were drooping, or he was staring at the fire.

In the evening, I sat with him while Ma went to a talk about Quaker work in Palestine, with a friend from Quaker meeting. I was brought up as a Quaker, but I'm not a Quaker now, although I'm in sympathy with what they stand for – peace, simplicity, integrity, equality, social justice. It's the God bit that I have a problem with. I only went to Quaker Meeting when Ma and Pa asked me to go with them.

Pa was fine while Ma was out. He was alert, and we managed to have a reasonable conversation. But his hearing was terrible.

When I switched on the telly for the news, he wanted it turned up loud. After the news, one of my favourite films was on – *It's a Wonderful Life*. The very first time I saw that film was with Pa, when I was a teenager. Ma, Megan and Steve were out at a New Year's Eve party, and I had flu and Pa stayed at home to keep me company.

The film made us cry then, and it made us cry now. When Ma got home from her talk it was at the bit where the hero – who had been on the brink of suicide – has just been shown by his guardian angel what his family and hometown would be like if he had never lived, and he says "I want to live again! Make me live again!" And then he finds his little daughter's petals in his pocket that he'd put there earlier, but had been missing when he'd looked before, and he shouts "Zuzu's petals!" and he knows he's alive.

Ma looked as us both, snuggled up on the sofa, sniffing, and said "What a pair of softies you are," and we laughed.

In the morning I woke up before Ma and Pa, got out of bed, and pulled on socks and a cardigan. I switched on the electric fire because they have no central heating upstairs. The fire is old and battered and has a wonky fire guard attached to the front with two old, fraying bits of string. The string had a crumpled look about it, and grubby ends, and I knew it would have originally arrived in the house around a parcel; Ma would have wound it up and saved it in her string jar for future use.

Hollycroft has two foot thick walls and small windows, so on a grey March morning it was gloomy in the bedroom. I wanted to make lists of jobs to be done when I got back to Ferndean Row. I switched on the bedside light. It had been my bedside light when I was little.

Everything in the room was the same as it had been since they'd moved there from the farm – the heavy walnut wardrobe with the chip in the mirror from when I threw a bottle of nail varnish at Megan in the middle of a teenage argument, the oak veneer chest that didn't match, the deep windowsill filled with books and needlework magazines and with carrier bags stuffed with old calendars and wrapping paper and "useful bits of cardboard" that Ma couldn't bear to throw away. The heavy velvet curtains were faded, the floral duvet cover in orange, yellow and brown was decidedly iffy, but the style of the bedlinen, it's functionality, the fact that it was cotton, the sewn-on ties at the opening instead of press-studs, plus my knowing that Ma had bought the material cheap from a market and sewn it herself to save money, all those characteristics gave it what I think of as essence-of-Ma. If I saw it in another house on someone else's bed I'd be thinking evil things about the nastiness of the fabric design, but in my parents' spare room it was not just acceptable, it was supremely comforting. Instead of making lists, I sat there and soaked up the security of home.

CHAPTER 4

The following week turned unseasonably warm. It was March, but the daytime temperatures were more typical of June, and the bookies were taking bets on whether the mercury would hit 21 degrees by the weekend.

On the Friday morning, I drove to the supermarket in a T shirt and jeans, with the window of my van rolled all the way down and my hair going wild in the draught. The Beach Boys were singing *Little Deuce Coupe* on the car radio and I was singing along with them at the top of my voice.

When I pulled into the car park on the roof of Somerfield, and got out of the van, there was something about the quality of the air, and the mood I was in, that took me back to when I'd lived in Italy, years before, and I thought about Giuseppe.

I lived in Vicenza, teaching English to Italian businessmen. That's how I met him. We dated for ages. He had an industrial design company and his offices were just across the piazza from the language school where I worked. He parked his open-top car round the back of his office, and when I finished work I would ring him, and go and sit in his car and look at the trees and dream, while I waited for him to finish his work and come out. His car was always locked, but I have long legs, and it was easy to swing one of them over the low car door, step onto the bucket seat and climb in.

So I was thinking about Giuseppe as I walked across the Somerfield car park, and then I saw him – *there* in front of me. His hair, his height, the loose-limbed way he moved – it was Giuseppe! He stuck a ticket on the windscreen of his open topped car and jogged over to the stairs and disappeared, as if he was nipping somewhere and would soon be back. And I climbed into his car to wait for him.

I shut my eyes, and the smell and the squishiness of the leather seat took me back to Vicenza, and all the good times we had, and I smiled to myself at the thought of his surprise when he got back. When I opened my eyes again on the Sheffield supermarket car park and the terraced brick houses beyond, it shocked me into hard reality – *Omigod, what am I doing? This is bananas! Why on earth would it be Giuseppe?* – and I was just about to climb out of the car and scuttle into obscurity, when I heard footsteps approaching, and my heart was thumping and I could feel myself blushing, and I wished and wished that I could shrivel up into nothingness.

"Who the devil are you?" he said. "What the hell are you…?" And as soon as he spoke I knew – well, of course – it wasn't Giuseppe. And I couldn't bear to turn round and face whoever it was. So I just sat there. I didn't turn round. I didn't say anything. My mouth had gone all dry.

"Well?" he bellowed.

I said, in a tiny voice, not looking at him, "I'm sorry. I've made a stupid mistake. I thought this car belonged to someone else. Please – don't say any more. I'm going." And then my voice flipped into this stupid American accent and I said "I'm outta here" and - still not looking at him - I turned in the seat and got onto my knees and made to climb out of the car.

"For God's sake," he said. "I'll open the bally door. I don't want you scratching the paintwork more than you have done already."

As soon as I heard the door lock clunk I opened the door and got out and I still couldn't bear to look him in the eye. I cast my eyes down to the paintwork, and examined it for scratches, and said, "If I've scratched your car, then of course I will pay for the damage."

"Too right you'll pay," he said.

"I'm really, *really* sorry," I said, still not looking up. "I saw you walk away from the car, and from behind, you looked the spitting image of someone I used to know. I was sure you were him."

"*He*," he said.

"Pardon?" I looked up. The guy had hazel eyes and tortoiseshell glasses. He looked nothing like Giuseppe.

"I was sure you were he, is the correct grammar," he said.

"Oh," I said. "I was sure you were he. And I thought I'd wait and surprise you. I so wanted to speak to you – to he – to him – again."

"If you had been planning on taking the car, I suppose you would have been sitting in the driver's seat," he said. And after that, the tension eased off a bit and I made a hasty exit, muttering apologies all the way across the car park. I got in my car and drove away as fast as I could and had to go back later to do all my shopping.

That night Elspeth and Viv came round to my house for a take-away Chinese.

"What kind of a car was it? How did you get in? Had he left it unlocked?" asked Viv. She was sitting on the floor, her back against the armchair and her legs stretched out towards my new stove. I'd lit it because the temperature had suddenly dipped, against expectations, and anyway, I couldn't wait to try it out. Unfortunately, it was emitting that hot chemical smell you get when you light a new stove, and the paint on the seals starts to burn.

"The car?" I said. "It was a shiny cerulean blue and it had a roll down sun top – that's how I got in. I *told* you – I *climbed* in."

"You climbed in?" said Viv. "How old are you, Corinne? What forty-something goes climbing into a stranger's car? And what on earth is cerulean blue?"

"Sky blue," said Elspeth. "From the Latin *caeruleus*."

"When I climbed in, I thought I knew him, didn't I?" I said. "Anyway, what difference does the method of entry make?"

Elspeth reached the end of a row of knitting and turned her needles round. "The style of entry can be crucial," she said. "There is a vast difference between knitting into the front of a stitch and knitting into the back of a stitch when you are decreasing for raglan sleeves."

"Thanks for that, Elspeth," said Viv. She turned to me. "Didn't anybody see you?"

"It was *really, really* early. There was just one white van parked in the corner, my car and *his* car."

"God, how embarrassing. So what happened? What did he say?"

At this point Elspeth's mobile phone rang and she answered it.

"I'm at Corinne's," she said. She listened a bit and then she said "Look, I am sorry, Jessica, but I cannot talk now.

I'm at Corinne's." More listening. "I know it is hard for you, sweetheart, and I am sorry." Gabbling from the other end. "No, I am at Corinne's." Response. "No, I cannot come down to see you tomorrow. You come home next weekend and you can tell me all about it…OK…Goodbye."

"Goodness," said Elspeth to Viv and me. "Why do they think I have no life of my own? Sorry, you two, do go on, Corinne. Where had you got to? Hang on – I will turn this thing off," she said, switching off her mobile phone and picking up her knitting again.

"What did he say? And what about you?" Viv was getting really hyper. I think she was in need of a smoke. She has tried to give up – that's how I first met her. Someone suggested she take up knitting so she had something to occupy her hands and she came along to the Stitch 'n' Bitch group that Elspeth and I were in. It was years ago, but I remember she knitted a scarf in pine green mohair, using needles as fat as her fingers. After that she lost patience with knitting, and now she's smoking again.

I took another sip of wine and continued the story, recounting the conversation I had with the guy, word for word, up till when he said *I was sure you were he was the correct grammar*, and Elspeth piped up, "*He* is not correct, Corinne. *He* is archaic. Awfully archaic. It's as passé as Bri-Nylon 2 ply."

"What did he look like?" said Viv.

"Nothing like Giuseppe. That's what's so stupid. He was tall, OK, but he had wavy chestnut hair and wore oval tortoiseshell glasses, and he didn't have that ruffled look that Giuseppe always had. This guy's hair was neatly combed. Giuseppe was always a bit dishevelled. Do you know – when I first read that word I thought you pronounced it *dis-hevelled* with a long e? It's like bedraggled. I used to think you said it *bed-raggled.*"

"*Bed-*raggled? Do you not have a decent dictionary that tells you where the stresses come?" asked Elspeth. She can be a bit pedantic. I don't know if it's because she lectures in English language or what.

"Belt up, Els," said Viv. "Let her get on with it, or you'll know where your stresses are without the aid of a dictionary."

"Anyway," I said, "this guy was neatly laundered and pressed, even if he was only wearing a polo shirt."

"Did the polo shirt have a little motif on the chest? You know, like Donald has on his? – South Antarctica Research Station…"

"For God's sake, Els."

"Oh go and cast off."

"I didn't want to look at him more than was absolutely necessary," I said. "He didn't smile – but then he *had* just found a strange woman sitting in his car. His eyes looked a bit crinkly, though."

"Do you mean the *skin around* his eyes?" asked Elspeth.

"Elspeth!" Viv and I said together in exasperation.

She dropped her knitting onto her knee and looked defiant. "Precision is essential, whether in language, or an Aran plait cable."

At that point my telephone rang, and I got up to answer it. It was Elspeth's elder daughter, Charlotte. I handed Elspeth the phone.

"Hello, is everything all right?…I am asking that because you are ringing me on Corinne's phone…Yes, I know it is switched off. I switched it off…Because I am spending the evening with my friends…Not important?…Is my social life not important?...No, no, of course not...Well, why are you ringing?...I really...If I can, but I do not have my diary with me. I will ring you back tomorrow...All right....Goodbye.

"Oh my. Can I never get away from them?" she said to us. "Do carry on, Corinne."

"There was something about him that was...I don't know...he had potential."

"How old was he?"

"Early forties?"

"You need to be careful, Corinne. He might be a serial killer. Or someone who uses glottal stops," said Elspeth.

"He spoke with a perfect accent. A little too perfect. It sounded slightly fake."

"There you are," said Elspeth.

"I'm desperate for a fag," said Viv. "I'm going outside your back door for a quick one."

"Do you mind if I get some more tea, Corinne? Do you want one?" said Elspeth.

"Great. Thanks."

They went out to the kitchen, and I got up and opened the door of the stove to put on another shovelful of coke. We're not allowed to burn wood in Sheffield because of the Clean Air Act. I checked my watch and programmed the video to record *Due South*, a comedy drama about a hunky but unworldly mountie. They were showing it every night that week. I had a thing about the mountie. I think it had something to do with his sculptured hat. Or it could be the red of his coat.

There was a loud shriek in the dining room. It sounded like Viv.

Elspeth came through the door carrying a tray of mugs, followed by Viv, saying "Ow, ow, ow, ow, ow. You've got to do something about that sodding table. I've only been through the dining room to the kitchen and back and I've banged my toe on it on both bloody trips. Ow, ow."

"Sorry, Viv. Do you want a plaster?"

"No. I'll suck it." She sat on the floor and bent her knee and pulled her foot up to her mouth.

"Gosh, you are awfully bendy. Is that what constant soaking in a hot tub does for you?" said Elspeth. "Maybe Donald and I should consider getting one. Maybe *you* should get one, rather than go in your neighbour's all the time."

"Watch this space," said Viv. "Corinne, what about counselling? Not that I believe in the stuff, but maybe you do."

"Counselling for a wounded toe?"

"Counselling for you, you fool! I was thinking about your bloody table."

"So was I. The grain on the top is awfully attractive," said Elspeth, putting down her mug of tea. She put on her reading glasses, and picked up her knitting.

"She's insane to think that an eight foot table fits into a room that size," said Viv. "What's the room? Eleven by eleven? There's not even room to fit chairs around it."

"You can at one side."

"Well, whoopee."

A tear rolled down my nose. Then another. Out of nowhere. I took a huge sniff, and Viv looked up from her toe, and Elspeth looked up from her knitting.

"There, there, Corinne. Here, have my hankie," she said, fishing one out of her knitting bag. "But would you mind not actually *blowing* your nose? It is Liberty Tana Lawn."

Viv reached over and rubbed my arm, consolingly. "Me and my big...What's up, babe?" she said.

"My parents gave us the table. I used to imagine me and Mark and our four children sitting round it for Sunday tea."

When Mark and I had moved in together, I thought I had finally found the person I was meant to be with. No, that's not really what I mean. I don't believe that there is one person you are meant to be with. I think that's crap. What I mean is that after all the unsuitable men I had been involved with over the years, Mark was…well…suitable.

We planned to have a family. But then we started having problems. We paced around the house lightly, him working late, me finding the most congenial place was the little back scullery where I stripped my furniture and did my caning and tinkered about with glass. I'd decorated it in the colours I wanted, with the pictures I liked on the walls. We didn't talk about the fact that we were drifting apart. Maybe I didn't raise it because the semi-detached life we were living didn't feel too uncomfortable.

One day, when he came back from New York, where he'd been working, and told me he'd met someone else, I just felt numb. I'd been feeling for several months that we weren't really suited. So I didn't argue. I just said "OK."

He signed over the house to me. He probably felt guilty. And he'd just had an obscenely huge end-of-year bonus.

By the time I decided to move, I felt fine about my split from him. Isn't it sufficient proof that I'd lost count of the number of men I'd slept with since he left me….actually no, I'd slept with five men. I just couldn't remember how many I'd been out with. When he left, it was the dream of a family life that was shattered.

"It is a shame," said Elspeth, patting my shoulder. "Though, actually, you should say *Mark and me.*"

"Maybe I should have married Giuseppe when I was 27,"

I said. I was in love with Giuseppe, but when he asked me to marry him, I couldn't face the thought of being so far away from home, forever.

"But the table," said Viv. "I don't want to sound unkind but…lots of kids? Now? At your age? It's not going to hap-"

"Things are not that simple, Ms Rationality," said Elspeth.

"Hey, hey," said Viv, obviously trying to change the subject. "You haven't told us about the guy who reclaimed you from the skip. Is he fit? What's the story? Spill the beans."

"He's fit in that he goes out on his bike all the time. Every time I see him he's in his cycling clothes. As to whether he's fit in the other sense – you'll have to decide for yourself. If you can get him to stand still enough to judge."

"What do you mean?"

"I mean that although I have tried to invite him round for a coffee, he always gives me the brush off."

"Have you seen any women going round there?"

"No, but I don't spend all my time peering over the garden wall."

"OK, so when have you asked him round? How many times? What did he say?"

"I asked him the first time I met him in the alley. That was just after I'd moved in. The next time I went round and asked him, he said he was sorry but he'd just got a commission from a new prestigious client and he'd got to work on that. But he was wearing his cycling clobber, and I must have looked as if I didn't believe him, because he said he just had to nip out to the art shop because he'd got to the end of his layout pad, whatever that is. But they've just opened that art shop at Ranmoor - half a mile away. He could have walked there and back in the time it took to get his Lance Armstrong costume on and off."

"Well, let's ask him round now!"

"But it's half past nine."

"I don't suppose it's past his bedtime."

"Let's not. I'm not in the mood."

* * *

I saw Rob Walker the following Monday in the supermarket. You couldn't miss him in his cycling gear – that day it was a luminous yellow over-jacket, black leggings and a peaked cap. I know he saw me when I waved because he blushed and immediately picked up a tin and pretended to study the label on it. But by the time I'd done a slalom through the pensioners and mothers with toddlers and reached the end of the aisle, he'd disappeared.

I knew he was at home at dinner time on Wednesday because I could hear his music through the bedroom wall when I went up to change my T shirt. Leonard Cohen. Unmistakable. I nipped downstairs and round to his house as quick as a cat and knocked on his door. I hadn't told Viv or Elspeth, but getting Rob Walker to come round for coffee had become a private obsession of mine. It wasn't that I fancied him – it was more a fascination with someone who was so determined to stay aloof.

He came to answer the door with a phone clamped to his ear. His other hand was fiddling with the neck of his jumper. He'd unravel the rib if he went on twisting the welt like that.

"Hang on a minute. That is *not* what we agreed," he said down the phone. "Look, hold on. No. Just hold *on*, will you? There's someone at the door," he said, and then brought the phone down from his ear and put his other hand over it.

"Sorry," he whispered. "I can't call them back. It's my agent and I've been trying to pin him down for ages and give him an earful. He needs to frame himself. Do you want something urgent?"

"No, no. It'll do another time," I said.

On Thursday I went round at tea time and he was on the phone again. I saw him through his back door window holding the receiver to his ear as he approached the door. I held up both my hands, showing him the palms in mock surrender, and walked away. It felt like a battle of wills. Maybe I should have respected his privacy and left him to his own devices, but I can't resist a challenge. I wanted to crack his defences and get him round just once, then I'd leave him alone.

✳ ✳ ✳

The washing machine clicked off and interrupted my worries about how much time I'd been spending on sorting out the house, and how little time I'd spent on taking photographs for my cards.

I took the wet clothes outside to hang them on the line. A breeze was blowing little clouds across a bright sky. The children at Nether Green School were whooping and calling in the playground, and it took me back to when Megan and I were at primary school. Ma would always take us to buy new sandals in the Easter holidays. The sandals would be *Start-rite* with patterns cut out of the leather, with crepe soles, creamy like Wensleydale cheese. We'd come home and prance around the garden doing handstands and cartwheels, as lively as lambs.

Today the wet grass was squishy under my feet, and the sun was sparkling on the drops of moisture between the blades. The strong light made the bark of the silver birches shine stark white, and the ends of the twigs were thickening up, ready to burst into leaf. It was like a painting of a spring day by Sisley.

When I'd finished hanging out the washing, I stepped back and gazed at the long line of T shirts, sweat shirts, towels and jeans and I had an idea. This would be much more original than my shots of narcissi spread out under the trees in the Botanical Gardens.

I went inside to get my camera and switched the kettle on for coffee. Back outside, I walked to the far corner of the garden and looked at the line from there. I took down two T-shirts and pegged them up again, swapping their previous positions. Then I exchanged the places of a pair of vivid lilac jeans with a navy sweatshirt, and stood back to assess the difference.

"Champion," said a familiar voice from the other side of the garden wall. "Now you've got them that way round the lilac counterpoints all the blues and greens. Nice."

I turned round. He was dressed in cycling clothes. Did he do nothing else but cycle? Was he a professional?

"I'm glad you don't think I'm mad," I said.

I walked over and leaned my elbows on the top of the wall.

"Did I say that?" He grinned. "Don't put words in my mouth."

"I love to see washing on a line," I said.

"Of course."

I beamed. "So what makes it so appealing? I mean – it's not just the aesthetics – the colours, and the way the shapes change when it billows in the wind, is it? Do you know that early Kandinsky painting of washing on a line?"

"It's the memory of Mam - my mother - hanging it out when I was little. And domestic order. The security that comes from that."

"Exactly," I said. "The essence of home."

"There's a continuity. When I'm hanging out my washing I feel, I don't know, what's that pseudy word? Grounded."

"And rotary driers just aren't the same, are they?"

"God, no," he said. "Completely different. Purely functional."

"And we haven't even touched on the feel and smell of the washing when you bring it in at the end of the day – the way it kind of links you to the elements. If the day's been hot, the dry washing is like a tangible memory of sunshine."

"You've lost me now."

The ivy on the wall was scratching my arms through my jumper. I stood back from the wall. "Do you fancy a coffee? And I've just made some parkin. Just tell me, though…what the hell is that black smudge you always have on your mouth? I can't wait until I know you better before I ask – it's so intriguing."

"Did you say parkin? I thought the smell coming from your back door was familiar. I haven't had parkin since my mother died. Years."

"Do you want some? I'm quite harmless. And the parkin's not drugged. Not this batch."

He laughed.

"I'll just get my key and put the sneck down and I'll be round, fast as Cippolini." He saw my puzzled look and said "A famous sprinter," and I raised my eyebrows, so he added "a cyclist."

I went back inside and made a cafétiere of coffee, and got down my favourite plates from the dresser. They're 1930s, with painted yellow and orange flowers and a fine black rim.

He tapped on the open back door and came in.

"OK," he said. "I don't like looking in the mirror, but I've checked, and the black mark is from my brush. I lick it to get a better point and there's no-one there to point out the smudge."

"OK. How do you like your coffee, then?"

He looked at the cafétiere and an expression that I couldn't fathom flitted across his face. "Black, please."

I lifted the warm cake tin off the cooling rack on the work surface and put it on a rush mat on the table, and found him a knife. "Help yourself to parkin."

"I won't have any, thanks. The smell of it is good enough for me."

I leaned over the cake tin and scrutinised it. It looked like a vintage parkin. "Have you seen something I haven't? It's not garnished with a hair, is it?"

"It looks grand. I just don't feel that peckish." He took a giant sniff of the parkin and then of his coffee and said "Hmm," and then looked around at my kitchen and said "You've already decorated, then. So you're not doing any alterations? Nothing new?"

"I've put a multi-fuel stove in the sitting room, and I've got a Velux lined up for the wash house roof, but I'm not sure what to do in here. I'm not keen on fitted kitchens." I had painted the walls in a light airforce blue which the paint chart called Winter Sky, but I knew I'd made a mistake - doing things in a hurry again. The kitchen window looked directly onto the wash house in the yard which blocked the light, so the kitchen walls looked gloomy.

"Good shade," he said. "But isn't it a bit -? Sorry…you never asked me what I thought."

"A bit what?" I asked.

"Dark?"

"I'm going to do it again in a warm white, and bring in my print of Matisse's *Snail* for a big splash of colour. Do you know it?"

"Doesn't everyone?"

"No. No they don't." It was so good to say 'Matisse's *Snail*' like that and for someone to know what I was talking about. None of my friends knew much about art, and neither had Mark. It's not as though I have esoteric tastes. I'm pretty mainstream.

I sat down at the table, opposite him, in my oak carver chair and clasped the warm wood arms. It still felt special to have it in my kitchen. Ma and Pa gave it to me as a house warming present when I moved to Ferndean Row, much to Megan's chagrin. She'd had her eye on it for years. It had been in the farmhouse kitchen before they moved to the cottage. Pa used to sit in it every meal time. I could still remember him sitting there carving for Sunday lunch. He had an electric carving knife now. Not as sexy as an ordinary one – like the difference between an electric razor and a safety one. The Christmas before had been the first time he'd used it and the knife made a real racket. Ma sat next to him, clapping her hands and giving little yelps "Hooray! Hooray!" as he began to carve, and he said grumpily "Be quiet," and she said, "I don't want to be quiet!" It was very comic.

"Tell me what you do for a job," I said to Rob. "Layout pads, paint brushes, clients, agent, you work from home...and yet, you're always out on your bike."

"It helps to combat the main professional hazard – cabin fever."

"So what do you do?"

"I'm an illustrator and cartoonist. You?"

"A cartoonist? How exotic! I've never met a cartoonist before."

He looked embarrassed. "What do you do?" he asked. "You seem to spend a lot of time at home."

So, he noticed my movements, did he?

"Where are your cartoons published? Will I have seen any?"

He shrugged. "It's mostly bread and butter stuff … drawings for calendars, cards, websites, corporate stuff-"

"Corporate? Like what?"

"Oh, cartoons to use in slide presentations, motivational stuff, in-house mags, health and safety, that kind of thing. *Oh God, what have I come to?*" He said this last phrase in a melodramatic tone, and then slumped face down on the table top. Then he looked up and grinned. "The thing is – *I'm drawing*, whatever else. And I'm my own boss. I don't think I could beat it." He took a swig of coffee. "What do you do?"

I told him about my painting and decorating for old people. That they trusted me, they liked the fact that I didn't smoke and didn't have the radio on full blast and I cleared up nicely at the end of the day, and I was happy to sympathise with their aches and pains. Then I told him about my recent change.

"That's brave."

"People keep saying that – brave. It always sounds like another way of saying 'stupid.'"

"You keep putting words in my mouth," he said, stroking his chin. "Maybe you should save your words for the verses in your cards."

The cheek! "They're not that kind of card," I said. "I'm aiming for the arty type…photographs – hence the washing

– but collages, hand-made crafty ones, anything that occurs to me, really."

"And selling them? Have you got a *Writers' and Artists' Yearbook*?"

"It's on my list."

"Well, if you want to check anything up in the meantime, I'm only next door. Think on."

As soon as he'd finished his coffee, he left, and I rushed to my computer to look for him on the internet. I found his website with a long list of his credits. He'd had cartoons in all the major daily broadsheets and three of the Sunday papers. I looked at the kind of work he did, and the jokes.

One that made me laugh was a doctor talking to a man in a hospital bed, "We don't have a diagnosis yet. We've done a bowel investigation but we've not got to the bottom of it."

And another one was a woman talking to her husband saying "Do I look funny in these glasses?" and the husband was saying "Compared to what?"

The last one that made me laugh was a woman saying to her husband "I hate looking old. I'd like to have cosmetic surgery." And the husband says "I'm afraid we couldn't afford sufficient."

CHAPTER 5

On Friday night I drove up to my parents' house.

When I walked in the cottage they were sitting by the fire. Pa was lounging on the sofa, resting his legs, and Ma was sitting with the folded newspaper on her knee. Usually she'd be knitting or doing needlework. I kissed her and she got up and said "I'll go and make you a drink."

"No, I'm fine. Sit down," I said and walked over to give Pa a kiss. His chin was rough with stubble, and for the first time ever he didn't say "I had a shave especially, so I could give you a kiss." It was chilling. I knew it was a milestone on a journey that I didn't want to take.

The next day he came down for breakfast wearing a jumper with a stain on the front, and Ma had to remind him to brush his hair. He looked frail and said he felt lousy. And he didn't want his daily four-minute egg.

"Do you know what's wrong with him yet?" I whispered to Ma. "What does the doctor say?"

"Nothing. He's referred him to the consultant at the hospital. We're waiting for an appointment."

"Why is he wearing jogging bottoms?" I asked her later, as we washed up the breakfast things. "He's never in his life worn those before. Where are his nice corduroys?"

"Joggers are so much easier to wash and dry. I got him those off the market because he wets himself so often."

"Come on, Ralph," she said to him before we went out. He was asleep in his chair and it was only half past ten in the morning. "Just have this cuppa and then I'll help you to the loo before Corinne and I go to Leyburn."

"Otherwise, more washing," she whispered to me.

We walked slowly round the supermarket, working our way down Ma's list, and every so often she would wince and lean heavily on the trolley. "It's just my hip," she said. "Is that a thick sliced loaf or a medium sliced one?" She couldn't see well because of her cataracts. It was impossible for me to judge how bad they were, and when I asked her about her eyes, she just said, "Oh, you know what it's like. I manage. I can't have them done at the moment, can I?"

She never complained about having to look after Pa. How did she keep it up? How could she go on from day to day with no time off? She needed a month in the sunshine with nothing to do but read and listen to the radio and knit the odd teddy.

I hated saying goodbye. Ma leaned on the gate and waved to me all the way up the lane.

CHAPTER 6

Viv liked working at the allotment because it gave her a feeling of control.

"Is there anything quite as satisfying as pulling a buttercup out of damp spring soil? They glide out. Dandelions are a bugger, though, but it's cathartic when you do manage to yank one out, root and all."

I liked the fresh air, and I loved digging. Deciding where to sow or plant things was stressful, but the huge pleasure I got from the repetitive nature of digging reminded me of how I'd liked stretching canvases and fixing them onto the frames, back in my art college days. That was a repetitive process, too. When it was time to start painting – making aesthetic decisions – that was the angst-ridden part. Now my aesthetic decisions were confined to my cards, my glass and my craft. For over a week I'd been shuffling patchwork pieces around on the back bedroom floor, trying to decide on the design I liked best.

We split the plot down the middle. Once we'd cleared it of weeds, we thought we might as well try to grow things. After all, that year was all about opening out and doing new things - at least for me. Viv sowed leeks, purple sprouting broccoli and courgettes, and she planted potatoes — with advice from other people on the allotments — and I sowed easy flowers that I loved, the ones that said on the packets they were suitable for children to grow — nasturtiums, cornflowers, poppies, and sunflowers.

Sometimes I went to the weekly meetings organised by the allotment dwellers, but Viv never did. "I go up there to be on my own, not to mingle with a load of spade-wielding mini-dictators. I get enough aggro at school, with all the bloody targets and regulations. I don't need people telling me what colour watering can to use."

One Saturday afternoon, I dropped into a workshop on organic gardening held in the big communal shed. Tim, a guy of about forty, was speaking. "...toxic chemicals..." (rant, rant) "...depleting the soil..." (preach, preach) "...principle of Gaia..." (impassioned facial expression).

I agreed with his views on organic gardening, from the little I knew, but I was irritated by the way he saw all the issues in black and white.

He stood there with his hands in the pockets of his little short shorts, staring into the distance, booming out in his hearty scout master voice and rocking back and forth on the balls of his feet, feet which were clad in thick white sports socks and brown leather sandals, and I had an urge to walk to the front and bop him on the nose.

I was standing at the back of the group, so it was easy to slip out quietly. I scuttled down the path, out of the allotments, and along Rustlings Road.

I'd made it half way to the shops by the time I realised I'd left my backpack behind. I stalled, dithering outside the new frozen yoghurt bar on the corner. When would be a good time to retrieve my bag? Now? Later? It would be perfectly safe where it was behind the rain barrel, but it would be a pain to have to traipse all the way back up the hill later on, when the meeting had finished and everyone had dispersed. I glanced along the road. *Oh no.* Tim was rushing towards me, half running with sure footed loping steps, and half walking with long, steady strides. Could I pretend I hadn't seen him and escape down the ginnel between the newsagents and the chemists?

Too late: he had put on a spurt and in a few seconds he was standing in front me, bent right over with his hands on his knees as he tried to get his breath.

"Oh goodness," he gasped. "Oh my."

"What is it?" I said, staring at the top of his head. He had thick and wiry blond hair. "Is there something the matter?" I said.

He stood upright. "Did you…leave the meeting…because of me?" he asked, his heavy breathing breaking up his sentences. "Something to do with me?…I sensed you felt differently…did I offend you?" He held his fist to his chest as he struggled for breath.

"No, I…" I hesitated. Why would he think that? He had looked as though he was aware of no-one as he stood there at the front, pontificating. And I'd only been in the shed for a couple of minutes.

"I did offend you, didn't I?" He continued to breathe heavily, though more evenly now. He no longer gasped.

"No. I wasn't offended. I felt…" I broke off. My face felt hot. How could I say that his tanned legs disturbed me and that when he started to talk about different composting techniques and to rock back and forth on the balls of his feet as he was talking, I had to curb an impulse to give him a shove so he lost his balance and fell over?

"I'm so sorry," he said. "It's not fair that you should leave because of me." He turned his head and looked at the door of the frozen yoghurt bar and then turned back and said: "Can I buy you a frozen yoghurt? I'd like us to be friends."

"Well…" I said. Why had I hesitated like that, and given him the impression that I was considering saying yes?

"Do. Please do. It's blistering – a frozen yoghurt would be just the ticket."

He opened the door of the yoghurt bar and it felt awkward to leave him there looking like a wally so I stepped in, and instantly knew I shouldn't have. I was doomed. I felt as though a trap were closing round me.

There was far too much furniture in the yoghurt bar: it was crammed full of glass tables and cane chairs and almost every one of them was occupied, making it difficult to manoeuvre between them towards the counter. I stood inside the doorway at a loss as to the best route to take.

"I wonder what health and safety would make of this little lot," he said. "What if there was a fire? Ah well, if you don't mind, I'll lead the way," he said, stepping in front of me and turning sideways to squeeze between two tables each with four people seated round them. I watched him, and my eyes were drawn to his tanned and muscly legs below the khaki shorts. I imagined smearing yoghurt over his solid gleaming quads like a marinade on chicken legs and then biting chunks out of them.

He was speaking. I tore my eyes away from his legs and looked up.

"Corinne, I was asking you which flavour yoghurt you'd like. Would you mind finding us a table? Look – someone sitting in the window is leaving. What shall I get for you?"

I was flustered. "I don't know."

"Well, would you like to-"

"Strawberry, please."

"Wouldn't you like to join me in something more exotic?"

Something exotic?

"Something along the lines of peach and pecan?" he said. "That's what I'm having. Or ginger and walnut? Pistachio and liquorice? Come and browse the menu with me."

I was amazed at his choice. He seemed like a meat-and-potato-pie kind of man. Once in an ice cream bar in Canada, I'd seen bubble gum flavoured ice cream on the menu. Could you get meat-and-potato-pie flavoured frozen yoghurt?

"I won't have anything fancy," I said. "I'll have strawberry. I don't like to mingle my flavours. I like to savour them singly. Focus on one at a time. Merge with it. Make it mine."

He jerked his head back like a startled pheasant. "It's only food, my dear."

My dear? My dear?

"I'll grab a table," I said, turning away and pushing between the crowded tables towards the window.

I sat down and looked out of the window. A guy cycled up the road, lean and sleek in Lycra shorts and a brilliant ultramarine cycling jersey. Rob Walker. He cycled out of my line of sight. Tim came back with the tray of yoghurt and cutlery and paper napkins. He rested the tray on the table and I helped to unload the items, and when everything was arranged and the tray was propped on the floor against the window ledge and he sat down, I was horrified to find that I could see his thighs beneath the glass table-top. His skin was satin smooth and so tactile that my fingers itched.

"It looks as though you've got real strawberries in there," he said. "The yoghurt's organic, but it doesn't say anything on the menu about all the added ingredients. Oh well."

"Cheers," I said, raising my first spoonful in the air between us before putting it in my mouth.

"Er, yes. If you like," he said. "Cheers. Down the hatch."

❊ ❊ ❊

Since taking the photo of the washing line, I'd been carrying my camera around with me all the time, no matter where I was going, snatching pictures like Annie Leibowitz.

I'd taken a sparrow's eye view from a footbridge in town, of people standing at a bus stop, all holding umbrellas, and I had taken some views of the city that I had never seen on local postcards. I'd also spent ages choosing some clothes to arrange in a pile on my bedspread for a photograph, thinking the bright sunshine would make the colours sing. I like to see a neat pile of laundered and ironed fabric. And if the clothes in the pile are ones I originally chose for their colours, then the composition can be as appealing as an abstract painting. But the lighting in my photo was wrong, and I didn't know why.

Many of my pictures had imperfections that needed editing out, but I'd never got to grips with all the facilities of my photograph software. And one day as I was struggling with the eye dropping tool, and then the slicer, I got the idea of asking Rob for help. I left my computer switched on and my sandwich half eaten and went to knock on his door.

When I explained what I wanted he said "I'll be round in a tick."

He arrived on my doorstep wearing his cycling clobber.

"You're not just off for a ride, are you? I don't want to interrupt your day."

"No, you're fine. Let's get to it," he said.

"But you were wearing jeans a minute ago."

He was patting the side of my dresser with the flat of his hand. And the muscles in his cheek were twitching, in and out, in and out. Was he grinding his teeth? I'd obviously touched on a sore spot, but hadn't a clue what it was.

"Look," he said, "do you want help or not?"

"Sorry. Please come in – my computer's on the dining room table, just for now. Through here." I led him through to my dining room and as soon as he stepped through the doorway he made an exaggerated, dramatic jump backwards.

"Whoa! A snug fit!"

It was true: there was just two foot six between my dining table and the wall.

"Yes, I–"

"That's a thumping great table. Are you expecting company?" he said.

"I know perfectly well that everyone thinks it looks daft." I was fed up with comments on my table, my beautiful table. "Can we concentrate on the pictures, do you think?"

"Fair enough."

I adjusted the chair for him to sit in and fetched myself another one that was tucked under the table further along.

"Look," I said, leaning over and clicking the mouse to display a photograph on the screen. "This is the one I'm having trouble with, but before we sort out the problem, would you mind looking at all of the shots in the same file and tell me what you think?"

He wasn't looking at the screen. He was looking at my

sandwich, and it was with such a look of longing that I thought he might pick it up and take a bite. But he pushed the plate away with a grimace. He pulled off his black ribbed arm warmers and laid them on the table.

"Right," he said. "Which picture was it?"

"Do you want something to eat?" I asked. "I've got some nice ham. Do you want a sandwich?"

"No, ta. I'll have a black coffee." He stared at the screen and said, "Instant, if you've got it. I can't stand that poncy… I mean, instant would be great." He clicked the mouse and became engrossed.

"Look," he said, when I came back with his coffee, "if you've got a wonky horizon like this one here, you select the ruler on the eye-dropping tool and align it where the horizon should be, and then rotate the image."

He shifted his chair to the side and turned to look at me. "Come on, you take the mouse and do it or you'll never learn. Grand," he said, as I followed his instructions, "now, you'll have to square it up by cropping the corners. Mind you don't take off too much."

While I enjoyed my sandwich, he pointed out changes I could make to other pictures, changes that I never knew were possible. "Look at this one you've taken of the window and the curtain blowing in the breeze. Were you thinking of that Gwen John painting? Any road, the composition's great, but don't you think it's got a nasty greenish cast to it? If you move the colour balance – like this – see? – towards magenta, you get a much warmer look."

"That's exactly how I saw it, when I took it."

"Yes, well, I'm going to undo my edits…there…there… right," he said, swiftly clicking the mouse and making changes on the screen so the picture was back to the original. "You do it now." He pushed the mouse over to me and moved his chair to the side so I could edit the picture myself. It was a relief to have someone helping with the computer who didn't take over with a million clicks of the mouse, with windows on the screen opening and closing as fast as blinking eyelids, someone who finished in a trice and then said – 'There you are, I've sorted it out but you'll know what to do next time, won't you?' *Well, no. Actually, no.*

"You've got a great eye," he said.

And you've got nice legs, I thought. Even if they are on the thin side. I leaned back in my chair for a better view – I hoped it was surreptitious. Then I shifted in front of the computer and took the mouse and got to work.

✳ ✳ ✳

Digging and raking were obvious, but I couldn't get into hoeing. It seemed slovenly just to cut the tops off things, ignore the roots and leave the weeds on the top of the soil to die. I'm not a perfect housekeeper, but on the odd occasion when I'd weeded the garden for Pa, I'd got a lot of pleasure from the clean and tidy appearance of the soil after I'd finished. Just to hoe and leave the debris didn't give me that same sense of gratification.

But hoeing the weeds – once the seedlings were coming up in rows - seemed to be de rigeur up there on the allotments, so I thought I'd better do it.

Albert was the one I usually asked for advice when I was up on the allotment. He was over eighty and as lively and smiley as anyone could want. I'd met him about four years before when I did some decorating for him and his wife.

"I feel bashful at getting someone in," he said at the time.

But he was recovering from a hip replacement operation. And his son said he would pay for Albert to have the decorating done because *he* didn't want to do it. Albert seemed to think it was a generous offer.

"He doesn't know which way is up, that boy." (His son is middle aged.) "But then he's got his troubles – his wife has just left him. Mary never took to her. She was bonny enough. But shiftless. Mary once asked her for a copy of a complicated recipe and Ginna sent it without the back page and kept saying she'd sent it all. As if Mary was gormless. Nah, Mary never took to her."

I walked over to Albert's allotment. It was perfectly ordered and clear of weeds, and every row of vegetables looked vigorous and healthy. I sauntered down the path and felt at peace: everything was as it should be – carefully tended, tidy, growing well. It made me feel calm and still, and a snatch of a hymn we'd sung at school came into my head – *Drop thy still dews of quietness, till all our strivings cease. Take from our souls the strain and stress and let our ordered lives confess the beauty of thy peace.*

But I couldn't find Albert, so I walked back to our less than perfect patch and asked Viv.

"Can you give me any tips on hoeing?" I whispered.

"God, woman, it's not a black art. Just get on with it. You can practise on my leeks when you've done your bit, if you like."

So there I was, hoeing between my rows of seedlings, when who should creep up behind me but locust legs. Tim.

"May I offer a few suggestions?" he said.

"Thanks, but I'll get the hang of it. I just need a bit of practice."

"To a certain extent that's true," he said. "It takes a

lifetime to learn how to hoe. But practice alone won't lead you to the correct technique unless you begin from a place of enlightenment."

"You sound like a horticultural guru."

"Oh!" He looked affronted. "Then I'll put it another way – practice is useless unless one has some pointers at the very beginning."

I sighed. I knew he'd be hanging around all morning if I didn't give him chance to spout. "OK," I said, handing him the hoe.

He stood upright and squared his shoulders, arranged his hands on the handle of the hoe with careful precision – in exactly the same position that mine had been in - and said: "First you must understand that one doesn't hoe with the hands and arms alone. One hoes with the whole person, the whole of one's body. One must feel it – so." He moved and swayed and the hoe was only a minimal part of the movement.

I suppressed a laugh. He looked as though he was demonstrating a new form of dance.

I said "Would you show me on that patch of leeks over there, on the other side of the path. I haven't attacked those yet."

He reeled back with a look of horror. "Oh no!" he said. "No! One doesn't attack weeds. One doesn't attack with a hoe. One caresses."

I snorted. "How can you caress something you're killing?" I said, hoping he hadn't heard the snort. "Unless you're into S and M."

He coughed with embarrassment. "Well perhaps caress isn't quite the right word. But the movement of hoeing is gentle and subtle – that's why I didn't like you using the word *attack*."

"Just show me, will you?" I was getting fed up. I only had another half hour before I had to leave, and here was locust legs trilling on about the subtleties of killing weeds.

He stepped over to the bed of leeks and began. I was standing behind him watching his hips sway and his little khaki bottom moving rhythmically, gently, in delicate circles. A rather nice little bottom, tight and muscular.

He turned round suddenly and I jumped. He passed me the hoe and said "Your turn. I'll just watch for a moment if you'd like me to."

"Oh, sure."

I stepped along the row of leeks and took over from where he'd left off. I certainly wasn't going to sway like him.

"No, no." He stepped up behind me and said "May I?" And before I could turn, or move at all, before I could say anything, he had his arms wrapped around me and was moving my hands on the hoe to a position an inch higher up. The touch of his hands on mine made a surge run up my arms. He must have been carrying a lot of static. Something to do with his polyester shirt. Or maybe it was static in me. I once got an electric shock from a pineapple.

His hands were warm and strong. The whole length of his arms, hard with muscle, touched the length of mine. He was breathing over my shoulder, and down the neck of my shirt. He was burbling on about something. I caught the words *tempo* and *pulse* and that was all. I was somewhere else, not listening. We held the hoe together moving it backwards and forwards. I was passive and wilting against him and had an unwelcome inclination to rest my cheek against his but I came to my senses just in time. *Oh lummy, this is locust legs, not George Clooney. This is Tim. Tim. What am I doing?*

"Thanks," I said, breaking away. "I've got it now. Thanks,

Tim. I'd like to practise on my own now. It makes me self-conscious when you're watching me."

"Of course." He stepped back, and something inside me lurched. Most odd.

✷ ✷ ✷

"You poor thing," I said to Mrs Galway, placing the fruit basket on her bedside table. "How are you feeling?"

Mrs Galway had slipped on a wet paving stone in her garden and broken her ankle. She was laid up in the Hallamshire Hospital.

"How am I? Nobbut middling. I'd be right as rain if they let me go home. Can you two talk some sense into them, do you think? Can't stand the staff nurse. She's stuck up. You should hear her put on a voice when she's talking to the doctor. All fur coat and no knickers."

Mrs Galway had started as a customer of mine and had become a friend. I was fond of her. And Viv liked her too, so she'd come visiting with me.

Viv said Mrs Galway was the only old person, not counting my parents, whom she could bear to spend time with. Viv had been an only child and when she was little her house had been full of old people. "An endless line of elderly relatives came to live with us. The house was *stuffed* with them. They had to have the gas fire turned up hot in the middle of summer. There was always one of them dying, or getting gangrene and having their leg off, just when I wanted to do something with my Mum. She never had time for me. The old fogeys thought they should get all the attention, just because they could do sterterous breathing."

I drew up a chair and sat down next to Mrs Galway's bed.

"Aren't they looking after you?" I asked.

"Oh they look after me, right enough. But the orderly's the only one with any gumption. All the others call me Marjorie – the cheek of it. Who gave them permission? I said to the last one – 'I don't believe we've been introduced. It's Mrs Galway, if you don't mind.' Anyway, what's in here?" she said, poking her freckled hand into the basket and feeling the contents. I could do with some prunes, next time you're in. Some of those ready soaked ones in the foil packet."

"Hark at you, Mrs G," said Viv. "You're getting expensive tastes. Have you had a win on the premium bonds?"

"Life's too short for soaking prunes. Some of us might be dead tomorrow. Come on, then, tell me the news. What's been going on? Any new men? Mrs French said she knew your neighbour…can't remember how, now… anyway, a chap who's keen on bicycling. What's his name?"

"She knows Rob Walker?" I said. They say Sheffield is like a village, and it's true. It's not six degrees of separation here, just two.

"That's it. Walker. A pleasant body, Mrs French said."

"I've not met him yet," said Viv. "But I've a feeling Corinne agrees with Mrs F. She likes his legs. I'm not sure she has an opinion on his body. Give her time."

"That's not what Mrs French meant by a pleasant body – and well you know it. So, he's a bit of all right, is he, Caroline?" She called me Caroline because she liked the name better than Corinne. She thought it was stately. "More fitting to someone like you, someone with character, someone with a bit of backbone," she said, the first time I did her decorating. It didn't seem important to pursue it.

"I think he's got problems," I said. "He always seems on edge. It's as if he wants to be friendly, but then if he catches himself relaxing, he clams up and retreats into himself. But he seems straight, you know, trustworthy."

"A man with no side?"

"Yes, that's the expression I was looking for. I've asked him to look after my spare key. It looks as though I could be spending a lot of time up at my parents' in the next few weeks, and he's going to keep an eye on the house for me."

"Are your parents not well, dear?"

I filled her in on the story.

"And what about the headmistress?" she said, looking at Viv.

"My news? I'm having a hot tub fitted in my back garden."

"I saw one of those on the square thing this morning. Usually the programmes are all about Spain."

"Huh! Spain!" said Viv. "Wash your mouth out, Mrs G." Viv's husband had retired early and gone to Spain to find a little place for them to buy, and he'd ended up moving in with the estate agent. Viv and he were now divorced.

"This one with the hot tub was a place up a mountain in Austria, near where Hitler used to stay. Do they think we want to hear about him any more? Daytime television! Pah! What I'd like is to be able to get a decent paper in here with a crossword designed for people with more than two brain cells to rub together. I reckon to do it every afternoon before *Alpha-Omega* comes on. But what were we talking about?"

"Hot tubs."

"But what are they for? Do you go in it on your own? Or with friends? Or is it for entertaining men?"

"Any of them. All of them. Personally, I wouldn't mind going in mine with the hot tub salesman. Come round to my house and have a go when you get out of hospital. They're fitting it next week. Corinne can fetch you in the van and we can all go in together."

"I'd better have a look at my Damart catalogue, then, and order a cossie," she said. "You don't have a sauna, as well, do you?"

"Give me a break. Why?"

"I was reading something in the paper about a wealthy businessman, Sir Derek something…anyway, he committed suicide by pouring rat poison over his sauna coals."

"Ah," said Viv. "That's when chemistry comes in handy."

❋ ❋ ❋

The allotment crowd had their own little social scene going on. There seemed to be an event of one kind or other every couple of weeks. The night they had their barbecue, I was sitting next to Albert.

"So what climbing rose would you recommend for the back wall in my garden?" I asked him.

He leaned back in his camping chair and closed his eyes and tilted back his head, a habitual pose of his. "Climbing roses. This is it…"

Tim swivelled round from the barbecue wielding a vege-sausage on a fork and said "New Dawn. Every time."

"Thanks for the suggestion, Tim, but I'd really like to know what Albert thinks. He's been growing roses for fifty years, haven't you, Albert?"

I turned to Albert. He had fallen asleep. His head was hanging forwards on his chest. Every other breath he took, he snored, and as he breathed out, he whiffled through loose leaf lips. What an old sweetie. There was a tiny dribble running from the left hand side of his mouth. I took the hankie peeking out of the top of his tweed jacket pocket, mopped up the spittle and returned his hankie to his pocket.

I took another bite of my beefburger sandwich and looked up to find Tim staring at me. "I suggested you might like to try New Dawn. It's a David Austen rose – pale pink, repeat flowering, idiot proof."

"Thanks Tim."

I got up and walked away.

Viv wasn't there, and now Albert was asleep I needed someone to talk to, someone who would make it worth my while to stay. I shivered. The sun had gone down. I walked over to my shed to get my fleece. I unhooked it from the back of my chair and pulled it on. I turned to go but leapt about a foot in the air because Tim was standing there, just outside the shed. He was holding a big bunch of flowers – I don't know their name but they were an impossibly ugly shade of yellow, the disgusting pastel yellow of cheap photocopying paper.

"Tim! You startled me!"

"I'm so sorry. So frightfully sorry. And I'm worrying that I've offended you as well. You were so short with me just now, and that's not at all like you."

"No, no, you haven't offended me."

"Please take these. They're my very best blooms."

"No thanks. I mean…I couldn't possibly. Don't you grow them for your mother? What *are* they?"

"She would want you to have them."

"But she doesn't know me."

"I've told her all about you."

Creepy.

I could hear the quiet chattering of the others round the barbecue two allotments away. I ransacked my brain for something to say.

"Oh, well, thank you, Tim. I was just about to leave." I *hadn't* been going to leave, but I was now. "I'll just lock up."

I grabbed my backpack and stepped outside the door, then pulled it to, and had to struggle with the padlock. Bother the fiddly thing – it needed oiling. I eventually got it to click together and turned round to find Tim still standing there, right behind me. Before I could think about asking him to move, he lurched forwards and kissed me. His hands were full of the awful flowers, so only our lips were touching, but his kiss was so urgent and the smell of him so surprisingly pleasant – Pear's soap - and the touch of his chin against mine so unfamiliar, I found myself kissing him back. When he stopped and withdrew his head I dropped my things and grabbed him, one hand each side of his face, and I pulled him towards me for another kiss, while a voice in the back of my head said "This is locust legs. You don't even like the man! Put the man down!"

CHAPTER 7

I avoided Tim for a week. It was easy. He was at work Monday to Friday – he worked for the council, something to do with roadside verges - so he was never up at the allotments during the day, and I made sure I didn't go up at evenings and weekends. I felt awful about what had happened. About my kissing him back. It was mean of me. Thoughtless and selfish and insensitive. He had a crush on me and I shouldn't have been so reckless. What could I say? *I'm really sorry, Tim, but I just got carried away – it's so long since someone kissed me when I wasn't expecting it, and it felt so nice. Plus I have a thing about Pear's soap. I didn't even know they still made it. But I'm sorry, Tim. It was a lovely kiss, but it wouldn't work out between us.* Did that sound all right? Convincing and definitive without being hurtful? I'd have to run it past Viv and Elspeth and…no I wouldn't. That would be pure procrastination. I decided to go up the following Sunday and find Tim and do the deed.

All that week Megan was staying with my parents and she rang me every night with bulletins on Pa's condition – which had worsened - and on how Ma was coping with all of it. "I think it's time I went home, though," she said. She lived in Bristol.

I was having a three-way conversation with her and with Steve – by email and by phone. Pa seemed to get worse - really, really bad, sometimes barely able to crawl up the stairs at night, and then he would have a day when he was *not* confused and *not* wetting himself, and able to walk without stumbling.

There was no way of knowing what was the right thing to do. Should we install a stair lift? Should we try to get him in a residential home? We had no idea as to how long the stage he was in would last. Was he about to die? When? That month, the next month, that year, the next year?

It was a strange thing that the thought of sending him to live in a home seemed worse than having him die. The half life of frailty and dependency and the shifting in and out of his old personality was unsettling and upsetting. He was no longer bossy, commanding, complaining or critical, and yet Megan said that when she was showing him some family photographs there was enough of Pa there to ask, in his typically critical way, "Why did you have that one taken in front of Safeway?"

❋ ❋ ❋

"Well, Corinne, this is me," said Albert as we arrived at the bus stop on Rustlings Road one teatime. We'd walked down from the allotments together. "I'll be catching the bus today." He placed his two bags of spring greens on the pavement and leaned his garden fork and spade against the bus shelter. He was taking them home to do something with the handles. Normally we'd walk up the road together. Albert would turn off into Cruise Road after a quarter of a mile and I would carry on up past the traffic lights and up to Ferndean Row.

"Let me carry something for you and then we can walk."

He shifted about on his feet. He adjusted the position of the tools.

"This is it. I need to do it myself, Corinne. Use it or lose it. That's what they're always telling us, isn't it?" I could tell he appreciated the offer, and part of him probably wanted to accept. I think it was his masculine pride that made him say no. "Any road, we've got to keep using the buses. It's use 'em or lose 'em, too."

I looked up the road, trying to decide whether to stay and chat while he waited for his bus. I didn't want to bump into Tim. A tall guy who looked vaguely familiar was striding down the road towards us. He waved to Albert and when he drew level, Albert said to him, "Where are you off to, lad? Mother will have got your tea ready. Have you seen the cake?"

"Won't be long. I've just got to nip down to get something before the bookshop closes." He turned to look at me and I realised it was the man. *The man whose car I'd climbed into.*

"Let me introduce you to Corinne," said Albert. "She's a friend of mine."

The man - Albert's son - was wearing a cream linen jacket with tortoiseshell buttons. He straightened his left arm and tweaked his cuff, and then he held out his hand to shake mine and said "A pleasure to be formally introduced," and our eyes locked. If we'd been in a Popeye cartoon there would have been long, straight, dotted lines between our eyes, to show the connection, and our pupils would be dilated to the size of coasters.

Albert chuntered on. "Corinne walks into gents toilets by mistake and has a yen for paint with an eggshell finish. Hates gloss."

"Albert!" I gasped. "What are you saying?"

"Well," he said, "This is it. I read an article last week in Mary's Woman's Weekly about how to introduce people at parties, and I thought I'd give it a go. Practise my introducing. You're supposed to tell each person two little tiddy-bits about the other, so they have something to chat about, so-"

"Are you going to tell me something about, about-?"

"Charles," said Charles.

"Now let me see." Albert closed his eyes and tilted back his head. Then he opened his eyes and said, "This is it. A couple of weeks ago, Charles found a strange woman sitting in his car when he came back with his shopping, and... um, yes, his ambition is to sail to Spain."

I squirmed at the memory of the car incident, but I brazened it out. "Are those two little fact-lets related?" I said. "Are you trying to get away from the strange woman by sailing to Spain?"

"Perhaps I am thinking of sailing away *with* the strange woman," he said. "I haven't decided. Would you like to tell me what you think? Only trouble is... I need to get to the bookshop. I ought to be off." He adjusted his glasses. "It would be awfully jolly if you came along with me."

He locked my eyes again and then turned and started walking down the road, turning round to look at me every few steps.

I picked up my backpack from the seat in the bus stop and hurried down the road after him, as if I was drawn by

an invisible force, calling over my shoulder "Bye Albert."
I caught up with Charles and we strode along, quickening
our pace with every step. He was walking fast and so was
I – perfectly matched paces – we could have tied our legs
together and been in a three legged race. It was as if we
shared an urgency to get away from Albert, to get away from
everything. Just to be two people walking into the distance
together. Just me and him. Or me and he.

There was a dream-like quality to all of this, and the dream
continued for half a mile, for as long as it took us to walk to
the bookshop, and for him to collect a book he'd ordered.
Something to do with techniques used to date Georgian
furniture. He told me he had an antique shop in Buxton and
he'd driven over to see his parents for the evening. It was his
birthday and they always liked to see him on his birthday,
"And I like to humour them."

Part of me was wondering as we marched along, perfectly
paced, if I could have imagined the episode with the car,
because neither one of us had mentioned it. We'd been
talking about how I knew Albert and why I had an allotment
and where I lived.

But as soon as we emerged from the bookshop and the
owner locked the door behind us, Charles said: "Do you make
a habit of climbing into strangers' cars?" and I felt as though
I was standing on the pavement naked, in front of Charles,
and in front of the rush hour traffic queuing up at Hunter's
Bar roundabout.

"No," I said. "Of course not." It seemed to come out in a
splutter. "I explained to you at the time why I'd climbed in.
Didn't you believe me?"

"I had you down as mad, I have to say. I thought it was
just my luck to have bagged a beauty, who on the surface of
it appeared to be a loon."

I'm not bad looking, but a beauty? I don't think so.

Loon or not, he asked me out to dinner the next night – Friday. He came to collect me in the famous car (a Mazda, he said it was). He knocked on the front door which opens into the passageway, and I shouted through "Please can you come to the back?" because the door stuck at the bottom and I hadn't got round to taking it off the hinges and planing it down. Then it occurred to me that shouting through a door on a first date is not very polite, and then I thought oh what the hell, I climbed into his bloody car didn't I, what did a little shouting matter? And then I thought about what I'd just been thinking and wondered why I was so self conscious that I had just gone through all of this rubbish in my head.

I think it was because of his style. I'd been living in dungarees and jeans for so long that I worried that going on a date with a man like Charles would be beyond me. Viv had once made a comment about how smooth Mark was, and I suppose he was, in a way, but really Mark was just Mark, and when we were together I never thought about whether or not he was smooth.

I opened the back door to Charles to find him straightening his tie and combing through his hair with his fingers, but he had this little curl at the front that fell straight back down again, onto his forehead, just touching the frame of his glasses. He was wearing an olive green linen jacket this time.

"Hel-*lo*," he said, emphasising the second half of the word. "You look gorgeous."

I was wearing the dark red silk Audrey Hepburn dress, and I'd plucked my eyebrows and shaved my legs and earlier on I'd popped round to Elspeth's so she could trim my fringe. Elspeth always cuts my fringe. Nothing else – just the fringe.

I like her precision and her attention to detail.

That day is hadn't been easy, though. Her daughter Charlotte had dumped her children on Elspeth while she went late night shopping. Minnie-May was three, and Honey-Lee was a baby, six months old. Elspeth had got Minnie-May sitting at the table doing fuzzy felt, but Honey-Lee was fractious, and every time Elspeth put her down on the blanket on the floor she started crying. As soon as Elspeth picked her up she stopped. In the end Elspeth handed her to me and I entertained Honey-Lee with my keys and tried to keep still for Elspeth.

"Do you think you might be making too much fuss about this date?" she said. "I trimmed your fringe three weeks ago. Look," she said, pointing to her calendar "7th April, 5 – 7 p.m. Minnie-May and Honey-Lee. 7.15 p.m. Corinne, haircut. Does the man warrant such fine tuning? If he is not bowled over by your creamy skin and your espresso eyes and your beautiful thick dark hair, is he worth the effort?"(Sometimes I wonder if I go to see Elspeth to have my fringe cut or to get my morale boosted.)

Anyway, there we were, Charles and me, standing looking at each other over the threshold of my back door, and the dotted lines were back, between his hazel eyes and my espresso ones.

A blackbird began to sing in my back garden and broke into the moment.

"That brown dress really suits you," said Charles.

Brown? *Brown?* The dress was red. Should I point this out, or ignore it?

I could have invited him in, maybe I *should* have invited him in, but I just grabbed my handbag and keys and my jacket and stepped outside instead. When we reached the car he walked round to the passenger door and unlocked it and held it open for me. I think it was gentlemanly behaviour, rather than a ruse to stop me from climbing into the car again.

I settled into the leather seat and did up my safety belt, and as I turned to smile at Charles, Rob wheeled his bike out of the passageway and over the cobbles.

He swung his leg over the bike.

"Hi, Rob," I called over the open top of the car.

He raised his hand and said "Evenin'" without looking up from the foot he was slotting into his pedal. Then he cycled off.

Charles had booked us a table at a restaurant in Calver, a Peak District village twelve miles outside the city. To get from Sheffield to Derbyshire you have to drive over a ridge – whichever route you take. You get to the top of the ridge and there is the Peak District spread out before you. Seeing the hills with their colours getting paler and bluer into the distance always reminds me of my art teacher at school, Mr Tasker, explaining aerial perspective.

Charles had chosen my favourite route via Froggatt Edge. At the crest of the hill I said, "Don't you just love the view of the hills from here?"

It doesn't matter what the weather is, or the colour of the sky, that view always makes me want to point it out to the person I'm with. I have said it so often to Viv that when we get to the top of Froggatt Edge she tries to say "Don't you just love this view?" in a soppy voice, before I do.

That evening, the sun was setting behind the hills and the duck egg blue sky was streaked with yellow and white.

"The view? Oh yes. Tip-top," said Charles, changing gear.

It was exhilarating driving with the top down. I hadn't been in an open top car since I had the 2CV, after I came back from Italy. I loved that car. It was such fun, despite the fact that when the hood was down it sounded like a mini-tractor. Riding next to Charles in his Mazda was a different thing altogether. Quieter, smoother, classier, more sensuous and more exciting.

As soon as we sat down at the table in the restaurant, Charles asked me what kind of water I wanted.

"Tap water's fine," I said.

"No, no. We must have the best." He ran his finger down the back of the wine list. "Now," he said, "I'm afraid they've only got two still and two sparkling at this place. Do you like still?"

"Whatever you like."

"Attagirl. Let's have still. The house water is Monkbar Classic Crystal. It's been filtered through ceramic earths. It's a good standard. Unpretentious. But the other one they have is Fiji water. My favourite. It's much more pert. It's so pure it makes other waters seem gloopy. Shall we have the Fiji?"

My God. And this was just the water. Had I made a mistake? I sat back and let him order the wine. I might as well see how the evening progressed.

Sitting waiting for our starters in the restaurant he said, "My father told me you've just moved house. Do you live on your own?"

"Yes." I took a sip of wine. "He told me that you're divorced. Do you have any children?"

"No, thank God."

"Thank God?"

"At least there aren't any poor little blighters deranged by a nasty divorce."

The waitress arrived at our table with my artichoke soup and Charles' paté.

"You haven't told me what you do for a living," he said, spreading butter on a wafer of curly toast. "I assume you don't have a private income."

Me? Monied? Ha. What an odd thing to say.

I told him that I used to teach art at a comprehensive school and gave it up to do painting and decorating, and now I was designing greetings cards and perfecting my skills at stained glass.

"But why give up a steady job like teaching in the first place? It's a profession, after all. More kudos than slapping on emulsion for pensioners, isn't it?"

"I liked teaching. I enjoyed the kids. I gave it up because Mark, my partner at the time, did a lot of travelling for work and I was sick of being left at home every single time he went away, and I wanted a job that gave me flexibility. The irony was that we split up only two months after I quit."

"Oh, bad luck," he said, putting down his knife and toast and resting his hands on the edge of the table. "Just when you needed some steady money."

"Yes, well…" I said, non-plussed.

"Have you thought about going back to teaching?" he said.

"No, that's another life, now."

"Good," he said. "What you're doing now sounds much more interesting."

We talked about his shop and about how he'd got into antiques. He'd started with house clearances and had a junk shop at first. But all the time he'd been aiming to get into quality antiques, and now he'd made it.

"Very impressive," I said.

"I have to admit that my wife's father helped in the beginning. Put up some cash, but I bought him out some time ago."

The evening flew by. He told me he had been learning to sail on a local reservoir and was getting the itch to sail on the open ocean.

"You'll have to come down next time we have a family day at the club," he said.

"Who would I be? Sister? Cousin?"

"The term family is used very loosely, you know." His voice was low and rich and warmed me from across the table. I liked the steady way he looked at me, the attention he paid when I was talking, as if everything I said was dripping with interest.

When we arrived back at Ferndean Row, he pulled on the handbrake and immediately leapt out of the car, walking round to open my door for me. I wondered how many times this would have to happen before I stopped thinking about the time I climbed in.

We walked down the passageway to my back door. Should I ask him in?

"Thanks for a lovely dinner," I said, my hand on his arm. I stood on tiptoe and leaned up and kissed him on the cheek. He smelled of cologne that was pungent but sweet, like lavender.

He touched the place where I'd kissed him with the tips of his long slim fingers, as if he was touching porcelain, and he smiled. "The pleasure's all mine. Can we have a rematch?"

"I'd love to."

We were back into the dotted lines again. *Should* I ask him in? It was obvious what was going to happen if I did.

The evening air was fragrant from the blossoming white lilac in Rob's back yard, just the other side of my wall. A few gardens away a woman called "Timmy! Timmy! Puss-puss-puss-puss! Come on!" and there was a faint rattling sound, like dried cat food being shaken in a box.

"Well," said Charles, "Saturday and Sunday are my busiest days in the shop." "But Carol – my assistant – comes in on Sundays. I could go AWOL. How about coming over to Buxton for lunch? I'll drive over and collect you."

"I have to be back by three."

"Or you turn into a pumpkin?"

"There's something I have to do on Sunday afternoon."

"Say no more. We'll make it brunch."

I didn't intend to say any more. My need to speak to Tim was an embarrassment I was trying to minimise by giving it the scantiest possible conscious attention. I hadn't even told Viv about what had happened.

"So," said Charles, leaning his shoulder against the door jamb, with his foot up on the step.

"So," I said, leaning infinitesimally towards him.

We were heading for something more intense and more urgent that a peck on the lips. I could see it in his eyes, and I could feel it in my gut. But before it could happen, footsteps pattered in the passageway and I knew it could only be Rob, and for some reason this flustered me - bugger Rob – and I said "OK, thanks again, Charles. See you Sunday. Ten-ish?"

Sunday was warm and sunny, but there were heavy skies on the horizon as we drove up the A6 to Buxton. The new spring leaves on the hawthorn trees were a fresh vivid green, the colour zinging against the intense blue-violet-pewter grey sky.

Charles introduced me to his assistant, Carol, and treated me to a tour of his shop – lots of Georgian oak chests of drawers with shiny brass handles, blanket chests, carver chairs, high-backed pews and leather-topped desks - and then we walked round the Spring Gardens in the sunshine. The miniature railway was running, and Mums with babies in pushchairs were standing waving to toddlers clutching their tickets, and Dads holding tight to the toddlers' coat hoods to keep them from falling off the sides of the tiny carriages. Lucky Mums and Dads.

We went in the Cavendish Arcade, a shopping mall based around the old Thermal Baths, now refurbished. It is bathed in light from a barrel-vaulted stained glass roof in a modern design in primary greens and blues and yellows.

"Is that the kind of stained glass you're interested in?" he said.

"It's clever, but it feels too modern and the design feels too cerebral. But I love the glass in the Opera House. There's a fantastic rose window inside, and the canopy at the front is so pretty and so full of character. Let's go and look at it."

I made him stand under the canopy and look outwards so he saw the glass against the sky, and got the full effect of the colours.

Then we had brunch in a pub near the Opera House. I *love* brunch. It's my favourite meal. I had crispy bacon and scrambled eggs and fried new potatoes still in their skins and scattered with rosemary. And they did that really rich hot chocolate like you get on the continent that looks and tastes as though it's best quality chocolate, melted and poured in a cup.

It was a peachy day – the best that Sundays can be.

When Charles dropped me off at Ferndean Row he asked when he could see me again, and I reminded him about my father's illness, and my need to go and stay at my parents' house. I said I would ring him when I got back.

At teatime I went to see Tim at the allotments and did the deed. I caught him on his own in his shed. He was waiting for his kettle to boil. His face lit up when I appeared, which made me feel even meaner than I did already. He listened with no comment and when I finished speaking he nodded.

"Thank you, Corinne. Thank you for being honest. If your feelings change, I'll still be here."

What a huge relief. It could have been so much worse.

That night I rang my mother.

"Having Megan for the week was marvellous," she said. "She worked so hard. She cooked, she did all the shopping, and she helped me to organise things. She took over and helped Pa to wash and to go to the loo, which meant I could have a bit of a rest. She's such a dear. You all are."

Megan is a star at being helpful and useful. When I spoke to her on the phone at her house, she sounded exhausted.

She said, "I'd been talking to Ed on the phone and I could hear he'd got the radio tuned to an alien station, not Radio 4, and I knew it was time to come home."

She'd given up a week of her annual leave to go to Wensleydale. It was time I pulled my weight.

I went up on the following Wednesday. I turned off the A1 at Leeming and drove up the dale, enjoying the new spring grass in the fields that last time I was there were a washed out, dreary khaki. Wensleydale is one of the broader Yorkshire dales, with rich pastures divided into a patchwork of fields by dry stone walls. It was a cloudy day, but a strong sun kept appearing, and on the hillside up ahead of me, Bolton Castle was lit up by a beam of sunshine like a spotlight.

I'd got as far as Swinithwaite when Ma rang me on my mobile phone. She was at hospital in Northallerton. She and Pa had gone in an ambulance for Pa's appointment and Pa had been kept in for assessment, so she was stranded. I drove twenty miles back down the dale to collect her and take her home.

The next day I drove to the hospital on my own.

When I walked into Pa's ward he looked dreadful: his face sagged like a bulldog's. He had a burst blood vessel in his right eye, glaring from under the lower lid. He had a drip and a catheter attached, and he didn't like either of them. His arm got sore when they stuck in a needle, because all his veins were shot, so bad that sometimes nurses couldn't manage to stick a needle in the right place and they had to get the doctor to do it. He kept on forgetting about his catheter, and would get up to go to the loo and trip over the bag and the stand, and pull the drip in his arm.

The first thing he said was that his cousin Robin Makepeace was a doctor in the hospital, and I was surprised, because as far as I knew Robin M was a consultant at St Thomas's in London. Then another doctor came and when Pa mentioned Robin, the doctor said "Oh, yes. Dr Robin is on another ward at the moment," and I realised that Robin was his surname and that Pa was confused.

He said: "There was a terrible downpour last night, and all my bed was awash with water that came through the hole in the roof, and a lady – she worked for the Chinese – stripped my bed and changed it, while I was lying here."

He could hear hardly anything, and he had been without his glasses for 24 hours: he was vulnerability personified.

"Have the doctors told you what they think the matter is?" I asked him.

"No. There were three of them standing at the foot of my bed this morning, having a confab, but they told me nothing."

They told *me* that Pa had some abnormalities in his blood and they were keeping him in to test it - to find out the cause. They were going to give him a kidney scan.

I took him for a walk outside in a wheelchair and he had a cigarette. It was upsetting to see him surrounded by strangers, in a strange and hostile land, not knowing what was happening, which hospital he was in, or why he was there.

As I wheeled him back to the ward I said "What would you like me to bring for you when I come tomorrow?"

"Ma and Steven."

The nursing staff were kind, but they had to shout to make him hear, and sometimes even then he didn't understand what they were saying. The physiotherapist came to fit him up with a walking frame, and she was "teaching him how to use it" but he couldn't hear what she said, and the instructions were so basic, the situation so demeaning, that it made me squirm. She said "Can you feel the armchair against the back of your legs, now put your hands on the arms of the chair, lower yourself down, no, not yet, do this…"

After she'd finished and left the ward, we sat quietly for a while.

Then Pa said, "Ma is worn out with looking after me. I tried to tell her how much I appreciate it. Do you think she knows?"

"Yes, Pa," I said. I gave his hand a squeeze.

I spoke to the staff nurse at the desk before I left. I wanted to explain that Pa didn't have Alzheimer's, that he understood things. It was just that he was deaf, and he was only confused because he was ill. She nodded.

I left in tears. I wanted to take him home. To be old and deaf and confused and ill and in the company of strangers is unbearably sad. However kind and patient they were, they didn't know who he was or what he had been, and they had no notion of what he was feeling. He ought to have been at home, being looked after by people who loved him, people who knew what an old sod he was, how loving, how mean, how generous, how critical, how caring, how sentimental, how much he loved his food and his home and the dale and mother.

On the way back up the dale to Hollycroft, I rang Steve to see where he was working. He farms the family farm and was working in the fields above the village that afternoon. He told me where to find him, and I went for a quick chat and a hug on my way back to Hollycroft. He gives good hugs.

CHAPTER 8

There was a loud rapping on my back door.

"Corinne? Are you there? Corinne?"

"I'm in the wash house," I shouted. I put down the glass cutter and the piece of expensive "cranberry" glass I was cutting for a poppy petal and sat back on my stool.

"What are you-?" Rob's face appeared round the door. "Oh...the famous glass." He came in and looked at the things on my work table and at the design I was following. It was a tall free-standing panel, about three feet six high and a foot wide: three poppies in vermilion, scarlet and crimson, against an eau de nil sky. I'd found a gorgeous bit of opaque brown glass for a corner of earth at the bottom - the colour of an old conker, but with faint creamy streaks.

"Mighty fine. I like the line of the three stems, that parallel curve," he said. "Very strong. But don't poppies have feathery leaves? Serrated?"

"Do they? I copied the design."

"What, freehand?" He sounded impressed.

"I've got an old overhead projector, and I beam the image on the kitchen wall, and draw round that. There's no way I'd be able to get the proportions right otherwise."

"It's going to be champion. Here, I brought you this." He handed me a jiffy bag. "The postman left it while you were away."

I looked at the label on the packaging. "My new soldering iron! Excellent." I ripped open the envelope, and took the thing out of its polythene wrapper.

"Why d'you need another one?"

"The guy at the glass shop said I needed a hotter iron to get better seams. I bought this cheap one, here," I said, picking up the old one to show him, "and it's useless." I swivelled round to reach a small finished piece off the shelf behind me. "Look at the bumpy seams on this – crap. I can't wait to try the new one."

He was standing in the doorway. "So. How was your trip up North?" He scratched his head. "How's your dad?"

I sighed. I smoothed the front of my canvas apron. "Not good," I said. "They've got him in hospital now, having tests."

I had been awake since four in the morning, tossing around and wondering what I could do. When Pa came out of hospital, Ma would need someone there all the time, not just for a few days.

At half past five I gave up trying to go back to sleep and took a mug of tea out to the wash house, thinking that if I did some glass work it might take my mind off things. It didn't. My glass cutting was rough and cack-handed and I cut myself.

"It's awful," I said to Rob. "They're trying to find out what's wrong with him. I think it could be the end. You know."

"I'm sorry," he said, and he came over and patted my shoulder. "I'm very sorry." The patting turned into small strokes.

I said nothing.

"What happened here?" he said, picking up my left hand

"I wasn't concentrating." The handkerchief I'd wrapped around my finger was soaked in blood and needed changing.

"Haven't you got any plasters?"

"Yes, but where? You know what it's like when you move."

"Back in a tick." He went out and returned a couple of minutes later with a black plastic case with silver go-faster stripes on the side.

"Would you like me to do it for you?" he said.

"Ta." I was perfectly capable of doing it myself, but it was comforting having someone look after me.

"Give it here," he said. He took off his cycling gloves, gently unwrapped the grotty hanky and examined the wound. He was leaning close. He smelled of shampoo and ironing. He smelled like home.

"It's a whopper," he said. "Looks clean, though. I'll soon get it fettled."

While he wiped the cut with an antiseptic wipe and dressed my finger with lint and microporous tape, I poked about in his first aid box with my other hand. "This is impressive. You've got everything that opens and shuts in here."

"Bella bought it. She came round once when I was trying to clean up a wound on my thigh. A car had cut me up on a bend and I skidded on some loose gravel." He laughed. "She was horrified with my first aid supplies and went right out and bought me this."

"Bella?"

"My daughter."

"You never told me you had a daughter, how old is she?"

"You never asked. 27."

"I like these plasters that look like strips of streaky bacon."

He chuckled. "She knows I like my bacon. There," he said, "done." He put everything away in the box and stepped away from my work bench. "So. Your dad. What do the doctors say?"

"Nothing. But he's 84, he's ill, he's weak, and he has abnormalities in his blood. I've never seen him so out of it. He's an intelligent, articulate man. He's never been like this before. He's always been in command. I think he could be dying."

"But if that's the case, what are you doing *here*?"

"What do you mean?"

"Why aren't you with him?"

I stared at him.

"You do get on?" he said.

"Of course. He's my dad." I felt a surge of resentment. What the hell had it got to do with him? A bloody neighbour?

"Thanks for doing my finger, and for bringing this" – I waved my hand at the new soldering iron – "but I need to get on."

He didn't move. He just stood there in the doorway holding his stupid crocheted gloves.

"If you don't mind," I said.

"Look, I know what it's like to lose a parent. You need to make the most of them while they're still here."

I said nothing. I picked up the piece of glass I'd been working on and placed it onto the pattern. Then I scored a line on the glass with the glass cutter, following the line of the design.

"Is this stuff more important than your parents?" he asked. He had his cycling gloves in one hand and was flicking them against his other palm. The fluttering movement at the edge of my vision was getting on my nerves. I picked up my grozing pliers and the piece of glass I'd just scored.

"Corinne. Did you hear what I said?" He paused. "Why are you sitting in your shed farting around with stained glass when your father could be dying?"

Who the hell did he think he was, to tell me what to do? What a cheek to think he knew anything at all about me or my family, or presume to give me advice!

"Mind your own business," I said without looking up. I concentrated on the curve I was cutting. It was concave – the hardest kind of curve. I snapped off a piece of the glass. That was OK. Then another. This one snapped off at a tangent. "Shit," I said. "Look what you've made me do now – I've wasted another piece of this expensive glass. Haven't you got a bike to ride?"

He pulled on his gloves and turned on his heel and left. I was steaming with anger and nearly threw my pliers after him as he retreated.

I was still looking towards the doorway when he stuck his head round the door jamb. He looked me in the eye.

"Think on," he said. And he left.

Think on. Think bloody on. Stupid expression.

"Sod bloody off!" I shouted, as loud as I could.

✳ ✳ ✳

His phone rang just once.

"Good morning. Elite Antiques."

"Hi Charles, it's Corinne."

I was sick of having the situation in Wensleydale going round and round in my head. In quiet moments, when I was sewing patches, or grinding glass, or digging the allotment, I thought of nothing else. I couldn't bear it any more, and I knew that Charles would be a wonderful distraction.

"Well good morning, madam."

It sounded like Charles – that low sexy voice – so why was he calling me madam? "Charles? Is that you?"

"This is he."

"I'm back. How are you? I'm ringing to invite you round to my house. I'd like to cook for you."

"That would be capital. May I get back to you?"

"Oh, I– you have a customer."

"Yes, madam. If you could just give me your number I'll ring back shortly."

※ ※ ※

"Corinne! I'm sorry about earlier. How wonderful to hear from you."

"Would you like to come over?" I said.

"Does the Queen like going to Ascot?"

"This week?" I said.

"It's not Ascot this week."

"No, Charles, would you like to come over this week?"

"You name the day. Although, having said that, I have a Chamber of Commerce meeting tomorrow night, and the next day I have a dental appointment in the afternoon. I don't want to come round if my face is still numb."

No, there wouldn't be much point.

"I wouldn't be able to do your cooking justice," he said.

Oh, the food. That was the least of it.

"Well, how about tonight?" I said. I didn't want to wait.
"Just tell me what time and I'll be there."

✳ ✳ ✳

"So…kitchen…and through here is the dining room, and
then there's this ridiculously tiny square at the bottom of
the stairs by the front door. Not exactly big enough for my
Christmas tree." I judge every hall by whether it's possible
to fit in a Christmas tree. "Then… here's the sitting room." I
sat down on the sofa and Charles did the same. "What shall I
get you to drink? I've got red wine and white wine. I've got
gin, whisky, loads of fruit juices."
"What are you having?"
"Valpolicella."
"Then I'll have the same. Tell me about the chair."
Charles had followed me through the house without
making any comments. Now he was looking round the room
at my furniture and his eyes had alighted on the chair I'd
inherited from Gran.
"Oh, that. It was my Gran's – she was born at the end of
the 1800s." The chair was a miniature upholstered one with
mahogany arms and legs. It was a perfect size for a toddler.
Coralie, Elspeth's grand-daughter, always rushed to sit in
it when she visited. "My Gran had polio when she was four
and had to wear leg irons. She used to tell us a story about
how she wanted to go to play in next door's hay loft with the
other children, but because she was lame she couldn't climb
the ladder. So the other kids tied some ropes round the chair,
and climbed up into the loft with the ropes and were trying
to haul her up when my great grandmother appeared just in
time to stop them."

"Do you mind if I have a look at it?"

"Go ahead. I'll get some drinks."

When I got back he was looking at my pictures.

"Mmm, modern taste, I see. Apart from the Scottish impressionist over there."

"Oh yes. That's precious."

"How much?"

"I mean – it's precious to me. My father gave it to me. He's a farmer. Retired. And he likes paintings. He has lots of paintings of beasts. That's the only one I ever liked. Look at the dappled light on the two cows under the tree."

"Mmm. Who's the artist?" He lifted the painting off the wall and examined the back of it. "Ah – him. Worth a bit, then." He turned round and I handed him a glass.

"Cheers," I said. I looked him in the eyes, as you're supposed to do when you say 'Cheers.'

He looked back into mine. "Tally ho." The evening felt promising.

He told me about his week. I gave him a snippet about my dad and – top marks to Charles – he offered me no advice.

Where shall we eat? At the dining room table or in the kitchen?" I said.

"Your dining table is a fine piece, but if I sit next to you – which seems to be the only option in there – I shan't be able to look at you. And that would be a shame."

As we walked through the dining room he ran his hand over the table. "Presumably you didn't get a good enough offer before you moved, and that's why you brought it with you," he said. "And presumably you decided you needed it erected to show it off to potential buyers."

"I–"

"It's not my period, so I won't offer to have it in the shop.

I could store it for you in my warehouse, though."

"Thanks, but I'm not selling it at the moment."

"But–"

"Shall we eat? Everything's ready. I don't want it to spoil."

He ate everything I offered him, and he ate with relish. I love to cook for people who enjoy their food – the greedier the better. Not that he was greedy, I don't mean that. But he did have second helpings of my home-made pork and apricot casserole and he tucked into the creme brulée as if there were a gold sovereign hidden at the bottom of the ramekin. I don't know the findings for men, but apparently, 70% of women (according to something I read) would rather have a crème brulee than sex. Not me.

"More wine, Charles?" I said, picking up the bottle.

He put his hand over the top of his glass. "No. I've had my limit. Don't forget I have to drive home."

I reached over and moved his hand. "You don't *have* to drive home," I said. "Have some more wine." He smiled and gave my hand a squeeze.

We didn't stay long in the sitting room. Charles is tall, and there's not a lot of floor in my sitting room, and I like my comforts. Call me bourgeois, call me middle-aged, I don't care, but why not use a king size bed when you have one?

✳ ✳ ✳

"I don't want to get up," said Charles, putting his watch back on the bedside table.

"You said that yesterday," I said.

"I don't want to leave you behind."

"You said *that* yesterday."

"Will you come with me?"

"To the shop?"

"Come and be my glamorous assistant."

"But you already have one."

"I'd hardly call Carol glamorous. Anyway, she's not there today. Do come, you could lure the customers in, then I can pounce and make the sale."

"What? Stand outside and smile suggestively?"

"Inside. On the merchandise. Like those models at the Motor Show drape themselves on the cars. You could give 'em a look at your legs, your delectable legs." He drew back the duvet and stroked my thigh and then leaned over and kissed each of my knees.

"But you don't have any chaises longues. What am I supposed to drape myself on?"

"On the settle, or the desk in the corner. It's got a leather top so you wouldn't be chilly. And I've got a couple of cushions in the office."

Would I have to talk to the punters?"

"If you like. Or you could just flash 'em your teeth. Did anyone tell you what a fine set of teeth you have?"

"My teeth?"

"That's the first thing I noticed about you. Your teeth are like apple blossom petals."

❋ ❋ ❋

"How about tonight, then?" said Viv on the phone.

"Tonight's a bit difficult," I said.

"Tomorrow, then."

"Mmm, not sure."

"Oh come on, Corinne. Mrs G has been dying for a girls'

night dip in the hot tub. She'll be really mad if we don't do it soon. She scares the knickers off me when she's angry."

"You?"

"Even me."

"You're bonkers. How can she go in a hot tub when she has a cast on her ankle?"

"She's going to put it in a plastic carrier bag and hang her leg over the side. She does have quite long legs. It should be just about feasible, if we take care to steady her."

"But she's 80. She has arthritis."

"She says she's got a really strong bag from the builders' centre. You left it at her house once, apparently, and she saved it. Knew it would come in useful one day. That's what she said. So when can you come? And what are you so busy with anyway?"

"Charles."

"Who he?"

"Do you remember when I climbed into that sports car and the guy came back and found me sitting in it?"

"Him? My God! Where did you run into him again?"

"You know Albert – up at the allotments?"

"It's him?"

"No, you dope. It's his son."

"Weird. Very weird."

"Albert's son. Isn't that amazing?"

"So bring him with you."

"I'm not sure he's ready to meet my friends."

"How long's it been going on?"

"Two weeks."

"Oh not long, then."

"Every night for two weeks."

"Bloody hell. In that case you can spare a night for us. Bring him round!"

"Not just yet," I said.

"Are you in love with this guy?"

"I love going to bed with him."

"Not the same thing, Corinne."

Well, yes. Did she think I didn't know?

✳ ✳ ✳

"I wish you didn't have to go," I said. I reached out my hand and tousled his hair.

"So do I," said Charles. "But I do. One of us has got to earn a living."

"I wish we could stay here all day. Maybe just until the sun moves to the other side of the chapel chimney?"

He kissed me. "How long is that?"

"I like being in bed with you."

"Ditto, dear lady,"

"Charles…"

"Yes."

"Why do you talk like that?"

"Like what?"

"Oh never mind. Come over here. I love the feel of your skin against mine. So smooth."

✳ ✳ ✳

"Are you in? Are you busy?" said Elspeth on the phone

"Why? I'm sort of busy for the next half hour. After that I–"

"Corinne, could I come round? The children are driving me to distraction with interruptions. When will it cease? How am I expected to get my work done? One might think that when offspring reached their twenties one could get one's life back. One might think that with Donald away in Antarctica and an empty house I would have endless time to do my research. But no. First Charlotte has a crisis with the little ones. Then Jessica wants me to help take her mind off her broken heart by going to Gap in Newcastle - the only Gap north of Birmingham she has not visited yet. And then Barnes rings to say he has broken his glasses and can he come round to borrow money for new ones because it is two weeks until he gets paid. Corinne! I am in despair! Trying to concentrate on the use of the subjunctive in seventeenth century poetry in the midst of my current life is like knitting socks blindfold and with only three needles."

"Well, I-"

"And I cannot sleep. And when I do sleep I have the most dreadful dreams. Last night I dreamed I had to measure vowel shift with glass tubes and grass cuttings."

"What?"

"Quite. An apt image for life itself. It summed up nicely the unpromising nature of the task."

"Elspeth, Elspeth, stop. Please stop. I can't talk now. I'm in the middle of something. You can come and work here. I will be doing my glass in the shed. You can work in the dining room. Come in an hour. Bye."

She arrived as I was saying goodbye to Charles, leaning over his car door and kissing him.

He drove away, and Elspeth and I walked down the passageway and in my back door.

"Sorry for being so long, Elspeth. I can't bear it when he leaves."

"There did seem to be an inordinate number of goodbye kisses. Obviously a bad case of oxytocin."

"What?"

"Surely you know, Corinne. When a woman makes love, a hormone called oxytocin floods her system, and that is what makes her feel bonded to the man. Pure physiology."

✳ ✳ ✳

The newsreader was recounting the latest estimates of the numbers dying in the African famine. I didn't want to hear about people dying. I switched the van radio off.

"What do you think's the answer to all this deprivation, Mrs Galway?"

"I dare say that in time pestilence, disease and famine will thin out the world population. That will make things a lot easier. Of course, I'll be well gone by then. Just pull up here, would you Caroline?"

"What, here? Is it the newsagent you want?"

"No, the off-licence. I expect you and Vivien will be drinking wine. I'd like to have some gin, myself."

She undid her safety belt and opened her door.

"You don't need to go. Tell me what you want. Which brand? What size bottle?"

"I reckon to get the cheapest." She pulled her door shut, and then she opened it again. "No, no. I'm sick and tired of relying on other people to do my errands. I want to get it myself."

"It would be so quick for me to nip in."

"I want to go myself."

"OK, OK. Let me hold the door open for you, then."

I got out of the van and went round to help her out. We were on our way to Viv's to have a soak in the famous hot tub. Mrs Galway still had a pot on, and she was using crutches rather than her usual walking stick to get around, but Viv insisted that we could manage to manoeuvre her into the tub. I wasn't convinced, but I was intrigued to see what Viv had in mind.

We were in the queue, and the man in front received his change from the assistant and left the shop.

"I'd like some gin," said Mrs Galway. "What's your cheapest?"

"It's the White Satin at £9.99."

"Oh, come on. You can do better than that."

"I don't think they do bartering in here," I whispered.

"Well they damn well should do. They need to keep up. I'll have to start buying it on Ebay."

I caught the assistant's eye and we both cracked up.

"You can't buy booze on Ebay," I said. "Anyway, what do you know about Ebay?"

"Don't be so patronising, Caroline. And you can shut up," she said to the assistant. "Give me the White Satin, then. And some orange cordial – the kind you let down. And be sharp. I have a hot date to go to."

"Mrs Galway, you are a hoot," I said as we walked back to the van. "The assistant didn't know if–"

"I *do* have a hot date. It had better be hot, anyway, or I'll catch my death."

We managed to get Mrs Galway into the tub by standing each side of her and hauling her over the brink, sans crutches. Viv goes to the gym and is super fit. She has muscles and everything. Once we had Mrs G installed, with her knee bent and her gammy leg hanging outside the tub, encased in the builders centre plastic bag, we climbed in ourselves and handed her a glass of gin and orange.

"Cheers!" said Viv.

"Cheers!" I said. I loved being outside in the fresh evening air, with the warm water lapping round my body.

"Bottoms up!" said Mrs G.

"Oh, Mrs G, can I adopt you?" said Viv.

"Pardon?" She steadied herself with the arm not holding the glass. "Adopt me, did you say?"

"My parents were always a dead loss. And now they're just dead. I'd like you for my Mum."

"Very well. I'll have to square it with Tina and Richard, but I don't see as they can complain. If they will insist on going to live on the other side of the world, they can expect to be supplanted in my affections – nice word that, supplanted, they had it on *Alpha-Omega* yesterday - especially when the person in question offers blandishments such as hot tubs. Blandishment. Another nice word. Are you impressed? That was on the day before."

She took a sip of gin and orange. Then she said, "What was so bad about your parents? Ooh, oh, the water's squirting up under my cossie. Oh, dear, can you take my glass from me for a minute, Caroline?"

She settled down and then said "What were we talking about?"

"Parents."

"Oh, yes, Vivien's parents. What about them?"

"They never had time for me," said Viv. "My mother told me that when I was born and my father went to visit her in the hospital, he walked past me and sat down and asked her how she was, and she said, *Well, go and look at the baby, then,* and he looked in the crib and said *You know, I'd rather have had a dog.*"

"Viv! That's awful!"

"Well, eventually he got a dog, so it all ended happily."

Viv put down her glass, and adjusted the jets. Then she said, "And then there was the Harry Corbett incident."

"Harry Corbett? That man with the hand puppet on television?" I said. "Sooty?"

"Yes. I loved watching *Sooty and Sweep* on children's telly," said Viv. "I had the replica puppets and did one-girl shows. Once, we all went to Southport for a day trip and I had my photograph taken with Harry Corbett and Sooty on the pier. We had to go back the following Sunday to collect it."

"Ah those were the bad old days when people had to wait for everything. Nowadays they would email it you. I dare say you could take the picture yourself on a mobile phone."

"Yes, Mrs G." Viv rubbed the back of her neck. "But I was ill the next week, and so my father went on his own to Southport and came back with a picture of Sooty with another girl. Not me."

"How could he do that? How could he not recognise his own daughter? It's not as if there was more than one of you. You're an only child, aren't you?"

"I bet your mother gave him a flea in his ear," said Mrs Galway.

"Oh yes. But in the middle of her telling him off, one of the elderly relatives had a heart attack, so it was all forgotten."

✳ ✳ ✳

"It's all go at your house these days, isn't it?" said Rob, standing on my doorstep. "People going in and out all the time."

"Well, just the one."

"I've seen two different cars parked outside quite a lot."

"Oh, yes. Elspeth." I opened the door wide. "Are you

coming inside?"

"No, I'm just off out. That guy with the Mazda – I know him. We were in the same class at King Ted's."

"What was it you wanted, Rob?"

"You gave me your key. Just wondered when you were going to see your parents. When I need to be on the alert, you know – keep an eye on your house."

"I haven't decided yet."

"Well you need to frame yourself and get yourself up there. There'll be plenty of time for lover boy later. He'll wait if he's keen."

I slammed the door in his face.

※ ※ ※

"You're a really bad influence on me," I said to Charles in bed.

"I doubt that. You seem to know what you're doing."

"No, I mean, I never get up before half past eight these days.

"*Do* people get up before half past eight?"

"I used to get up at seven, and be working by eight."

"Even this year – on your year off?"

"It's not a year off. What makes you call it that?"

"Well, doing craft work, stained glass, photography. It's not exactly a proper job, is it?"

"It will be a proper job when I get established. I'm not going to get established the way I'm carrying on at the moment though, am I? The way we're carrying on…"

"Is there time for a quickie before I go?"

"Oh, several I should think." We kissed. "See what I mean about you being a bad influence?"

✳ ✳ ✳

"Are you going to put in a decent power shower some time?" said Charles. He leaned back in the bath.

"Maybe. Haven't decided yet. This is quite cosy, though, isn't it?"

"I'm not sure those two words go together. Cosy bed, yes. Cosy bath, no. I need a bit of room. I'm not a dwarf."

"Don't you think I've noticed that?" I said, climbing out onto the bathmat and wrapping myself in a towel.

"When are you coming back from your parents?" he said as he stretched out into the space I'd left.

Pa was still in hospital, and I planned to drive up to Wensleydale the following day. The denial was wearing too thin. Being in bed with Charles every night was the ultimate distraction, but now the worry about Ma and Pa was continually breaking through, as was the guilt about leaving Steve to support them both. And I'd finally admitted to myself that what Rob had said - two weeks before - was true: I should be spending time with my father, while I still had the chance.

"I don't know how long I'll be staying," I said to Charles. I sat on the loo seat and bent over to dry between my toes.

"Do you have any idea?" he said. "Two days? A week? I need you here, not a hundred miles away." He climbed out of the bath and took a towel from the rail.

"I know. I want to be with you, too." I stood up and kissed him. "But I need to see my father." Kiss. "I *want* to see my father." Kiss. "He's not getting any better." Kiss. "And my mother. I want to see her. I'll ring." Kiss. "I'll ring you often."

He put his arms around me. "I need you here. I need you in person. In the flesh. Every bit of your body."

"My teeth." I smiled.

"Ah, your teeth." He ran the tip of his index finger between my lips, and along my front teeth. "But sweetheart, if I had to choose, I'd take your softer parts over your teeth."

❆ ❆ ❆

Dear Rob,

I feel really embarrassed about slamming the door on you. I'm very sorry.

I am going to my parents' tomorrow and don't know when I'll be back. My friend Elspeth has a key to my house, as well as you, but she will only be coming round to work here on Wednesdays and Thursdays. Apart from that, the house will be empty, and it would be great if you could keep an eye on things. You can ring me if you need to, on my mobile or the landline I gave you.

Thanks,

Corinne.

p.s. It's very good of you to do this, and I do appreciate it.

CHAPTER 9

I drove up the A1 and instead of turning west at Leeming
Bar to drive direct to my parents' house up dale, I went east
and visited Pa in hospital in Northallerton. There's a stretch
of cherry trees along that road and last time I drove along
it they were in full bloom. The blossom is not a shade of
pink I like – it's dirty and dead-looking like those ancient
candlewick bedspreads you see at jumble sales. That day half
the petals had fallen off and were dusting the grass verges
and the edge of the tarmac.

I found Pa in a different ward from last time. He didn't
have tubes or a catheter attached and was sitting sideways on
his bed in his pyjamas and maroon dressing gown.

I kissed his cheek and he smiled. He hadn't got his false
teeth in, so I found the pot containing them and showed it
to him.

"Why don't you put these in?" I said.

He looked at them as if he didn't know what they were.
"There's a man in Leyburn who will fix them for me," he said,
as if they were broken. Then he put them in his mouth.

I tucked him up in the wheelchair with a blanket and took him outside for a cigarette. We went in the tiny enclosed garden, in the middle of the building. It has gravel and shrubs and hostas and small leafy trees. It's a nice attempt to give a space for people to sit, but there was no sunshine and no colour in the sky and it was draughty, so I took off my fleece and wrapped it around Pa's shoulders.

There were some nasty, spooky, life-sized statues of children playing - a child with a hoop, a boy kneeling down with marbles, a child sitting with a doll. Their clothes were coloured brown. The figures were like those figures of children with leg irons holding charity donation boxes that used to be outside shops when I was little.

Because it was cold, I took him inside again and we sat in a broad corridor, which seemed to be the only place to be private away from the ward. I tried to talk to him, but his confusion and his deafness made it hard. I would say something to him, trying to make conversation, and he would respond with words I either couldn't make out or I couldn't understand, so I gave up trying, and just responded when he spoke to me.

"I keep thinking that the boy is here," he said.

"Which boy? Steve?"

"Steve or one of his lads - Matthew or Jake."

I took him to a window so he could see a distant view of countryside and hills.

"I'm not sure which direction we're looking in. Do you know?" I said.

"South."

"Thirsk must be down there, then, where Frank lives," I said.

"Frank died two or three years ago."

"No, he didn't, Pa. It was his wife who died."

"Oh yes, that's right."

"Have you finished reading that book about Dickie Bird yet?" I said.

"No, I'll be going home shortly."

I wheeled him back to the ward, and as we passed the nurses' station he said "I hope in a couple of years I will have forgotten all about this place."

"Yes," I said. "You will."

Before I went home I asked the staff nurse if the doctors had decided what exactly was wrong with Pa. She said an X ray had shown up a shadow on one of his lungs, and they were considering giving him a bronchoscopy to investigate further.

"But we'll consult the family before we do that," she said.

When I got back to Hollycroft, Ma came to the door to greet me. She sat me down and gave me a cup of tea. When I told her about Pa's lung and the bronchoscopy she put down her cup so roughly, the tea spilled into the saucer.

"I won't have them giving him one," she said. "He's not well enough. It would be awful for him, and what would be the point? It's not as if he's strong enough to cope with an operation, to sort out whatever the problem is."

"I'll tell them tomorrow," I said. "Don't worry – they said they wouldn't do it with out our, your permission."

When I walked into the ward the following day, Pa was sitting in his pyjamas in his chair, with his bed stripped. He was dozing, with dark marks under his eyes. I kissed him on the cheek and sat down, with my hand resting on his, and he opened his eyes and smiled at me.

"How are you feeling today?" I said.

He leaned towards me and whispered. "Quick, let's go, before they change their minds."

Then he told me he needed a pee, so I fetched his walking frame for him and he got out of bed and went tanking off to the loo. On the way back he stopped before he got back to his bed.

"Take me out for a cigarette, will you?" he shouted across the ward.

I got up and rushed over to him and laid my hand on his arm. "Come back and have your dinner first, Pa. Come on, it's shepherd's pie and it looks quite good." I had to speak loudly, to make sure that he could hear.

He pulled away from me. "I'm not coming back for that dinner."

"Well, come and have some of my beef sandwich, then."

"It had better have some fat on it. It had better have some flavour."

"Do you think Ma would buy a piece of beef without any fat?"

"All right," he said.

He did have some sandwich, but not very much.

I took the lid off a jam jar full of melon that Ma had cut up and sugared, and I handed it to him, along with a spoon. When Ma had put it in my bag that morning she'd said, "That'll be a way of getting rid of a jar," and I laughed.

I popped out to the loo and when I got back, I noticed that Pa had got something floating in his tea. He'd put two pieces of melon in there. I fished it out. It was mouldy, though in fairness to Ma, you couldn't tell, unless you looked closely.

I went off to ask the nurse, on Ma's instructions, if Pa had had a shower.

"Yes," she said, "I gave him one myself. He wasn't happy about it. He was chuntering all the way through, so I gave him the shower head to hold, and he darn well soaked me."

(When I reported this later to Ma she said "Serves her right for giving it to him." Very robust. Very Ma.)

I had asked to speak to the house officer, and finally she arrived. She was young and bouncy, scrubbed and neat, and she had her blond hair scraped back into a bun. She was a young soldier doctor from the local army camp at Catterick. She was all dressed up in uniform trousers and shirt.

She took me to the nurses' tiny room, sat down and crossed her legs, and I'd barely got my bum on the seat of my chair when she said in a breezy tone, "Your father has a tumour on his lung, and we think the cancer has spread to his liver, because there is evidence of abnormal liver function."

"Oh," I said. *How could she just blurt it out like that?*

"We don't really want to operate because of his general ill health, and anyway it's probably inoperable." She re-crossed her legs and then moved her dangling foot in circles, as if she were doing warm-up exercises. "We could have a look at it if we gave him a bronchoscopy, and then we'd know for sure, but-"

"We don't, I mean my mother, none of us…the family… wants him to have a bronchoscopy. It would be too painful and unpleasant for him. He's old, and what would it prove?"

"Well," she said, straightening a paper on her clip board, "If you're all happy for him not to have a bronchoscopy, then we're happy not to do it." She got up, then, as if to go.

"How long do you think he will live, if nothing's done?" I said.

"I'd say he has weeks to live rather than months." She had her hand on the door knob.

"How do you know?"

She sighed and sat down again.

"That's easy," she said, as if I'd asked her a question in

an oral exam. "It's because he's deteriorating week by week. When we're judging how long it will be before a patient pops his clogs we look at the speed of deterioration."

Pops his clogs? Pops his clogs? Why did she think it was all right for her to talk like that? Did the woman assume that because we did not want them to operate, we would therefore not be upset at his death? Did she assume that because I was calm and rational, because Pa was old and confused, did she think I didn't need sensitive handling?

She got up again. "Now, the social worker wants to talk to you about the care package."

The social worker took me to her room, to talk about continuing care for Pa. The room was all done out in subtle, tasteful greens and blues. There were matching sofas, a pine dresser, a coffee table, and a telly up on a bracket in the corner of the room: a stilted attempt at homeliness, but welcome, even so.

She told me what they could offer in the way of care for Pa. Ma could choose between a hospital bed for him, or a nursing home, or care at home, though the social worker was not sure about exactly how much care there would be in the last option. She didn't think it would be 24 hours a day. Ma might have to cope for a few hours every day on her own.

"Is this the first time you've had the diagnosis confirmed?" she asked.

"Yes."

"And has anyone offered you a cup of tea?"

"No," I said, and crumpled. A show of kindness and sympathy is fatal when you're trying to stay tough and defended and calm. She handed me a box of tissues from the dresser, patted my shoulder and left the room to find a cup of tea.

When she came back, I told her about the family support there was - that Steve lived locally but Megan and I lived further away, but that we all wanted to do our bit, and to help.

"Your parents brought you up right, then," she said.

"They're both wonderful," I said, "but especially Ma."

"You and your brother and sister need to cherish each other," she said.

I went back to see Pa and he asked me when we were going home. I said he couldn't go home yet because we weren't ready for him. We were working out how we were going to look after him. I brought over the wheelchair and wrapped him up in two blankets and took him outside for a quick cigarette. When he flicked the ash it fell on his blanket and I had to keep shaking it off. I hardly spoke to him because there was no getting any kind of sense. And anyway, what could I say?

Back in the ward I sat and held his hand while he talked gibberish - entertaining gibberish, I have to say. I was sorry I couldn't catch all the words. He told me about people in the ward. "I suspect that this man here," (surreptitious pointing) "is a murderer. He wears murderers' clothes, he looks like a murderer…"

Then he said "The doctor is called Dr Day. He's also called Mr Day. And he's called Mr Sunny Day, Mr Bright Day…"

All of his statements, all of his nonsensical talk, was peppered with his own particular verbal tics that I knew so well e.g. "I suspect" "For some unknown reason" "Apparently."

"Apparently," he said, "this hospital was closed today, and so was the hotel next door."

I rang Megan from the hospital car park to tell her the

news. Then I rang Steve to tell him, and to ask him where he was working, because I needed a hug.

"People are going to wonder who the strange woman is that you're hugging on grass verges up and down the dale," I said, when I saw him.

"The locals know you, of course," he said. "But I've had a comment from a couple of incomers. That's fine. It'll enhance my reputation."

When I got home and told Ma the diagnosis, she didn't cry. She's a stoic. She is warm and kind but she rarely shows her feelings. If my parents' roles had been reversed and I'd been telling Pa that Ma was going to die, he would have wept.

I explained about the three options of care for Pa, and asked her what she wanted, she said – without hesitation – the nursing home. This made it very easy. But I have to admit that when she said it there was a catch inside me, at the thought of his not coming home again – for his sake. But Ma didn't hesitate, and it was she who had been caring for him for the last 58 years. Who was I to say what should happen?

That night Steve came round for a chat and a cuppa. Ma wanted him to move the bureau to the side wall in the sitting room, so that it stood underneath the bull picture – the huge Robert Nicholls pastel of a bull standing against lush May vegetation. I guess she had been wanting to do this for a while, but Pa had objected.

Steve moved it. And that meant that other furniture needed re-arranging. "What shall I do with this coffee table?" I said. "It's in the way, now."

"Oh," she said, "Let's get rid of it. It's a monstrosity. I've never liked it. We'll put it in the porch for the Age Concern collection."

Although it was dark, we hadn't drawn the curtains,

something that Pa always insisted on. He would say, "Draw the curtains, and keep the black pigs out," which is an old rural Irish saying that he got from his mother.

"I don't care about that," said Ma, when I mentioned it. "Leave the curtains." The first whiskers of liberation.

And no jelly to make. No egg for breakfast. No more meals to make if she didn't feel like it.

The next morning over breakfast, Ma and I talked about how to tell Pa that he was going to be moved to the nursing home.

I don't think Ma wanted to go to the hospital again, but she felt she had to go to thank the staff and to take them some chocolates. Steve rang to tell us he was at home that morning, doing some paperwork, so why didn't we call in to see him? We dragged our heels with errands in Leyburn and then we called at the farm. We admired his garden and sat on his garden bench in the sunshine drinking coffee, and then eventually we hauled ourselves off to Northallerton and the hospital.

Ma wanted to go to the loo before going up to the ward. She washed her hands with soap and water, and then her face, and dried them with paper towels. It seemed a strange thing to do – to wash her face - but then I remembered how when we were little and fell over and hurt ourselves she would cuddle us and then say "Now go and wash your face and make yourself feel better."

We went upstairs to the ward, and Ma stopped at the nurses' station. She asked if anyone had told Pa that he would be moving. No-one had.

She thanked them for looking after him and gave them the chocolates, saying they were for everyone, every one of the staff, signalling to include the orderlies and the clerk, as well as the nurses.

The staff nurse was kind. I hadn't seen her before. She laid her hand on Ma's shoulder and said "Thank you," and "you're welcome," and something else, and Ma started to cry, and then stopped herself.

We went round the corner to see Pa and he was as far away as I'd seen him. He was like a baby.

When his lunch arrived, the orderly had to cut up his food for him and Pa ate it with a spoon - great lumps of baked potato mashed up with baked beans. A month ago he would have scorned such a meal if we'd offered it to him at home. Though 'scorned' is too meagre a word.

He ate a banana and Ma said she couldn't remember the last time he'd eaten one. There was a piece of fruit cake in a cellophane wrapper. He struggled unsuccessfully to open it, and resorted to putting it in his mouth to rip the wrapper with his teeth, but couldn't do it, and then he must have forgotten what he was doing because he absent-mindedly put the whole thing in his mouth and tried to bite it.

I gently took it out of his mouth and opened it for him and put it on his plate.

"Look at all the cherries," said Ma. "Are you going to have some of it? You like cherries, don't you?"

"No, I don't want it," he said.

"Are you tired? Would you like to go to sleep?"

"Yes," he said.

It was painful to see her sitting next to him. She did not hold his hand. Eventually she laid her hand on his thigh. She hated the lack of privacy in the ward. I went off to ask the nurses to put him into bed. I leant against the door frame of their room and as I spoke I wept. The kind nurse took me into her room and asked, "Would you like to sit down? Are you all right?"

I wiped my eyes and struggled not to cry any more, and said "I don't want to cry in front of my mother."

They settled him in bed and we said goodbye and left. I had dreaded telling him we weren't taking him home. But in the event, Ma just said "They're going to move you somewhere else tomorrow, and it's too far for us to push you in the wheelchair." He smiled at this. "So you're going in an ambulance, and we'll meet you there."

"Will you?" he asked.

"Yes."

He seemed to accept it. So it was not too hard.

✳ ✳ ✳

The next day Ma and I went to the nursing home first thing, to introduce ourselves - as Ma put it - and to look at Pa's room. It was only a five minute drive from Aysgarth, the other side of Thornton Rust. It was a large Victorian country house with a sweeping drive, set in large lawned grounds with mature trees everywhere. On the front steps were some pots and in them the very same, unusual tulips – white and a delicate and pretty pale pink - that Pa bought last year as bulbs, and which Steve planted for him in the garden. That felt like a sign. I picked up the two petals that had fallen onto the step. They were satiny smooth. I kept them in my hand as we walked through the door.

The matron had been at school with Steve. She was brisk and breezy and jokey, and Ma seemed taken aback. She showed us round and then we drove home.

The hospital had promised to ring us when Pa set off in the ambulance to go to the nursing home, so that we could be there when he arrived. We had gone home and had lunch and still had not heard from them by two o'clock so I rang them and they said the ambulance had already taken him.

I was furious they hadn't rung us and warned us, and upset that we wouldn't be there to welcome him, and I rushed around grabbing things to take for him, such as the Heaton Cooper print which hung in the window recess by the chair he always sat in, in the dining room.

When we got to the nursing home, he was already installed in the easy chair in his room, munching his way through a bag of chocolates and sweets. He had chocolate dribble down the front of his jumper. We could not understand what he said, nor get him to understand us. I worried that his hearing aid wasn't working, but I think now that he was just confused.

He tidied his little table compulsively, setting things straight, neatening his book and his cards, and placing his glasses on top of the television remote control. He would pick up tiny specks of tissue and shreds of sweet wrapper and put them in the bin. And he would pick at tiny marks on his jumper or pluck at the chair piping where it had gone white. I didn't recognise this as Pa-type behaviour.

I showed him the Heaton Cooper. "Look, I've brought this for you," I said.

"Very nice," he said, as though he hadn't seen it before. My father collected pictures. He visited galleries and exhibitions. He knew his artists. He knew his art. *Very nice?* I hung it on the wall, opposite his chair.

We left him sitting watching television with the sound turned off. He was calm.

That night I slept until 1.30 a.m. and then spent three hours tossing and turning, unable to sleep. I gave up for a while and listened to the BBC World Service and eventually dozed off.

When I got up I felt like a wreck and decided to have a bath, though I never normally have baths at Hollycroft because the bath is so huge that you can't lean against the end. When I lay back in the bath, it was so big I nearly drowned. I rang Viv on my mobile. She was sitting in the shed at the allotment.

"How's it going, babe? How is your dad? How's your mum? And you? Are you coping all right?"

"Just about. It's nice to hear your voice."

She told me that Elspeth hadn't been using my house for a refuge in which to work, because Barnes, her son, had been attacked outside a nightclub and so was staying with her until he felt robust enough to go back to work.

"Hey," said Viv, "You know that goofy guy up here with the nice tanned legs – Tim?"

"Ye-es?" Oh, God, what was she going to say?

"He asked me why I never go to the meetings. He said there'd been mutterings about our plot. A couple of them said we should be made to replace our grass verges."

"But there weren't any when we took it over. What are they on about?"

"I told him that, and he said he'd put them straight. I told you they were a weird lot. You can just imagine it if we dared to buy the wrong type of compost bin, can't you? They'd think we were plotting an anarchist revolution."

"You didn't say that to him, did you?"

"No, no. But it was strange, because the next thing was, he was asking me if I was interested in being a guerrilla gardener."

"What's that?" I said. Had Tim got hidden depths?

"Oh, sorry babe, can't talk now. Someone wants to borrow my kettle. I'll tell you later. Look after yourself. Bye."

I rang Charles. "I'm in a bath," I said. But he was opening up the shop and couldn't talk. He said he'd ring back later.

The bath water was getting cold, so I topped it up, and lay back, resting on my elbows, to stop me from slipping under the water.

"Are you all right, Corinne?" called Ma from outside the bathroom door.

"Do you want me to come out?"

"No, you stay there as long as you like. No hurry."

Before I faced the day, I needed to talk to someone else who was friendly but was outside the situation. I checked the time on my mobile. Rob would be getting ready for his morning ride. I rang him.

"How are you?" he said. "How's your dad?"

I told him what had been going on and he listened like an old friend.

"The nursing home is as nice as can be. But I wish he was here," I said. "I wish he was home. I wish he was himself. He's turned into someone else. I can't bear it. I've started waking up in the middle of the night. I lie there with everything going round and round in my head and can't get back to sleep."

"I don't sleep well, either, so when you get home you can text me and I can come round and give you a Photoshop tutorial on your computer. I've bought you a little A5 hardback notebook so you can write down all the instructions – I know you never remember them."

"That's sweet."

"Yes, well, on second thoughts, you probably won't need me to come round in the night. I know you have someone else who's up for that."

Megan arrived in the middle of the morning. It was such

a relief to have her there that when I met her at the door and gave her a hug, my eyes filled with tears.

"I have waited and waited for you to come," I said, as if I were Jo in *Little Women*, waiting for Marmee to come home when Beth was ill with scarlet fever.

Megan is cheerful and matter-of-fact like Ma. She bustled about, bringing in things from the car, like a little box of raspberries for Pa because he likes them so much, and bottles of wine and nibbles from Marks and Spencer for us. And she brought a huge cool-bag full of frozen meals for Ma that she'd prepared at home.

She said we should all go out that night for a meal, and Ma said she was happy to go, so they rang up and booked a table at the Fox and Hounds in West Burton.

Emma, Megan's older daughter, arrived later. Megan has two boys and two girls, late teens and twenty-somethings.

All through the day I was tearful. When Steve called in and gave me a big hug, I cried. He had taken his dog George to visit Pa, and he said Pa's eyes had lit up at the sight of George.

After lunch Megan and Emma were going to the nursing home so I found Pa's large book of Carl Larsson prints for them to take for Pa.

"Did he look at it?" I asked when they got back. "Did he seem to recognise the pictures?"

"He wasn't good. They've put him back to bed," said Megan. "He was wandering around in the night so they've moved him to a room downstairs."

It felt odd to go out for a meal that night, with Pa lying so ill at the nursing home, but no-one else seemed to think it mattered. It wasn't too bad, not all of the time, anyway: Emma entertained us with funny stories about life in her office.

Just before I went to bed I checked my mobile for messages. There was a text from Charles: *When are you coming back?* I didn't text back.

I slept in Pa's room at Hollycroft that night.

In the morning I intended to go back to Sheffield for a few days, so I went to the nursing home straight after breakfast to say goodbye to Pa, but he looked terrible. He was lying in bed with his hair all ragged and his eyes were wild. I know he recognised me, but he couldn't speak. I sat with him and fed him a few of Megan's raspberries with my fingers.

The matron came in and drew me over to the other side of the room.

"Your Dad was struggling in the night and I sat with him," she said. "I don't think you should be going home. I know the signs. You need to be ringing your family."

Megan drove up straight away with Ma.

The doctor came later on and examined Pa, and told Ma he wanted a word with her. Matron signalled to me and to Megan to come out too. We all trooped down the long corridor to her office. The doctor sat opposite mother and leaned forward close to her, his head ducked down, his voice calm and serious, making close eye contact all the time, and said "He's not going to get better. And it looks as though it's going to be fast."

"It's better if it's fast," said Ma.

"And you don't need to worry," he said, "we'll make him comfortable. We won't let him be in any pain."

One or other of us sat with Pa all day. I didn't want him to be alone.

Later in the afternoon we were all there together. We got the staff to move his bed over to the window so that we could have chairs on both sides of his bed and Steve sat Pa up in the bed so that his lungs could drain. He also lit him a cigarette, and we fanned the smoke out of the window, though the matron had said that as he was in a room on his own she really didn't mind about his smoking.

Megan stayed with Pa that night. I slept in Pa's bed again, at Hollycroft, and had a nightmare which woke me up. Pa had woken up from a deep untroubled sleep and punched back the covers and leapt out of bed. He was fully dressed in corduroys and a shirt. He messed up an arrangement of patches I had laid out on my dining room table, trying to work out the design for my quilt, and then he started climbing the walls and acting like a mad thing.

I gave up trying to sleep at two o' clock, and read a book of Pa's - Katharine Whitehorn's *Observations* – an old collection from her columns in *The Observer.*

The drive between Aysgarth and the nursing home was lovely, with sweet cicely and cow parsley lining the hedgerows and a couple of stray lambs always on the road by a particular gate. Was it the same lambs sneaking out to play every day? The next morning they had a third with them, and one of them was springing up vertically on its stiff little legs - so comical I laughed out loud.

The next night Steve spent the night with Pa. Steve said that every 45 seconds all through the night Pa stopped breathing, and then would panic and wake up and start breathing fiercely again.

I took over from Steve. I sat there waiting for the matron to come down and give Pa some morphine, because Steve said it was a while since Pa had had some.

He was grabbing the cot side and struggling, and it was difficult to concentrate on anything but him.

His cheeks were sunken, his cheek bones protruded. His

nose looked big and beaky. His hair was fluffy and stuck up on top. His eyes were sunken with huge sweeping circles of purple bruise under and around the eye socket. His eyes were cloudy and grey, like old faded heather, and I didn't know whether he could see anything when he opened them.

He looked like the father of the butler in the film of *The Remains of the Day* – the archetypal old, dying man. He didn't look like Pa any more. If they told me to look around the home to see if my father was there I would say that he wasn't. Except for his hands: those hands could only belong to Pa.

When he opened his eyes fully I talked to him, though he couldn't answer. I told him about all the people who had asked after him and about all the people who had sent him their love.

Outside the window was a conker tree and more than enough blue sky to make a sailor a pair of trousers. I could hear a wood pigeon. It was beautifully peaceful in the room, though there was a lady across the hall who rang her bell or called out a lot for the nurses to come, and whenever they did they were unfailingly patient.

Megan, Steve and I were keeping in touch on our mobile phones. The reception wasn't good from Pa's room for talking, and anyway it would have been a shame to talk and disturb him, so we sent each other texts. It was unobtrusive. We could tell each other how Pa was, and if there was any change in his condition. We could say how we were feeling – if we were tired and wanted a break, lonely and craving some company, or sad and needing a hug. All without leaving the room or disturbing Pa. It was like magic messaging, like the lemon juice invisible writing we used to do when we were little.

Pa's eyes had been closed for an hour or so, so I moved to

the spare bed and sat there propped up against the wall. His breathing was shallow and rattling and it sounded as if he was gargling in the back of his throat. The man in the next door room started calling out the same phrase over and over. Every day he had a phase of doing this. Just then he was calling "My dinner, my dinner," on a falling note. He used a falling note in all of his phrases.

Pa's room was peaceful, but it was a mess. There were four sets of single width drawers, painted cream, a wardrobe, a wash basin in each of two corners, a high backed chair in green upholstery with wooden arms - most comfortable - and a chair with no arms, a dining chair, an invalid table and a spare bed. Everything was higgledy piggledy, and I had no energy to make it straight. Feng Shui would be having kittens if he'd been there. Pa was in the corner of the bagua to do with fame. Maybe he should have been in the part of the bagua associated with the elders, or with contemplation.

His face was so unlike the face I'd known all my life. His cheeks were so sunken and his cheekbones stuck out so much he was beginning to look like a rosy cheeked skull, with a crown of white fluffy hair, and his lovely bushy eyebrows in grey and white.

Pa died the next morning at 8 a.m.

CHAPTER 10

Megan spent Pa's last night with him, and Steve had gone up early after breakfast, so they were both there when he died. I was getting ready to go to the nursing home when they rang with the news.

Ma stayed at home, saying she had said goodbye to him the day before. So I drove up on my own.

When I opened the door of his room, Megan and Steve were sitting by his bed, and so were the matron and a nurse. It felt like an intrusion. Why were they there?

I looked at him from the doorway, called "Pa" and rushed over and kissed him, crying. Then I turned round to the matron and said "Are you sure?"

"Yes, darling. I'm sure."

She and the nurse left then, and we sat for a while and talked. Steve kissed Pa goodbye and left. He had to go and deal with a cow with mastitis. Megan and I stayed. She sorted Pa's clothes and left them folded on the chair. We packed up all his other things to take home, but when I bent down to pick up his slippers, my head started swimming. I thought I must be ill, so when we went down to the matron's office to talk about funeral arrangements, I asked her to check my blood pressure. She humoured me and did it, and it was fine. Of course.

As we were leaving I asked the matron, "Will he be all alone? In his room?" I didn't like the thought of him being there all alone.

"We'll leave him there and you can come back to see him any time you like today. You might feel you need to come back. Some people do."

When we got back to Hollycroft, we talked to Ma about local undertakers and which one to use. In the end, Ma insisted that we asked the one from the village, so Megan rang him and arranged for him to come in the afternoon to discuss arrangements.

Then Steve arrived and said he was going up to the nursing home to see Pa again and to tidy him up, so I went with him. I sat and held Pa's hand - which was still warm - while Steve brushed Pa's hair and clipped and filed his nails. It was reassuring to be there with Steve: he was calm and practical and focussed, and we even shared a joke. When he put Pa's teeth in - with a little difficulty, and with some help from me - I said the Morecambe and Wise phrase "What do you think of it so far?" and then I made Pa mouth the answer "Rubbish." Pa had gone.

Back at Hollycroft, Megan was itching to sort stuff out. She was Pa's executor. She began mowing her way through the papers in Pa's bureau drawers, putting some in the bin to her left, and some to her right in a pile to keep. Steve and I crept in and sat silently behind her on the floor, and as Megan put something in the bin to her left, Steve took it out, passed it to me for inspection, and I would then put it in the pile "to keep." Eventually, we packed her off to sort out the pantry, something we considered could do with clearing out.

We then loaded everything back in the drawer for looking at later - without Megan. Megan was a whiz with power of attorney stuff, but we didn't trust her to make decisions about sentimental papers. Even Ma has a notice in her room (for when she dies) saying that nothing is to be thrown away without Steve's and my permission.

The undertaker came after lunch, and we all sat around in the sitting room - mother, Megan, Steve, and me - to decide on what to do. Somehow it had been agreed - when I wasn't there - that we were going to have a private family burial on the Saturday (three days later) at the Quaker Meeting House in Carperby - where Pa had had a plot booked for twenty years. Then we would have a memorial service for everyone to come to the following week.

The arrangements were a funny mixture. On the one hand we wanted simplicity, as is the Quaker way, with no minister, no flowers, other than one bunch from us. And Megan insisted we didn't need any bearers. She wanted to be one of them, with Steve and his two sons.

And yet we had very particular tastes as to fixtures for the coffin. We wanted an inexpensive coffin, so it would have to be veneer. We asked for a light wood with a prominent grain, with wooden handles. The undertaker told us he had run out of wooden handles and offered chrome. A chorus of disgusted groans ran round the room. Steve said "You'd better get your router out, then," and Megan said "Perhaps you could order some."

On top of the coffin we wanted a plaque inscribed with RDM, Pa's initials. This was my suggestion.

When the undertaker had gone, I rang some florists to order a bouquet of sweet peas to come from mother and from the sibs (this is my pet name for the three of us – the siblings.) I really wanted to get some flowers that Pa would like. But none of the florists in the dale could promise to get sweet peas in time for Saturday. At that time of year it would have to be a special order and there wasn't time for this. So then I tried to get some yellow roses with a fragrance - because Pa liked his Arthur Bells so much, but no-one could get those either. So we had to make do with a sheath of unscented red roses, pink ones with a fragrance, foliage and gypsophila. In the middle of the phone conversation with the florist I started weeping and couldn't speak, and Megan kindly took over from me. We asked for a label to say, "All our love, from Mary and the chundies" (Pa's name for the three of us).

The Friend from Quaker Meeting in charge of the burial ground was having difficulty getting hold of the plan of the graves, which he needed in order to tell the undertaker exactly where Pa should be buried. Not only were there other graves to be avoided in the tiny plot - there was a drain pipe, too. There were several phone calls between him and Megan, and we tried to keep from mother the difficulty he was having, and the uncertainty about whether it would be sorted out before the burial on the Saturday.

All through the day Ma and we sibs lurched between tears and laughter in a way that was both comforting and liberating. It felt as though we all knew and accepted that each was upset, and we didn't have to be proper, or to make any kind of pretence. The closeness, the intimacy, the warmth and the comfort from being all together, with no hangers on in the shape of spouses, partners or children, felt special. A special kind of special. It was the first time we'd been all together with no-one else like that since we were little.

But late in the afternoon there was a time when it got a bit sticky. We were sitting in the dining room and Megan and Steve were talking about the arrangement of the furniture and someone suggested moving the book case, and then someone said yes, and what about getting rid of *this*, and *that*, and *so on*, and I told them to stop it and shut up. It felt unseemly to be talking about changing anything - whatever it was - when Pa had only died that morning.

At the evening meal the hilarious hysterics returned when we were eating Megan's Bolognese sauce with pasta penne, and mother burst out laughing.

"It's the penne," she spluttered. "It's just like the drain pipe in the burial ground that runs near the graves, that the gravedigger's going to…" she couldn't finish her sentence for laughing, and we all joined in.

We told her about the flowers we'd ordered and the message – All our love, Mary and the chundies.

"And you can put something else on there: p.s. I'll see you later, Mary."

Later on, after Steve had gone home and we'd washed up, Megan and I went out to get some air. We walked up the road towards Thoralby and stood at the crest of the hill looking over the gate towards Pen Hill. We stood apart. It felt lonely then. It felt as though we were each entombed in our separate griefs. We shivered in the chilly evening and heard the curlews calling and Megan said it made her think of Pa and his birdwatching. It made me think of the curlews in a watercolour he had hanging on the landing.

I fell asleep quickly that night, but then I awoke at three in the morning with my mind alive with stuff about Pa, and about us clearing out his things, and generally about throwing things away, and how our family is hopeless at it, except for Megan.

The next morning I thought Ma would be desperate for some peace, so I persuaded Megan to go out and do some shopping and some errands and I would stay home and answer the phone. There were oases of quiet, but the phone rang constantly.

We all wanted a small number at the burial - just family. But really and truly a part of me just wanted Ma and the sibs, because I only wanted people there who loved Pa without reservation. He could be selfish and rude in his latter years, and irascible because of the pain in his legs. It's understandable that chronic pain from the deep vein thrombosis frayed his temper. If I were not his flesh and blood who had known him and loved him from childhood, I would not have had the little patience I had with him. What I wanted for the burial was to have only people there who loved him.

Viv and Elspeth kept texting me little messages and that was a comfort.

✳ ✳ ✳

Ed, Megan's husband, arrived from Amsterdam the night before the burial. He'd been away on business. He drove up from Hull feeling rough after his ferry trip, with severe indigestion, and we packed him off to bed.

Megan came downstairs and said "He always gets the collywobbles when he's upset. Have you got any nux vomica, Ma? That's what I give him at home. Did you know it's derived from strychnine?"

Ma looked in her box of homeopathic remedies but hadn't got any. "Here," she said. "Give him some arsenicum."

"Well, doctor," said Megan, laughing, "we didn't have any strychnine so we gave him arsenic."

Steve and Martine came over to join us for the evening meal. It was roast beef, Pa's favourite.

That night, I slept at the next door neighbour's house to make room for Ed. But I woke up at five in the morning and crept back to Hollycroft. I sat in Pa's reclining chair by the dining room window, swaddled in a blanket, feeling sad.

All week there had been a succession of sunshine and showers and a gusty wind. It was the same that morning. We kept looking at the sky to see if there was enough blue sky to make a sailor a pair of trousers, but there never was.

At half past eleven we took two cars to Bainbridge to meet the hearse. Megan's husband, Ed, drove Ma and Megan in the first car, and I rode with Steve and his family in their car. The dale was looking lovely, and the river was running a full pot. The rain on the new May leaves made their freshness glisten. There was cow parsley and sweet cicely billowing on the verges all of the way, and the may blossom coated the hawthorns with cream. Lady Hill, Pa's favourite hill, looked its best, in his honour, with the cluster of pine trees on the top silhouetted against the misty, rainy distance. On the green at Bainbridge the leaves on the big copper beech were fully out, but still new enough for their colour to be at their richest intensity. Pa would have commented on the tree.

I wept silently for much of the short journey, and Steve or Martine kept reaching out their hands to comfort me.

We drove back down the other side of the dale to Carperby. Waiting there was a man, John, who was there from my parents' Quaker Meeting, to introduce the service.

Megan, Steve, and his two sons carried the coffin from the hearse up into the tiny burial ground. I stood close to Ma on the road. She had her arm linked through mine. She carried a small posy from the garden – two different small purple flowers, lilies-of-the-valley, variegated leaves, and three of Pa's yellow Arthur Bell rosebuds, barely open.

When they had lowered the coffin into the grave, the rest of us went up the steps to join them. I hated the flowers on the coffin. The pink roses were a deep, disgusting, synthetic, dolly-mixture pink, which Pa would have loathed, and I felt I had let him down.

The rain stopped and the sun came out and we could hear the birds singing. There was cow parsley behind the grave and it all felt right. John began the Quaker Meeting for Worship by reading something written by William Penn, and we had ten minutes silence. Then we shook hands. Ma shook hands with everyone. After the morning of tears and tension it was very calming. It felt complete. We talked quietly and then went back to Hollycroft, where we had a buffet lunch in the dining room. We put Ma's posy in a vase in the middle of the table, and for the tea we used the silver teapot that Pa's grandfather had won at the Birmingham Cattle Show in 1868.

It was a comfortable meal. One of the quiches was leek and Stilton, and I missed Pa saying "as good a Stilton as I've tasted in years." But anyway, it probably wasn't.

CHAPTER 11

I arrived back at Ferndean Row at tea-time. It was a chilly May, and I planned to light the stove and snuggle down on the sofa under my knitted blanket, watching old videos of *Due South*, the series with the mountie in it. It was times like this that I wished I was going back to something warmer than a knitted blanket. And I don't mean a cat.

As soon as I opened the door, I could tell someone had been in the house. When I go away I always intend to leave the house tidy but never quite manage it. That's because I always forget something and remember it as I am driving off and I stop the van, leave the engine running and rush into the house to grab what I need and rush back to the van as fast as I can. If the something I've forgotten is at the bottom of the drawer, then the drawer is left open. If the something is in a cupboard, then the cupboard door is left open. Usually I forget at least three things, so a trail of untidiness greets me when I get back.

Today, all the cupboard doors were closed, the post was neatly stacked on the table, all the surfaces were tidy and wiped, and someone had washed out the plastic washing up bowl in the sink and turned it on it's side, and they'd rinsed the dish cloth through and hung it on the tap. And I could swear they'd cleaned the smudges off my chrome kettle and toaster. Elspeth. Of course.

Also, the house was warm. I walked through to the sitting room, and yes, the fire was glowing. I opened the draft a bit, threw on a shovelful of coke, and went back to the kitchen to make some tea.

I sat in the carver chair, waiting for the kettle to boil and thought of Pa. I don't think I ever described him as "a wonderful father" but he was my father and I loved him. All my life I felt as though I sailed in a sturdy ship, my family, looking down on other mortals whose ships were not so handsome and fine as mine. When he died it was as though someone had blown a hole in the side of our craft. I sat and snivelled.

The kettle clicked off. I poured boiling water onto the teabag in my mug and automatically reached over and opened the fridge door before I remembered that I'd been away and there'd be no milk.

But there was. How sweet of Elspeth. But maybe it wasn't Elspeth. Viv said she hadn't been working at my house because of Barnes. So it must be Rob, because he had my other spare key.

Maybe he'd bought bread as well. I lifted the breadbin lid and peeked inside and there was a wheaten loaf from Rose the Bakers.

I drank my tea, and then went to thank him.

When he opened his back door he was wearing jeans, a

grandad collarless shirt and a Fair Isle tank top. I mention what he was wearing because it was only the second time I'd seen him in something other than cycling gear. And that time he had been at home in his kitchen, too. Every time I saw him outside his house he was wearing Lycra.

He opened the door wide. "Come in."

I stepped inside, wiped my feet and took in the minimalist kitchen. It was the first time I'd ever been inside his house. He had an eclectic mix of streamlined techno stuff and retro chic, such as the brown glazed teapot in a tea cosy knitted in yellow and red and white, the teapot sitting on a black granite work surface. On the wall above the breakfast bar was a framed print of a cartoon.

"How are you?" he said, before I got chance to read the cartoon caption. "How did it go? Here, take a pew…well, stool." He pulled out a stool from under the breakfast bar.

"Rob. Thank you. Thank you so much." I continued to stand.

"I'm sorry about your dad." He reached out and touched my shoulder, a brief, quick contact.

"Thanks for making the house so welcoming. Buying me bread and milk. How did you know I'd be back tonight?"

"Some strange woman accosted me outside Somerfield when I was locking up my bike. I've no idea how she knew I was your next door neighbour."

"What was she like?"

"Noisy."

I laughed. "No, what did she look like?"

"Dashing. Blonde streaks. Green eyes. Lots of slap. Tight jeans. Crisp white shirt. Boots."

"That's Viv," I said. Gosh – he thought Viv was dashing – I'd have to tell her. She'd be really chuffed. "Well, thanks,

Rob. I really appreciate it. Especially as the last time I saw you I slammed the door in your face. I–"

"Forget that. I just thought that…well, coming home to an empty house after a …" He scratched his head. "Have you got everything you need?"

✳ ✳ ✳

"My lovely lady. Is it all done, now? Can I come over? I don't think I can wait any longer." I had rung Charles to tell him I was back.

"I'm not–"

"I've missed you. I'll jump in the car now. I'll be with you ASAP."

"Charles, I don't think…I'm not sure…I–"

"What is it, lovely lady?"

"I'm a bit tired. You know, drained. It's been a long day."

"Of course. What am I thinking? Tomorrow?"

"Maybe. I'll give you a ring."

✳ ✳ ✳

The next night I opened the door feeling flat inside. I knew it would be Charles, and I didn't feel like seeing anyone. Not even him.

"Hello," I said. I tried to smile warmly. I'm not sure I managed it.

"For you," he said, flourishing a big bunch of roses he'd had behind his back.

"Oh. Scarlet. My favourite colour." Did I sound sufficiently pleased?

He stepped inside the kitchen and put his arms round me

without giving me chance to put down the bouquet and he kissed me, a deep, passionate kiss, but then he stopped, mid-tongue, and drew away.

"There's not much heart in that," he said. "Have I done something wrong? Am I in the dog house?"

"No. No, of course not. I just feel a bit, well, I'm just… I'm…"

"Yes?"

"Sad."

"Of course you are.

"I never expected to feel like this. So bad, I mean. It's not as if it was sudden. He was 84. He's not been himself since Christmas. He was ill for the last two months, but–"

"Eighty-four? He had a good innings, then."

"A good innings? I know he was old." From Pa's point of view, it was good he'd had a long life – but that didn't stop it hurting for the people who were left behind without him. "It's me I feel sorry for," I said, "not him. I don't want him–" I couldn't bring myself to say the word *dead*, "not here."

"I'm sorry for your loss." He sounded like a vicar in a movie. Something like that. He didn't sound like himself.

"Why do people have to die?"

"What did you say?"

"Why do people have to die?"

"Pardon?"

"You heard."

"Steady the buffs, now, don't jump down my throat. Let's sit down and talk. Let's just go in your room and settle down a bit. Go flop bot. Is a chap allowed to have a drink?"

"Of course, of course. I'm sorry." I laid the flowers carefully on the sink and poured him a glass of wine from the opened bottle in the fridge. Then I half heartedly looked in the cupboards, trying to find a vase that was big enough to hold two dozen long stemmed roses, two sprays of gypsophila and oodles of greenery. I knew it was a lost cause, but I went through the motions, and then ended up filling the sink with cold water and standing the bouquet in there, leaning against the taps. I knew Charles wouldn't like it if I put them in my galvanised bucket in the shed, though actually it could look quite trendy. "I'll find something later to put these in." I said, turning round, but Charles had taken the wine bottle and two glasses and gone into the sitting room.

"It will take time, of course," he said, as we sat together on the sofa. "A week or so. I understand. But now you have the ceremony over you'll-" He had his hand on my knee. I got up and rearranged the cushions on the sofa and then sat down again, out of his reach.

I said, "There's the memorial service yet - I thought I said - it was just a private family burial, but we're having a memorial service for everyone next week. I'm dreading the drive up there on my own. I was wondering if… I wondered… are you doing anything next Wednesday?"

"Oh, now, yes. Yes I am. I'm sorry, sweetheart." He shuffled up the sofa, nearer to me, and reached out and smoothed a strand of hair off my face, tucking it behind my ear. "Awfully sorry."

I shook my head and my hair fell forwards again. Then I got up and stood by the stove, facing him, my hands in my jeans pockets.

"Is it important?" I asked him. "The thing you're doing on Wednesday?"

"I can't actually put my finger on what it is, but I know there's something in my diary. I'm sorry. But you drive up there all the time. What's the problem?"

"It's just that I don't want to – you know – drive on my own – it's all so hard."

"Why don't you go on the train, then?" he said, completely missing the point. Was he being obtuse on purpose?

"We're talking rural transport, Charles. The nearest station is 25 miles away."

"How about if I spring you for a taxi from the station?" he said, as if money was what I was after.

❋ ❋ ❋

The next morning I wandered disconsolately into the wash house to see if I could drum up any enthusiasm for my glass work. I sat on the stool, and looked at the current pattern I was working on. It looked as meaningful to me as a design for a space ship. I picked up a piece of cobalt blue glass and held it up to the light. I did the same with one in sap green.

I heard someone's steps in the yard.

"Hello," I called.

"Hi," said Rob, coming into the shed.

"I just came round to tell you about this software package that I should have shown you before – Picasa. I think you'd find it useful for editing your photographs."

"Thanks," I said. I put the green glass down. "Do you think I'll ever want to do this again?" I said. "Do you think it will get better after the memorial service? I'm dreading it. And Charles can't drive me up."

"Why isn't lover-boy going?"

"He's got a meeting, and do you have to be so rude?"

"I know him."

Sometimes Rob got on my nerves. "Yes. You said. You were at school with him."

"He was a right poser, even then. Why does he have to act as if he's from the minor aristocracy?"

So it wasn't just me who thought the way Charles talked was odd… but I wasn't going to admit this to Rob. I folded my arms.

"When did you say the service was?" said Rob. "Wednesday? If your van is insured for other drivers, I could come up with you – drive you," he said.

"That's kind, but Viv offered too. And it is kind of you, but, well, she has been up there before, you know, met my parents, so–"

"Right enough. That makes sense. I'm pleased you have someone who cares enough to…any road, must be off…it's a bit too parky today to be standing around in shorts."

✳ ✳ ✳

Viv and I agreed that I would drive up to Wensleydale in my van for the memorial service, and she would take over afterwards and drive us back to Sheffield at the end of the day.

"Do you want to chat… or be quiet?" she asked, as I slowed down at the traffic lights on the Parkway at the junction with the M1.

"Tell me what's happening in allotment world," I said. "You never explained what a guerrilla gardener is."

She told me that Tim and two others from the allotments were in a group who found neglected public spaces in Sheffield and planted them with shrubs and flowers.

"You know, little plots of scrubby soil built into pavements, ones that have never been planted, or where there was originally a sapling and it's died. That kind of thing. *We have a six point plan*, he said. I thought he was going to get a laptop out of his rucksack and do me a Power Point presentation."

"I never imagined Tim could be so...so interesting. So what is the six point plan?"

"Clear litter. Clear weedy growth. Add new soil. Plant stuff. Go to pub." She counted on her fingers. "Oh, that's five. Whatever."

"Are you going to do it?"

"Nah. Can't be doing with the hassle. I'm amazed to find that I actually like gardening. But it's about being peaceful. I get enough rushing around at school, and plenty of aggro."

"What? From the children?"

"The kids are fantastic. Did I tell you they really love that introductory philosophy I'm doing with them? No, the aggro is from the education department. So, I don't need any adrenalin rushes in my leisure time." She reached into her bag for her flask and poured a drink. "Plus," she said, "Tim said I ought to get some wellington shoes if I was going to join in. Apparently they're less conspicuous than boots. As if I'd be seen dead in something so naff. Shall I pour you a drink?"

"I'll wait until we stop for your fag break, thanks."

I drove through Carperby on the way to Hollycroft so I could visit the burial ground and leave some flowers on Pa's grave. I had bought some yellow roses the day before and they'd been standing in water in a bucket in the wash house, to keep them fresh. They didn't have a fragrance, but at least they were the right colour. Viv walked up to the end of the village and back, having a smoke, while I went into the tiny burial ground.

When we arrived at the cottage, Megan and her husband Ed were outside in the garden, dead-heading tulips. They both gave me a giant hug and I introduced Viv.

"We were just having a laugh about Jonathan," said Megan. Jonathan is their youngest. "He had absolutely nothing respectable – and I mean *nothing* – to wear. I never realised the true state of his wardrobe till this morning. He has only one tidy T shirt and that has a skull printed on the back – not exactly suitable for a memorial service."

"Where is he?"

"Inside chatting to Steve's two. He doesn't look too awful. In the end he chose his least shaggy trousers and a polo neck jumper which he gave to Ed as a cast off a couple of years ago. Funny, isn't it, that nowadays it's the parents who wear the children's cast offs?"

I wouldn't know. The only kids I know well are Elspeth's three, and there was no way she would want to wear any of *their* clothes. Elspeth was a Marks and Spencer woman, Barnes was a Goth, Charlotte was nearly thirty but she still had strong punk tendencies, and Jessica was half the size of her mother, in every dimension.

My parents' house was stuffed full of family and extended family, with someone sitting in every chair, and huge adult grandchildren all dressed in black lining the walls like gigantic bats in a cave. It's at times like these, at extended family gatherings, that I feel most alone. So to have Viv there was a comfort. It felt so different from the Saturday before, on the day of the burial. The atmosphere had changed: it was becoming a public event, with people expected to behave in constrained and respectable ways.

Viv and I were hungry, so after a few desultory introductions, we went into the kitchen to find something to eat. Megan had saved a plateful of remains from the cold lunch they'd all shared, but the quiche tasted of dishwater and I left it.

The service was at the Quaker Meeting House in Bainbridge, a few miles up the dale. It was built in the 1700s and has high windows and austere lines, and a raised platform at the front for the elders, and benches to sit on, and polished wooden floorboards. Even the loo is decorated in impeccable plain taste with bare white walls and a rag rug on the floor. I sat for five minutes in there after I'd finished peeing, just looking at the rug. I wanted to examine the construction to see if the maker had used the same method as me. But when I came out of the loo I couldn't remember anything about the rug, not even the colours.

Ma wanted the family and extended family to sit on one side of the Meeting House, with her and the three chundies sitting on the front row. We all walked in together from the hall, and when we sat down she held the hands of the two who were sitting next to her - Steve and me. She had asked that the service be only half an hour long, rather than the full hour, because she wanted the children who were there to be able to sit through the service without fidgeting. I don't go to Meeting often, only when I am staying with my parents, but I was disappointed with the length of the Meeting. How can you give thanks for someone's life in half an hour?

In a Quaker Meeting for Worship, you're supposed to attend "with heart and mind prepared" so that when the Spirit moves, you are ready to listen. If you feel moved by the Spirit to get up to speak, you do, but otherwise you sit, and stay silent. There is a little leeway for funerals and memorial services: sometimes people go with something prepared… but only minimally.

We had agreed the week before that Megan should read Pa's poem that he wrote about a farmer who'd lost all his cattle to foot and mouth disease, because we think the poem is one of his finest, and also because it's moving.

Steve got up to speak after Megan - something about the similarities and differences between life and farming. He ended up with that quote "Live as if you'll die tomorrow, farm as if you'll farm forever."

Then I got up and told the riddle that Megan's daughter Emma had made up about Pa when she was three. "What bellows but loves people?" Several people chuckled. Whatever else he had been, he had been very loving, and none of the family was in any doubt about that.

We - the chundies - were all too upset to launch into a full spiel about his life and his contribution. There were one or two local Quakers who got up to minister, but all Pa's close friends were dead, and I felt that no-one who really knew him and appreciated his unique and special personality, his achievements and his talents, got up to share their memories.

I was sitting there feeling more and more agitated with the passing minutes, thinking that the service was about to finish and no-one had got up to say anything substantial about Pa, my father, the special man whom I loved and admired.

Then, in the nick of time, Melanie Carter, the daughter of Pa's oldest friend Jack (who died years ago), rose to her feet at the back of the room, directly opposite us, and spoke about Pa's farming expertise, his wit and intelligence, his charm, and so many other characteristics which were so especially him. My heart was full. She spoke warmly and sincerely, and I was so very grateful.

Then the elders shook hands. The service was over.

We had tea and cakes in the Meeting House with a hubbub of people chatting in an atmosphere that was a mix of seriousness and jokes. And I met a couple of elderly cousins, one of whom said I looked just like Pa's mother, Edie. That really cheered me up. It was strange, because usually I hate to be told that I look like someone else.

Viv and I didn't go back to Hollycroft after the service. We drove to look at Aysgarth Falls, from the bridge, and drove back to Sheffield from there. On the way back I spent a long time thinking about the burial, because for me it was so much more special, moving, real and soothing than the memorial service. It was a beautiful occasion, and one of the people in our family who would have appreciated this would have been Pa. He was the reason and he was the focus, but he wasn't there. He missed it, and I yearned to tell him about it. So when I got back I wrote him a letter and described how special his burial day had been: what had happened, how we had arranged things, how everyone had been and behaved.

The letter was easy to write. It came from the heart. But the week that Pa died, Ma asked if I would write an obituary for the *Darlington and Stockton Times*, and that task hung over me like some awful homework essay.

When I first sat down at my computer to write it, I sat there for ten minutes with an empty screen. I couldn't bear to begin to type. If I was writing his obituary, it meant he was dead, and I did not want him to be dead.

Then, when I finally started typing, I hated it because I had to write the thing in a formal tone, in a set format, and I couldn't say all the human, trivial stuff that described Pa, that said real things about him

The paragraphs about his schooling, his farm, his successes and his triumphs described the public man - Ralph

David Metcalfe. He sounded like a thoroughly accomplished chap (as he was) but I hated that obituary. The required style constrained me. I could say that he was brought up a Quaker, but not that for the last ten years of his life he would lie on the sofa every afternoon watching the racing on telly. I could say that he was a keen hockey player but not that he had a passion for Stilton cheese and Craster kippers and home grown raspberries. I could say that he sometimes wrote poetry as a hobby, some very moving poems, but I could make no mention of his sometimes less than happy use of words - that his criticism could be scorching, his rudeness outrageous, or that his acerbic tongue could reduce a sensitive grandchild to a pulp.

And I couldn't say how fervently he loved his family, how sure we were of this, and how much we would miss him sitting smoking in the corner being crabby, and then at the end of the evening asking for a goodbye cuddle. And there was that last time I visited him at home when I knew he was ill because it was the first time he didn't say "I had a shave especially, so I could give you a kiss." That couldn't go in the obituary either.

When Megan, Steve and I were little, we would roll our eyes when he told us, yet again, about his great-grandfather's heifer which won first prize in the London Show, and then "was roasted whole for the poor of Chelsea." With him gone I saw all the dog-eared stories of his farming forebears as weighty anchors to our family history.

When cousin Marjorie at the memorial service said that I looked like Pa's mother, it made me feel like a link in a long, long chain stretching back into the past, even if I had no children to link me to the future. My father was gone, but he was still a valid link. He might no longer sit at the head of the table repeating his catch-phrase "As good a Stilton as I've tasted in years," but at future family gatherings one of us could say it for him. And now I can hear Steve inside my head saying – "Only if the cheese merits it." Ah, that critical gene again.

CHAPTER 12

In the days that followed, I tried to get back into the routine I'd established before Pa died, before Charles and I had that wonderful wicked fortnight: get up at seven, be working at craft or photography or stained glass by eight. Stop at one, and then after lunch do a different activity from the one I'd done in the morning. Twice a week, if it was fine, I'd been going up to the allotment in the afternoon.

I could manage the mornings, but the afternoons were hard. By three o'clock I was flagging and unable to do anything sustained. I had this space to do things – and so many different options - but I couldn't settle to any of them. All I wanted to do was sit on the sofa. If I felt like this, how must Ma be feeling? I couldn't even knit because it was impossible to concentrate on the complicated pattern I was doing at the time – scores of miniature knitted Christmas trees for hand-made Christmas cards. Because I was trying out different designs to find the best one, and making them all up as I went along, I had to be aware of every stitch. It wasn't like a scarf that you don't even have to look at because you know you're doing it right. Having given up the idea of knitting, I tried getting out my current rag-rug-in-progress and shredding fabric to weave into that, but the shredding mirrored what I was feeling inside, so I stopped.

One day I dragged myself up to the allotment and did some desultory weeding, but people kept coming over to me and saying they hadn't seen me for a while, and was everything all right? Where had I been? And then when I told them, they would say hideously unhelpful things like *Well, he's out of his suffering now*, or recite sickly, inadequate poems and quotes about death that meant nothing to me, and made me feel worse than if they'd said nothing. If anyone else went on about Pa being *just in the next room*, I thought I might throw a spade at them. Even Albert said "This is it, Corinne. Death is part of life." *Well, it damn well shouldn't be*, I felt like shouting back. *It's completely outrageous.* I was screaming it inside my head as he stood there, and he, oblivious, patted my shoulder and said, "It won't always be dark at six."

I knew they were all of them trying to be kind, but they weren't reading how I was feeling, tuning in to what I might need – they were just spouting clichés. After two trips up to the allotment when I'd slunk away after just an hour because I couldn't hack it any longer, I rang Viv and begged her to take over my share.

"But I'm not sure I've got time to do any more," she said.

"What can I do, then?"

"OK, OK. I'll do it for a couple of weeks. Then see how you are."

❄ ❄ ❄

I wasn't seeing much of Charles. He was out every night for the first week I was back, on a special intensive evening class in sailing theory – a Day Skipper course, I think he said. But on the Saturday he persuaded me to go out to dinner with him. At first it felt like a relief to get out of the house and to be driven away to somewhere different, with the wind in my hair. He drove us up to Fox House, a pub on the ridge between Sheffield and the Peak District, overlooking the hills, and we sat outside in the fading sunshine.

He wolfed down steak and chips and I picked at a goat's cheese tartlet. He talked non-stop about sailing. He burbled on about pilotage (whatever that is – I didn't ask) and navigation, safety at sea, boat handling, engine maintenance, and the different characters on the course – some of whom "Don't know their longitudes from their bally latitudes" – and then he rambled on about the kind of boat he was going to buy when he persuaded the bank to give him a loan. I bailed in and out of concentration and contributed little. He was awash with excitement, and I got by with smiling and nodding and asking a question every now and then. But by the time he'd finished his main course and was asking if I wanted a pudding, I was exhausted with the effort of being sociable and smiley. I longed to be home on my own.

"Can you just hold me?" I said in bed later.

"I thought that's what I was already doing."

"No. I mean…can you just hold me and nothing else."

"Are you feeling a bit below par?"

"Just sad."

"You poor sweetheart." He held me to his chest and stroked the hair off my forehead like Ma used to do when I was little and had a fever. "Maybe tomorrow," he said.

I doubted that I'd feel any different the next night.

I didn't.

On Monday morning he was up by eight and sitting on the bed putting in his cufflinks. I lay there with my head resting on my arm on the pillow, watching him. Now he was fiddling with his tie. I'd made it from a piece of silk I'd decorated with batik. "Awfully jolly," he said when I gave it to him. He was standing in front of the mirror, fiddling with the knot to get it precisely as he wanted it. Did he appreciate that I'd made it from my very favourite piece of fabric?

"Maybe it's a good thing I have my Day Skipper practical next week," he said, combing his hair.

"How do you mean?" I asked, but I knew what he meant. He meant that as a lover I was currently useless. Not fit for the purpose. Not as (previously) described.

He turned round and looked at me. "Think about the last two nights we've spent together."

What was there to say?

He went on. "I'm sure you'll feel better by the time I get back. Then we can make up for lost time. You're a lovely lady." He leaned over and kissed me and I felt a tingle, but it was more of a bicycle bell than a gong.

I fumbled for something to say. "I hope you get a good wind." I'd gathered one thing from all the sailing talk: when he was deciding whether to go down to the reservoir Charles always looked at the wind.

"It's not yachting this time. I thought I'd explained. The basic course next week is on a motor cruiser. I told you all about it last night. At sea."

"Oh yes." I knew all about being at sea.

❋ ❋ ❋

I did up my safety belt and turned the key in the ignition. I loved my van. When I decided to leave teaching and go into painting and decorating, Steven told me I should buy a van from a motor auction – I saw the adverts every time I drove up the A1. Mark was away in Japan on business at the time, and anyway I knew full well he wouldn't have wanted to come with me. He was a car snob and thought I should be getting a new something-or-other-XJwhatsit.

Steve was happy to come and give me the benefit of his advice, and anyway, he wanted to check out the Land Rovers. He thought I'd got a bargain with the ex Post Office van I bought, but then said I'd missed the point when I paid to have a full respray and to have an advert for my business put on the side. Cream paint, black writing, 1940s type font. I washed it once a week – more often than I washed the kitchen floor.

"Sanctuary! Sanctuary!"

Elspeth had appeared from nowhere and was banging on the passenger window of my van.

"What the hell's the matter?" I shouted. "Come round to this side and tell me. I don't have electric windows."

She scuttled round the front of my van while I unwound the window. Her frizzy, salt and pepper hair was looking ready for its bi-annual perm, the fastener of her seed pearls was swinging at the front, half open, and her reading glasses which always hung round her neck were tangled up in their chain. Viv and I occasionally suggested – gently and tactfully – that maybe she'd like us to give her some fashion tips, or a make-over. Last time we did, she said: "Thank you, but I have always been content to follow my own sartorial imperatives."

She looked as desperate as if she was fleeing from a gang of hoodies. "Can I come with you?" she pleaded.

"But you don't know where I'm going."

"I do not care. I simply need to escape."

"But Elspeth, you've got a key. You know you can come in and work whenever you like."

"Work? I cannot face another subjunctive clause. I cannot look one in the eye."

"Then why do you need sanctuary?"

"Neither can I face another one of my offspring demanding something from me. If I come with you – where are you going? Never mind, I do not care – if I come with you they will not be able to track me down. Even with satellite navigation – which none of them currently have, though they might be planning to get it just to follow me around – even with that they would not be able to trace me. I have hurled my mobile phone down the cellar."

"What?"

"Jessica sent me a text at half past four this morning saying *I've locked myself out.* I did not respond. The girl lives in Birmingham and she is 25. What am I supposed to do about it? Then, at half past five she sent me another text – *Why have you not texted me back? You and Daddy don't seem to give a shit.* Not only had she been pestering me in the middle of the night, she had sent a text to poor Donald six thousand miles away. It was the final straw."

"Blimey." Perhaps I hadn't been missing anything not having kids. "Well, I'm going to Wath-on-Dearne, to Kansacraft. You can come if you want."

"What is that?"

"It's where I get my glass supplies. I need more lead. H profile, heavy gauge. Come if you want, but hurry up and get in. It's taken me ages to drag myself out as it is." I had felt like doing nothing but sitting on the sofa with a mug of tea all morning, but had given myself a kick in the butt. "I don't want to lose any more of the day," I said.

"Oh, that is better," she said with a big sigh five minutes later, as I changed into second gear and edged down the steep hill to Rivelin Valley Road.

"This hill is 1 in 4 in places and Rob cycles up it, isn't that amazing?" I said.

Elspeth took out her knitting from the bag she always carried, arranged the four needles in her hands and made a stitch. "I feel easy, now," she said, clicking busily at an argyle sock. "Simply being in another valley provides a little distance."

"What on earth's got you into this state? Surely it's not just the texting?"

As she knitted, she spilled out a long tirade about how each of the children was driving her mad and what were their particular sins of the previous week. I can't remember now what they were. She was always moaning about them, and the complaints that morning just joined the others already in the slurry pit.

She doted on all of them, but she could not cope with their incessant demands. Her husband Donald was away for months at a time in Antarctica doing meteorological research, and this had been a pattern for the last ten years. Maybe the children felt they never got enough attention, and that was why they were always in her face, in her space.

If she was at work at the University they left constant messages on her voicemail. The department secretary had been instructed not to put through personal calls to her office. I'd given up trying to get hold of her through normal means. She had instructed Viv and me to text her on her mobile if we wanted to get in touch, and then she would ring us back.

"But why aren't you working?" I said as we drove past the Superbowl.

"I hate my work."

"What?"

"I *hate* my work. I loathe the study of language. I despise the students. I abhor the department politics. I detest the need to justify myself with constant publications. It is a cynical game. Do you know, I have just churned out five different papers for five different academic journals all based on the same flimsy piece of research, merely written from varying angles. I hate my work. I hate – oh bother, I slipped a stitch at the beginning of that last needle instead of knitting it." She began to unpick her knitting. She was using three colours, and long loops of wool were everywhere.

"Hell's teeth, Elspeth, your wool's wound itself round my gear stick." There was nowhere to park on the main road so I pulled into a side street and parked, and when we'd sorted out the problem, I set off again.

"But your work. You've worked so hard to get where you are."

"It is true."

"Everyone goes through periods when they get fed up with their job, Elspeth. Everyone. I bet even David Hockney sometimes tires of the Californian sun and doesn't even want to paint Yorkshire landscapes – just sit in a deckchair on Bridlington beach with his trousers rolled up and a daschund on his knee and his feet in the water. Even paradise must become tedious sometimes." It didn't sound very convincing, I admit. Although when Megan and Ed had lived in San Francisco for two years (with Ed's work) Megan moaned about how she would do anything for a decent bit of rain. "I want a nice English autumn," she said. "It's Thanksgiving.

Why is the bougainvillea still in flower? I'm so desperate for fallen leaves, I've been making little heaps of any I can find on the sidewalk and stomping on them."

Now Elspeth had her knitting problem sorted out she was back in full flow. "This is not a temporary disenchantment, Corinne. I know what I want to do. I feel it with every fibre of my being. It is what I have wanted to do since I was seven and knitted my first dolls twin set and won second prize in the village show. I want to run a wool shop."

We were stopped at traffic lights, and I turned to look at her to see if she was joking. A tear was rolling down her cheek.

"Elspeth," I said, reaching out my hand.

There was a loud hoot behind me. I looked ahead and saw the traffic lights were green and the queue in front had moved away. I let off the handbrake and followed.

"I expect you think I am mad," said Elspeth.

"No, of course I don't."

"I have wondered myself. I have worried about it. But yesterday on Radio 4 – it was a programme about vocation – I heard someone interviewing a chip shop owner in Skipton. She said she had wanted a chip shop since she was at school. She *adored* her work. Frying fish was an art form, she said. She could hear the fish singing to her when they were frying. She could tell if they were happy or not. She said she tried to make every fry better than the time before. Each time she fried a batch it was the chance to make them the perfect fish."

"There is nothing better than Yorkshire fish and chips," I said. "At least that used to be true, when they still fried them in beef fat."

"I feel you are wandering from the point, Corinne."

"What does Donald think about it?" I said.

"He thinks it is a temporary insanity."

"But you've just said it's what you've always wanted."

"Yes. I told him on our very first date. But he never took it seriously. That was 1975. I remember it perfectly. I imagine one always does remember one's first date. He had just begun his PhD on cloud formation. He wanted to research changes in the ozone layer, but his supervisor had discouraged him. I was doing my finals, and when he asked me what I planned to do afterwards I said I wanted to run a wool shop. He laughed so heartily that he choked on his prawn cocktail and I had to get up from the table and rush round and do the Heimlich Hug on him. Then when he had recovered and was breathing easily he said 'I love your sense of humour,' and the moment passed. I did not want to ruin my chances with him by explaining that I was not joking, so after my finals I began an MPhil and then I got pregnant with Charlotte and gave it all up anyway. And being at home I could indulge my knitting fetish as much as I wanted - it seemed a perfectly natural thing to do – to other people, I mean. And then when all the children were at school, we were short of money for a period when Donald's research funding ran out, and I started teaching. And then it just went on and on, and I sit before you, in an ex-post office van – yours, admittedly – at the age of 53, still yearning for a shelving unit full of wool, a display carousel with patterns on it and a drawer full of needles."

By this time we'd arrived in Wath and were approaching the stained glass warehouse. I pulled the van into the yard and switched the engine off.

"Elspeth. You have to do it. You have to follow your bliss."

"What kind of modern self-centred new age nonsense phrase is that?"

"Oh come on, you're just putting on the fuddy duddy act now. I know you are."

She laughed. "Come on. I want to see what they have in here. Will I be able to see all the different kinds of glass?"

"Of course. And you can help me look through the box of scrap, and see if there are any tasty bits in there. But let's sit here for a bit and talk about you."

"No. Now is not the time. We can do that later." She was already out of the van and slamming the door.

✻ ✻ ✻

It was Ma's birthday coming up. I looked at my card designs to find one that fitted the situation and couldn't. Not surprising, really. I don't suppose anyone's done a category of *Birthday card for your mother when your father's just died.* Though if they did, maybe they could put Munch's *Scream* in there.

Nothing I had would do, and I did have quite a store. In the end, I traipsed off to the card shop in Broomhill to see what they'd got to offer, and I still couldn't choose. I wanted the perfect card, of course. I looked at everything that was vaguely suitable but wanted none of them. Eventually, the woman walked over to me from behind the counter and said "Is there something particular you wanted?"

"No" I said. I welled up with tears and turned my face away. Then I turned back and told her that my father had just died and it was my mother's birthday. She said, "Oh I am sorry," and bustled about, picking out flowery cards with no message, so they were pretty (she thought) and yet none of them were too upbeat. It was kind of her, but all the ones she picked out were disgusting flowery nothingnesses.

When I got back to Ferndean Row I met Rob wheeling his bike over the cobbles in front of our terrace. He asked me how things were going and I told him about the card problem. He said – "You've got some grand photos that you've taken for cards. Would you like me to come in and make some suggestions?"

He spent half an hour sitting in front of my computer saying, "What about this one? What about this one? That one's champion. This one's mighty fine." And when I gave him a reason why each of them just wouldn't do, he didn't try to persuade me, he just said, "OK."

"I wonder if I've got something at home," he said. "I have a box of cards – odd ones I see in shops that I like and bring home for later."

He brought me a card that was a print of a five barred gate dividing two fields, with a deep cloudy air-force-blue sky behind it and a faint streak of a rainbow slanting off steeply at the side. The style looked familiar. I turned it over to look at the back. It was called *April Shower* and was by a Wensleydale artist called Piers Browne. There were several of his prints hanging up at the cottage.

"Perfect. Thanks." I was so relieved I kissed him on the cheek and immediately felt embarrassed, and he made an excuse to leave.

❉ ❉ ❉

That weekend I went up to stay with Ma. Megan's lovely daughter Emma had stayed for a week, and then Ma had had a week on her own.

On the way up the dale I dropped in on Steve for a hug and a chat. He was sitting outside, just about to go off and do the milking. I stood and looked at his garden. All his poppies were out. It was a visual feast, and Pa wasn't there to see them.

There were crimson, vermilion, magenta and I think some white ones. And carmine lupins, and hardy geraniums in too many shades of blue and purple to count. I stood on Steve's back door steps, just to the left, and cast my eye the length of the border that leads down to the farmyard and the milking parlour. It was beautiful: no other word will do.

On the Saturday, Ma asked me to clear out Pa's bedroom so that she could make it into a guest room for us all, with a new carpet and a double bed. She wanted to make use of the lovely east view and the morning sunshine. I was anxious to support her with whatever she wanted to do, but why the indecent, inhuman haste? It felt brutal.

I slept heavily that night. There were four full black bin liners crowding the room and it felt as though the weight of everything was hanging in there, and the pain of it lay on me all through the night.

In the morning, I rang Mrs Galway. I couldn't talk to Ma about it, and I needed to discuss it with someone.

"We oldies don't have the luxury of time, like you whippersnappers do," is what she said.

"I don't know what you mean," I said.

"How old is your mother?

"Eighty-four."

"She has to get on. She hasn't got much life left. And I seem to remember you telling me that your Ma was clearing things out some time ago...when was it?...and wasn't that before your Pa became ill? This is probably just a further manifestation of that. Yes – manifestation - it was on *Alpha-Omega* yesterday."

"I think she said that Quakers are supposed to leave things in an orderly fashion for people when they die. But it's not Ma who's dying."

"It doesn't mean anything about her feelings for your Pa."

"But you still have Mr Galway's coat on the back of your kitchen chair." Mr Galway had been dead for ten years. "That is his jacket, isn't it? That tweed one?"

"It is. And then there's Vivien's caretaker – Edgar Wibberley – he positively doted on his wife - he was a fool for her - but he wanted all of her things cleared out whilst he was at her funeral, because the man couldn't bear to come back to the house afterwards and see them. Everyone's different, Caroline."

She was probably right. But speed was anathema to me.

Added to that there was everything I found in there. Raking over the remains of someone's life felt like being ripped open. I was faced with the pain and the sadness woven into the everyday fabric of people's lives.

As I sorted through the papers, letters and photos in his desk I saw all the stages of his life documented, all the major traumas and turning points set out, as if there were a virtual calendar, a long ream of monthly tables, with all the events marked on it. Going through his papers made me think of his life, of everyone's life, as a series of choices, triumphs and disappointments.

There was a bundle of airmail letters I'd written to Ma and Pa from Italy, loads of other family letters, and there were formal records of significant events, happy ones like the scrolled marriage certificate of his and Ma's Quaker wedding with all the signatures on it of those present. And there were public notices of sad ones, tips of icebergs of a hidden mass of heartache, like the printed notice of his mother's memorial service in 1956.

There was the wallet he'd taken when he went on his three month tour of the USA with the National Farmers Union, and in it was a photo of the farmhouse, one of the cows walking in for milking, and one of all our family sitting on the garden bench - the photo we all have in our albums now.

Clearing out his things, sorting through his letters and photos and significant papers he kept - I got the long view. I saw all the turning points and critical life events and what came after. I remembered the foot and mouth outbreak when I was little, what it was like as a child, the way they would send us out from the kitchen after tea to the sitting room and say "You chundies go next door while we discuss our financial difficulties."

I looked back on his successes – the Dairy Show triumph – and representing the NFU – and the sadnesses of the difficult decisions like deciding to give up the pigs. And I wished he was there to discuss it all – but would I have been able to do this, anyway? The last year he was too deaf, and not well from Christmas onwards.

Life is too hard, with too many difficult choices. And then there was all the stuff about the impact of someone's life and how they lived it and whether the overall impact was good or bad, positive or poor…I had to start thinking about that as well.

CHAPTER 13

When I got back to Ferndean Row, I rang Elspeth to invite her round for supper so we could talk about her wool shop. She was keen, but she had to stay home because Minnie-May was sleeping at her house for a couple of nights. Charlotte had gone to see a friend in Paris. She'd taken the baby with her. Presumably if she hadn't still been breastfeeding, she'd have dumped the baby on Elspeth as well.

I'd been in the wash house doing glass all day, and when I came out at tea-time to bring the washing in, the evening was so balmy that I decided to walk to Elspeth's house. It's about a mile and a half from my place to hers. She lives in a big Victorian house off Ecclesall Road.

I rang her bell, went in and shouted "Hello," and she came out of the sitting room to meet me in the hall.

"I have told Donald about my dream," she said.

"How did he react? Was he shocked?"

She took my denim jacket and found a place for it on top of all the other coats that were hanging in her airless hall.

"Hey, Elspeth, is this yours?" I said, fingering a coat in the latest style in a fabulous magenta. "It's very trendy."

"You know that I have never been an acolyte of sartorial whimsy. I assume it belongs to a friend of Jessica. She must have left it here last weekend."

We went into her sitting room, which has magnolia walls and ready-made Marks and Spencer curtains and matching cushion covers in a subdued floral print. At the top of the walls there's a matching border. She has books everywhere, not just on the shelves in the alcoves, but piled on the coffee table, on the floor at each end of the sofa and in the corners of the room. There are also piles of knitting patterns and back copies of *Needlecraft* and a knitting basket with a lid to stop the cat from climbing in. There's a china cabinet made of a dark polished wood with leaded glass doors. It's crammed with crystal. She has no interesting paintings on the walls - just family photographs, and a framed poster of Monet's garden at Givenchy above the fireplace. Very dull.

Elspeth picked up the knitting she'd left on the sofa and sat down. "Tell me what you think of the new seat cushions. They are fibre wrapped foam."

I sat down on her olive green dralon sofa. "Very squishy. Are *you* pleased with them?"

"I find it a very interesting sitting experience. It positively buoys the buttocks."

"So," I said. "Donald. What did he say?"

"He thinks we have got to the stage in our lives when we should do what we want. He is ready to retire. He says he can understand the lure of the simple pleasures of neighbourhood commerce after a life in the cut-throat world of academia."

"Does he want to help you? You know – run the shop with you?"

"Oh no. He would like to spend his time researching his family history. He does that on the internet at the moment. But now he has got back as far as the early 19th century and the digital data has run out. He needs to go in person and inspect parish registers and other primary sources."

At that point the front door slammed.

"Barnes," said Elspeth in a low voice.

Barnes stuck his head round the door. He was all black leather and facial metal. I am always taken aback by how many piercings he has.

"How's it going?" he said, but before either of us could respond, he said "Anything decent to eat?"

"I am sure there is plenty," said Elspeth, and Barnes disappeared before you could say Black Sabbath. "I think he has forgotten he has a flat of his own. Still, I have taken the opportunity to teach him to cook. He wanted to know how I made my Bolognese sauce, to which he is partial."

"What do you put in it?"

"Onions and tomatoes, of course, like everyone else. But he abhors them and when he found out that they are essential ingredients, he said he had not been so disappointed since he discovered the truth about Father Christmas."

Catty Fassett nudged the door open that Barnes had left ajar, and strolled into the room, his tail high. He saw Elspeth's ball of wool on the carpet, pounced on it, and began to chew the strand of wool that led to Elspeth's knitting.

"Get off," she said, picking up the wool and placing it out of his reach. "Desist, you bad cat."

I picked up Catty and cuddled him. Cats are such a comfort. I thought for the umpteenth time that maybe I should get one. "Isn't he gorgeous?" I said.

Elspeth reached across to rub him under his chin. "There

you are, there, there. You like that, don't you my sweet?" She sat back and continued with her moss stitch.

"And to think," she said, peering at me over her reading glasses, "he will go through the whole of his life, completely oblivious to meta cognition."

At that point there was a distant thump upstairs and a piercing wail, followed by a scattering of quick light footsteps on the landing,. Elspeth threw down her knitting and left the room, knocking over a pile of books on the way. I restacked the books and then followed.

When I got to the top of the stairs, Minnie-May was screaming and jumping and flapping her arms up and down, and Elspeth was trying to get close enough to see what the matter was. There was a stream of blood and snot dripping off Minnie-May's chin, forming a big, disgusting stain on the front of her nightie. When Elspeth got close to her, Minnie-May screamed louder and pushed her away, and Elspeth turned to me with an anguished face.

"Help me! Can you get behind her and grab her and hold her arms down and then I can get up close and talk to her?"

Poor Minnie-May.

I moved behind her and lurched forwards and held her tight and Elspeth knelt down and placed her hands firmly each side of Minnie-May's face and talked soothingly to her, and the frenzy stopped, Minnie-May wilted and I let go. She threw her arms round Elspeth and then shrieked again as she bashed her wounded face on Elspeth's shoulder, and when Minnie-May pulled back, Elspeth sat on the landing carpet and gently took Minnie-May onto her knee, finally getting a chance to look at the wound.

It turned out that Minnie-May had got up to go to the loo, slipped on the bathmat and fallen against the bath. Her chin had caught the top of the bath side, and she'd bitten right through the flesh below her lip.

I didn't have my car, and Elspeth didn't want to drive hers to casualty because she wanted to comfort Minnie-May, so we went in a taxi.

We checked in, and a nurse examined Minnie-May's wound. She gave her a wad of cotton wool soaked in something to hold against it, to numb the pain, while she waited for it to be stitched.

The waiting room was nothing like the ones I'd seen on the television on the hospital soaps. It was quiet. Maybe that was because it was half past ten on a Wednesday night and because we were in the Children's Hospital, not the Northern General casualty department full of drunks and druggies and car crash victims.

There was a man with a young teenage boy who had what looked like a strip of old white sheeting wrapped around his shin. There was a young woman clad entirely in pink – pink vest, tight pink jeans, pink high heels – with a little girl all in violet, who had her hand on her ear and was moaning, while an older woman on the other side of her cuddled her and told her to "Shush, Chelsea. Everyone's looking at us."

Minnie-May had been whimpering for the last half hour, but this had diminished to the occasional sniff. She was sitting on Elspeth's knee, leaning back against her shoulder, with Elspeth stroking her hair.

Elspeth and I had chatted for a bit when we first arrived, but now we were silent.

I was staring at the wall opposite, thinking about Pa. He was handsome when he was young. On his wedding photo he looks like James Stewart in *It's a Wonderful Life:* a 1940s double breasted suit with big lapels, thick brown hair parted and slicked back with Brylcreem, long smooth face with even features, nice eyes and a smiley, slightly open mouth because he's just about to say something.

And he looked dashing in his farming clothes when I was young. I liked his tall black wellington boots.

I remember him trying to teach me to dance the quickstep at a Christmas party when I was small – showing me the steps and letting me rest my feet on top of his highly polished brogues, dancing around the room with me. He came to watch me play netball and tennis at school. He bought me my first Rowney watercolour paintbox at the Yorkshire Show, and he once wrote me a poem for homework because I couldn't do it. And when he was old and retired and I went up to stay at the cottage, he walked up the road to Thornton Rust with me, every fine evening after tea. Why did I love him so much when he was such a grouch, when he could criticise for England, and he could be so hurtful and so rude? Like the time I gave him a crocheted blanket a couple of years ago to wrap around his legs when he sat outside on the garden bench, and he said "What do you think I am? A refugee?"

When we were children he composed a treasure hunt for one of Megan's birthday parties. He hid the clues all over the farm and garden. Each clue was a verse, and each verse had a missing letter. The clue told you where to look for the next clue, but you had to collect all the missing letters, because they were an anagram and the solution was the prize: Smarties. A big box of them.

Sometimes on Sunday afternoons he would take us out digging for treasure, and we found flint arrowheads. He played table tennis with us when we went on holiday in a Quaker hostel. He taught us to fish for trout, and then how to gut our catch, and how it tasted best for breakfast when fried with streaky bacon, and how the tenderest part of the fish was the cheek. And he took us out looking for mushrooms, which he also liked in his breakfast fry-ups.

I think it was his passions that made him so attractive. I can list his passions – field mushrooms, raspberries, pictures, racing, good food, Stilton, kippers, good sausages, jelly, sweet peas, Arthur Bell roses, his children, his home, his dale, his family history.

It was stuffy in the waiting room, and I was drifting off, near to dozing, despite the hardness of the hospital chair. Even under the bright lights it was a struggle to keep my eyes open, so when a mountie on a unicycle glided round the corner I thought I was imagining it. *Yes – a mountie!*

He came from the right and cycled past us to the swing doors on the left. He struggled to open a door, teetering and jerking, his booted feet doing little pedals and back-pedals, but he managed to get one door open and to get through the doors without falling off. I had to be imagining a mountie, didn't I? Just in case I was, I didn't point him out to Elspeth. She was having a whispered conversation with Minnie-May.

Then it happened again. He came lurching back through the swing doors on the left, glided smoothly across my line of sight and disappeared round the corner on the right again. I sat up and looked around at the other people sitting in the waiting area to see if they were as gobsmacked as me. Yes. People were whispering and nudging each other and pointing towards the corner of the room round which the mountie had disappeared. The woman in pink was gabbling across Chelsea to the older woman, and the lad with the hurt leg was pointing to the door and talking to his Dad. Others were chatting too. Everyone was sitting up now, alert and expectant in case he should return, but when after a few minutes nothing happened, there was a slumping back down into seats, and a return to waiting for the nurse to come and call out a name for treatment.

I wasn't going to leave it at that. I asked Elspeth if she wanted a cup of tea and I went off ostensibly in search of a drinks machine, but really in search of a mountie.

I scurried round the corner and through a set of swing doors and down the corridor, looking right and left all the time to make sure the mountie wasn't lurking in a corner. I went past the chapel and a drinks machine and the pharmacy and another drinks machine and the end of a short corridor leading down to toilets, finally coming up against a set of doors that said *No public entrance - Staff only* and I wondered whether to go through them anyway, and turned round to see if anyone was watching me. But just then the mountie emerged from the end of the corridor on the left that led to the toilets. He cycled to the drinks machine and hovered and back-pedalled and jerked to keep his balance while he tried to get a coin from the pocket of his jodhpurs, one of those tiny pockets that men's trousers have for coins, tucked in tight near the waistband.

Whenever I see a man getting a coin from his waistband pocket, I see James Stewart in *It's a Wonderful Life* when he's 'mending' his little daughter Zuzu's flower. Two petals have fallen off it and she tells him it's broken and will he mend it? He pretends to paste two petals back onto her flower, while hiding the petals in his little waist pocket. I love that scene with Zuzu's petals.

I hurried over and stood behind the mountie, but to the side of him, so as not to get in the way as he wheeled back and forth, and then he muttered "Sod it" and dismounted from the unicycle, and leaned it up against the wall. Then he held the long flap of his jacket out of the way with one hand while he fiddled in his pocket to get the coin out with the other. I couldn't see his face because of his hat. Was he as good looking as Fraser in *Due South?*

He shoved a coin in the machine and when the spout stopped gushing coffee he carefully lifted the plastic beaker from the machine. He turned round and raised the drink to his mouth, and at the very same moment I saw it was Rob, and he saw it was me and he jumped and said "Whoa!" and spilled a great swirl of coffee on the floor.

Rob! I was so amazed that I just stood there with my mouth open, unable to speak.

"Here," he said. "Hold this." And he rushed off in the direction of the toilets, coming back with a fistful of paper towels. When he had mopped the coffee up off the floor, and thrown the soggy towels in the bin, he took the beaker back from me and said "Are you going to speak, o silent one? Are you going to say hello? Sorry for making you jump?"

He took a sip of coffee, then, but his eyes were on mine all the time.

"What are you …? But…"

"Yes?"

"At least I'm not in fancy dress."

He looked down at his jacket – such a fab shade of red – at his midnight navy jodhpurs with yellow flashings and his brown leather knee high boots, as if he had forgotten he was wearing them.

"Oh."

"And I have a bona fide excuse for being here. I'm with an injured child. Elspeth's grand-daughter. We were baby-sitting and she bit her lip right through. They're down there," I jerked my thumb towards the waiting room, "waiting for it to be stitched. You?"

"I come a couple of times a week to cheer up the kids. No-one knows I come here and do this – apart from Bella, she's a nurse here – so you'd better keep mum."

"You cheer up kids in the Children's Hospital at eleven at night?"

"OK, not usually as late as this, obviously, but one thing led to another. It's been one of those days. Bella had a little girl on a side ward who couldn't sleep for pain, and–"

"You come here twice a week? As a mountie? Always a mountie?"

He nodded and took another sip of his coffee. "This is disgusting stuff," he said. "I don't know why I always forget how vile it is. Every week I have one and every week I end up throwing it…what? What are you looking at me like that for? It really is repulsive stuff…here, have a–"

"Why a mountie?"

"No reason."

"There must be a reason!"

"Truth is I first went to the Joke Shop the day before Hallowe'en, and this was the only costume they had left that was suitable for cycling in. Then after a while it became a kind of trademark – the unicycling mountie – you know how it happens…"

"Oh yes, it happens to *me* all the time…"

"Yes, and so the Friends of the Children's Hospital bought me a costume so I didn't have to keep on hiring one. Oughtn't you to be taking a drink back to Elspeth?"

"Elspeth?" Who was *she?* "I've met a mountie running loose in sunny Sheffield and you're suggesting I abandon him and take someone a beaker of hospital tea? I'm bloody not, the mountie might disappear."

He blushed. "Don't be so daft."

He was right, though. I ought to go back. I'd solved the mystery of the mountie, and the mystery was the man next door. So I got two drinks from the machine and left him sipping his.

When I got back to the waiting area, Elspeth and Minnie-May were being ushered into a room by a nurse with an angular haircut, and Elspeth signalled to me to follow.

Minnie-May was lifted onto a high bed and Elspeth and I stood one each side of her to comfort her and try to keep her still while the nurse injected anaesthetic into her lip. Minnie-May screamed and squirmed and another, younger nurse talked soothingly to Minnie-May. The nurse with the needle heard Elspeth stifle a gasp and looked at Elspeth, and seeing the tears in her eyes, said curtly "If you're going to faint you'd better go out."

"I will not faint," said Elspeth, and sniffed. The younger nurse reached out to squeeze Elspeth's arm sympathetically, and then went back to holding Minnie-May still. I held one of Minnie-May's hands and with my other one I stroked Elspeth's empty hand until the stitching was finished.

Soon we were outside the hospital again with a taxi. Elspeth and Minnie-May had already climbed into the back seat and I was just about to get in when I saw Rob emerging from the hospital.

"Will you be OK, now, do you think?" I said to Elspeth.

"Absolutely fine," she said.

"OK, well I'll walk back with Rob. Bye."

The taxi pulled off up Witham Road, and I rushed after Rob who had slipped down the side of the building. I got round the corner and found him unlocking a bike from the railings. Of course – he'd be cycling home. I turned to go.

He spotted me. "Are you going home?" he said. "I'll walk with you."

"No, you'll be wanting to ride."

"Come on," he said. "I'm just as happy to walk, it's such a grand night, warm and still. I've been inside since dinner time and I'm starved of fresh air. Anyway, once we get past the shops at Broomhill and the road flattens out, I can give you a ride on my crossbar."

How could I refuse a crossbar from a mountie?

I examined his bike. "This isn't your usual bike, is it?"

"This bike is the one I stopped a mad woman from chucking in a skip. Just a bit of TLC, and a bit of brass, that's all it needed."

It was shiny and sound. New tyres, new brakes, everything polished.

When we got past that last little uphill bit by the *Oxfam* shop and we'd passed the traffic lights, he said – "Hop on. You've got long legs so you'd be best on the seat, not the crossbar. I'll stand on the pedals. Best option."

So that's what we did. I clutched the edge of the broad old fashioned seat as best I could, while his nice little bum swayed from side to side in front of my face. I felt insecure and precarious, and it was hard to keep a firm grip on the edge of the seat, so I steadied myself by grabbing his brown leather belt.

"You're pulling me down," he said. "Can you hold onto my trousers instead?"

So I grabbed the stripes on the bulgy side bits of his jodhpurs.

As we cycled along Fulwood Road, his Stetson fell off backwards and swung by its string round his neck. We cycled past the halls of residence, past the Ranmoor Inn, where a bunch of students were still lounging at the tables outside, and laughing at us as we wobbled on, past the chippy with the enticing smell wafting through the open door, through the traffic lights and along past the new block of flats on the left hand side, past the garage, and on, and just as we were turning into the little lane that leads down to Ferndean Row, wobbling precariously on the turn, a woman standing on a doorstep with a dog on a lead shouted into her open front door – "Neville, there's a mountie on a bike – come quick and look! – and he's got a woman sitting behind him grabbing his britches."

But we weren't hanging around for Neville, and Rob was juddering down our lane, coming to a sudden halt as we reached the cobbles. I was falling forwards into him and he was toppling over onto the handlebars and then to the side, and I grabbed him to stop him falling. I clambered off the back of the bike, and he cocked his leg over the crossbar; we were still both laughing. I was laughing so hard I couldn't stand up and had to hold on to him. He led the way up the passageway between our houses, holding the front wheel up in the air like he always did when he wheeled his bike through the gate, and I was holding onto his belt to steady myself, and when he got through his gate, he leaned the bike against the wall and turned. We were very close.

He said, "Mad to ride home in this garb, on a night like this. Red serge! God, I'm hot." And he undid his belt and unbuttoned his jacket and revealed a tight white T shirt and braces. And I was standing there thinking that there is nothing as sexy as a fit man in braces, when he pulled me to him and kissed me.

Then he said "No, sorry. Shouldn't have done that," and stepped away, but I pulled him back and put my arms round his neck and brought his head down to mine. I could smell the wool of his jacket, and ironing, and sweat; I kissed him back, and he tasted salty. He was kissing me as if he'd been on a six month expedition through frozen Alaska with nothing for company but a couple of huskies.

His hand was on my neck, and all I could think about was his thumb, stroking my ear lobe, and after half a minute we came up for air. I looked into his eyes and said "Being kissed by a mountie is even more exciting than I imag-" and he interrupted me by kissing me and then said, "How long have you been fantasising about mounties, then?" and he kissed me again, and then I said, "Ever since we did the Commonwealth in Miss Bilton's class at Redmire Primary, and I chose Canada for my special project." And he was kissing me again, and I was inside the roughness of his open jacket, but after only a few seconds, oh, I couldn't wait and oh, I like my comforts and oh, like an impatient fool, I said, "Are we going to stand here all night?"

And he looked at his watch and said "Blimey, I'm catching a train in the morning at six o'clock. Better go," and my stomach caved in.

"Are you?" I said, failing to keep the rush of disappointment from my voice.

"Going to London to meet a new client. Can't afford to get the train at a reasonable hour – can't afford the *Master Cutler*. Have to get the early train. I'll have to love you and leave you." Now he kissed me as if he were a husband of twenty years, leaving for the office.

"Good night, then," I said.

It was as sudden as that. Quick and surprising and wonderful, and then it was over.

I padded away, feeling like a dog that's been told off and sent to its corner. He'd been my neighbour, then my friend. Was it different now? Did I want it to be different?

And what about Charles?

CHAPTER 14

When I woke up in the morning and remembered what had happened, my first thought was the same as always, and it had nothing to do with Rob - *Pa is dead, so what's the point of getting up?*

I did get up, though, and followed my usual routine: glass work, craft work, a boring tea of scrambled eggs, work on *Photoshop* on the computer in the evening, and then bed. All through the day my mind was on Rob and Charles, spinning round and round and trying to work out what the night before had meant to me, and what it had meant to Rob. I heard him come home late from London. I heard his footsteps in the passageway.

The next day I woke up with a bad headache. It subsided once I was upright, but then I felt woozy. It was often like this in the mornings that summer. Some days when I woke I saw flashing lights as well. And I'd been having weird vibrations in my head during the day. It felt as if miniature railways were running up and down the side of my head. I thought it was something to do with grieving for Pa, but that week I'd been worrying about having a brain tumour, so I'd booked an appointment with the doctor.

He took my blood pressure, and examined my eyes, and said, "I'm certainly not worried about a stroke. Have you been under any stress lately?" and I told him about Pa.

"Then I don't think we need to worry," he said.

"So it's just psychosomatic."

"Just?" he said, "It's still unpleasant."

He wanted me to see a counsellor to talk about my bereavement, maybe just once or twice. It felt polite to say I would think about it. But I didn't want to talk to a counsellor. Grief is natural. I wanted to talk to someone who knew me and knew Pa and knew our family.

All the way back from the doctor's, I thought about Pa. It would have been easy to slip into a romantic and idealised grief where Pa was a perfect Pa instead of the selfish, critical person I knew he was. But he wasn't *just* selfish and critical. He was affectionate and generous, too; and I liked the way that he obviously enjoyed having a family, the singing in the car, the photos he took of us. I remember him at the bottom of the stairs shouting up to us to tell us that there was going to be a new series of *Wonder Woman* starting the next week, and he couldn't wait to watch it with us.

I was going to drive up to Wensleydale in the afternoon, so I tidied the house and packed. I wanted to see Rob before I went. When I'd woken in the night feeling sad, yearning for comfort, it was Rob who'd come into my mind. But before I had chance to call on him, he knocked on my door.

When I saw him standing there, I felt steadier than I had done all day.

"I need to talk to you," he said.

I leaned towards him and touched his arm. Was it all right to kiss him? But then I noticed the two little notches between his eyebrows, and how pale he was, and that his cheek muscles were twitching in and out, in and out, and I stepped back.

"Come in."

He came in and hovered. He patted the kitchen table with the flat of his hand. He scratched his head.

"Sit down, then," I said. "It's so *lovely* to see you. Did you have a good day in London?" I sat down at the table facing him but he remained standing.

"I need to say…" he said, and stopped.

"Yes?"

"I need to say that I shouldn't have kissed you and I'm-"

"But why?"

"Please, Corinne. Would you mind if I finished? This isn't easy."

I rested my chin on my hand, my elbow on the table, and looked more carefully at his face. Why did he look so tense?

"I'm just not up for anything other than friendship," he said. "I'm sorry. I really like you, and if I was looking for someone…well…if I was, which I'm not…I would have thought I'd found her in you."

What a sweet thing to say. *I'd have thought I'd found her in you.* But he wasn't really saying it, was he?

"Why?" I said. "Why? I haven't seen you with anyone else."

"But *you're* with somebody else."

I'd forgotten about Charles. "Is that it? Is that the reason? I mean, we're not…" *What are we not?*

"It's not that," he said. He was leaning with his back against the fridge - as far away as he could get from me.

"Because if it is…" *If it is, what?*

Before I could think of what to say, he said: "I don't want to get into all this heart swapping, souls touching, dependency, vulnerability, the possibility of damage kind of stuff."

Someone must have definitively stomped on his heart.

"Was it your wife?"

He folded his arms and the movement dislodged a magnet from the front of the fridge. It fell to the floor and he bent to pick it up.

"Oh no," he said. "Oh Corinne, I'm so sorry – I've broken your Tigger. His tail's broken off. I'll get you another. Oh, I'm sorry."

"Please - why don't you want to be with me?"

He looked out of the window and didn't answer. A cat was sitting on the sill; he often came. Sometimes I gave him some left-overs in a saucer by the back door.

"I don't want to go into it," said Rob.

"Don't you think you owe me that?"

"I don't owe you anything."

I flinched, and he saw me flinch. He walked over and came round to my side of the table, and squatted down so he could look into my eyes. His gaze was steady. His eyes were kind and troubled. He picked up my hand from my lap and held it. His fingers were hot.

"I'm sorry, Corinne. I don't know where that came from… I…" He dropped my hand and stood up straight and put his hands into the pockets of his jacket. "Look," he said, "I don't want to get into lots of personal stuff, but, well…" he had moved away and was leaning against the kitchen sink now with his arm stretched out along the work top. He was fiddling with the corkscrew lying next to the kettle. OK," he said, "when my wife moved out and went to live with someone else she didn't just do it out of the blue, she had already as good as left me eighteen months before, and all that time I was trying to win her back, hoping it would pass, thinking if I just held on then she'd realise – you see, I'm doing it. Getting into all that stuff again. I don't want to."

I sighed. Part of me was thinking, no not thinking, it was as if my brain was flailing about in distress at what he'd just said. The other half of me was exhausted. I felt as though I was peeking out of a cage of weariness. I was staring into the turquoise of his cycling jumper, but my mind had wandered away from what he'd just said. I looked at his face and saw his eyebrows raised as if he was waiting for me to say something.

"Why is it that every time you leave the house you're in cycling clothes?" I said. "Don't think I haven't noticed."

He didn't look surprised at my non sequitur. "That? That's part of it. It's something she once said to me."

I waited for more, but it didn't come.

"Well?" I said.

He still didn't answer the question, but he came and sat down opposite me and stretched out his hand towards me on the table top, his palm open. "Can we go back to being friends?"

"What? I suppose so," I said, without enthusiasm. I was feeling so tired. I folded my arms on the table, leaned forward and rested my head on them.

"Thanks, Corinne." He touched my shoulder and made to leave. Then he turned round and said "I didn't ask you how you were feeling. I know this is a really hard time for you. For anyone."

"Yes, well, you don't think you've made me feel any better, do you?"

"Sorry."

"I have one good day and one bad day. Wednesday – especially Wednesday night at the hospital when I met a gorgeous mountie – that was a good day." He opened his mouth to say something but didn't, and I continued. "At least it was a good day for me. Today is a bad day. I start off OK in the morning, but by late afternoon I start to flag and feel miserable and weepy and all kind of heavy inside. I am comfort eating, and I ache all down my right side from the waist down. Shall I tell you more? I could go on."

"Poor you."

"I wish he hadn't died. Death is a very bad idea. I don't approve of it. And don't come out and tell me that death is a part of life, or–"

"It doesn't help."

"No." A tear rolled down my cheek and then another and then I couldn't stop.

"People shouldn't die. It's too hard for those who are left behind," he said.

He passed me the box of tissues from the dresser and waited for me to dry my eyes.

"After my mother died, my teeth hurt all the time," he said.

"Really?"

He made to leave again. "Any time you want some undemanding company, you know where I am," he said, shutting the door behind him.

That was the trouble. *I* wanted to be demanding. I wanted to demand he stay with me and put his arm around me and tell me that he loved me and that Pa wasn't really dead.

The door opened again and his head popped round. "Don't worry – I'll get you another Tigger."

"Bugger Tigger. Get me an Eeyore."

✻ ✻ ✻

The journey to Wensleydale was dreary. I hadn't the heart for motorway driving, and I stayed in the slow lane for much of the time, chugging along at 50mph, slowing down every time a car came on from a slip road, instead of staying the same speed and moving over to the middle lane.

I hated arriving at Hollycroft to find Pa still not there and no hope of his coming back. And everything was different – his chair gone from the dining room window and the table moved in its place instead, his bedroom changed to a pristine white room with a new deep pink carpet, and all the pictures dusted and the double bed in there, and the sitting room with not a trace of him. His hat still hung in the porch, though. That was some comfort.

All of Saturday there was a heavy feeling. Ma was depressed, and I didn't manage to make her feel better. We went for a drive over the hill to Cray where, in spite of it being July, the hills looked barren under the grey sky. It was cold and dull and windy, and though we tried a little walk on the top it was too cold, and Ma was as fed up as me. Driving back through Hawes she asked "Do you want to go and have a cup of tea at the dairy?" and then she dithered and said she couldn't be bothered.

On Sunday I was determined not to be a wimp – if Ma could be brave then so could I, and I would help to do more clearing. But at breakfast we were talking about who should have what – the silver presentation tray that Pa got when he won the trophies at the Dairy Show, for example – and my stiff upper lip crumpled and I said "I don't want anything. I just want Pa," and I cried.

Ma got up to put her arm round me and said "Yes, especially now when he could help you" – which I took as a reference to my attempt to start a new business. But that wasn't the point. I didn't want him there so he could help me. I just wanted him there because I wanted him, and because that's where he belonged. And I know it sounds like a cliché – *I don't want anything. I just want Pa* – but that was exactly what I felt.

Anyway, we cleared out one more desk drawer, and it wasn't too hard. I found another bundle of letters I'd sent Ma and Pa from Italy. What a long time ago that was.

And I found a small cutting from the *Farmers Weekly* from the 1960s, called Wensleydale High Yielders, where he was standing talking to a group of farmers, and he was moving his hand, holding his hand, in the distinctive position that I know, that I recognise from all of my life. Ma said I could have the clipping.

After lunch I was desperate to get out, so I asked Ma if I could take some Arthur Bell roses from the terrace to put on Pa's grave. She said yes and helped me to tie up a bunch of them with raffia.

I walked over the fields to the falls, choking up on occasion with tears, and while I walked I felt like an archetypal character in a rustic drama – walking across the fields to the next village to visit her father's grave and leave a bunch of his favourite roses picked from his own garden. And there were tourists around – visiting the falls, even though it was a wet Sunday teatime and the falls were looking dry and not up to their best at all. What did I look like to them? A lone woman in a Barbour jacket, jeans and wellies, with a mournful look on her face, carrying a bunch of fine yellow roses.

I walked past the gate we used to drive through with

our Austin Countryman loaded with children and camping equipment – to camp there with Ma and Pa, Megan and me, with Steven a baby who would sleep in a drawer. Pa always had some excuse about a crisis on the farm that needed sorting out, and he'd leave Ma to settle with us in the tents, and he often didn't come back till the morning, because he wanted to sleep in the farmhouse in comfort.

It was raining, and I thought about *Wuthering Heights* and all the other melodramas in which death figures strongly, with people throwing themselves on graves and weeping, and how it's always raining in dramatic funerals.

When I got to the burial ground I walked up and arranged the roses on the grave. The card was still there saying "All our love from Mary and the Chundies." I sat on the wet bench on the opposite side of the path and wept a little and wondered if the people who live in the house at the back would see me and wonder who I was, and again I stood outside myself and watched me. I probably spent ten minutes there, though it seemed like longer. When I walked back I felt better. I felt calmer, and I'm sure the exercise did me good quite apart from the cathartic effect of visiting his grave.

I walked in the cottage to find Ma had a visitor from Quaker meeting, so I jumped in the car and drove over to Preston-under-Scar to see Steve. He'd just brought in the cows for milking.

"Nip in the house and borrow one of my boiler suits," he said. "I think Martine's will be too short for you. Any road, they're hanging in the scullery. Martine's not there. She's over at her mother's."

I found one of Steve's boiler suits and took it into the kitchen to put it on. The kitchen was huge. In summer holidays when it was too wet to play outside, Ma would sometimes load all the chairs on top of the table, and take up the rugs and let us roller skate in there.

I stood in front of the Rayburn. It wasn't cold, but that's not always the point. There's something inherently comforting about old fashioned stoves that are kept in 24 hours a day. When I was little, Ma looked after orphan lambs in cardboard boxes in front of the Rayburn. Sometimes, when they were really tiny, she put them in the stick oven with the door open. We fed them with a bottle. I remembered their warmth and the feel of their short fuzzy coats and the smell of the sweet powdered milk we gave them.

Steve was standing in the pit when I got back to the milking parlour, with ten cows each side of the parlour already hooked up. I stood with him, taking care to dodge the muck and the pee from the cows that were being milked. He usually had the radio on, but today he didn't. It was peaceful. The cows standing waiting to be milked were quiet. I breathed in the smell of chlorine and cowshit. There was no mooing, but one or two near the front of the crowd pushed and nudged each other to make sure they got in first when the next lot were let into the parlour. They wanted their cake.

"How are you doing?" I asked. I didn't want to mention grieving for Pa specifically, but that's what I meant.

"Not bad," he said. "Now."

"What do you mean - now?" I said.

The teat cups unit jumped off the udder of the last cow on my right, and swung at the side of my head.

"Hang on," said Steve.

He grabbed a sprayer hanging down from a pipe and sprayed the cow's udder with iodine to disinfect it. All ten cows on that side had finished milking now, and Steve opened the far barrier to let them out.

The cows left the stalls and walked through a footbath back into the cubicle house. Steve cleaned where they'd been with water from a wide-bored yellow hose, then he opened the far barrier and another ten cows walked into the stalls without prompting, the automatic gate shutting behind the last one. He then hooked all the new cows up to their teat cups, pulling each of the cow's four teats to squirt out a bit of milk to make sure it was flowing before he fitted on the cups.

He reached up and turned a handle to dispense cake for each of the cows. "I couldn't afford to have an automatic feed dispenser," he said. "Now," he said, coming near to me, "what were we talking about?"

"I was asking how you were. You know…"

"I've had a couple of disasters. Mind not on the job, sort of thing."

"What?"

"The week after the memorial service I forgot to turn off the tap after the tanker driver had taken the milk from the tank so that next time I milked, the milk was fed into the tank but drained out the other end because of the open tap." He slapped his forehead. "Stupid. Pa would have given me a right rollicking if he'd been here. All that waste. All that money. Then last week, I forgot to connect the water pipe from the pre-cooler so it went all over the floor…annoying, but not a catastrophe."

The cows on the other side were all finished milking now, and he went through the same procedure again and then came back to talk. "How are you, then, Corrie? Nobbut middling?"

"Sad. But all the better for seeing you." He put his arm round my shoulder and gave me a squeeze. I stayed till the end of milking. The quiet routine, the contented cows, and Steve's no-nonsense steadfastness were comforting. As long as he was there, Pa wouldn't be far away.

CHAPTER 15

It was the kind of hot, August afternoon designed for lying in a hammock in an orchard gazing at the pattern of the leaves against the sky, or for sitting in a summerhouse curled up in a sagging, horsehair-stuffed armchair reading a favourite book – *Homestead* for me, *It's not about the Bike* for Rob. But we had no hammock, no orchard, and we had no summerhouse. Have you noticed how I'm using the term "we" as if we were a couple? I longed for Rob and me to be a couple. I ached for it. But we weren't a couple. We were friends.

But Rob was just the right kind of friend to have around when you're feeling miserable. I was spending a lot of melancholy afternoons that summer sitting in the sun with him, and he didn't demand anything from me in the way of conversation: he read his book, or more often he drew, and every now and then he looked up and asked if there was anything he could do for me. *Just stay with me*, is what I thought, but didn't say. What I said out loud was "Don't worry, I'm OK."

The day I'm talking about I'd been to town in the morning and had my first glimpse of the end of summer peeping darkly over the blue horizon when I went into M&S and stumbled into one of those horrid *Back to School* displays, with child-sized mannequins dressed up in grey pleated skirts and synthetic blue V necks and pale blue poly-cotton shirts and shiny black clompy shoes. I always get a suffocating feeling when I see a *Back to School* display and find myself rushing to the door to escape from the stuffiness into the fresh air outside.

When I got back from town, I sunbathed in the back garden on my steamer chair, but now the sun had slid behind the houses and I was knocking on Rob's door in my bikini top and shorts, wanting company.

He was upstairs working on illustrations for *Teach Yourself Hungarian*. I had a look at some of them. He draws in pen and ink, sure and spare. The men in this set of cartoons were mostly chubby, with a worn look on their faces. His women were slim and sharp, with hatchet faces and big hair.

I stretched out on his sofa and opened my book of stained glass designs. I was trying to find an Art Nouveau one that I could make. Rob sat on a high architect's chair at his drawing board with his back to the open sash window.

There was no hint of a breeze: warm air outside and in. Still. There were faint bursts of traffic noise from Fulwood Road, and Aidan, the toddler two doors down, was splashing and squealing in his paddling pool, with his mother's soft murmurs interspersed between his yelps.

"Is that futon OK?" said Rob, his head bent over his work. His anglepoise light caught the grey hair at his temples, shining it silver. "Bella always moans about it when she comes to stay."

"The futon's comfy but the canvas is a bit itchy," I said. I rubbed the back of my thighs. "But that's OK, I'm not sleeping on it."

"Oh yes?"

"Damn, I thought you hadn't noticed." Was it significant that he'd been watching me?

"Your breathing changed and your eyes were closed."

"It's so embarrassing to nod off. It makes me feel – hey look at this design! It's more like a Mackintosh than a Mackintosh."

"What are you on about?" He hopped off his chair and came over to look at the page I was holding open.

"Do you like it? I love the way the leaves curl into the frame like that."

He was bending over me to look at the page of the book, his head an inch from mine, and I could feel every molecule in my body buzzing. I could have turned my head and kissed him, just like that. He might have switched off his attraction to me, but my feelings for him were fierce. I loved his kindness, his sensitivity, his – sometimes painful - honesty. I loved his patience, his straightforwardness, his Yorkshire accent. I even loved his bloody accent! And I fancied him rotten.

"It's OK," he said, "but I prefer Art Deco really. Aren't you sleeping well?" he asked as he went back to his desk.

"Not too bad," I said.

That week I felt brighter inside my head - the migraines and miniature railway effect had gone - though every morning when I woke, my body had a new ache or pain. Whenever I met Rob the first thing he said was "What's the symptom of the day?" which made me laugh. I was trying to cultivate a stoical approach: ignore the pains, not mention them, and just get on with it. I didn't want to be forever complaining.

"Well, that's another reception desk in the bag," he said. He put down his pen and stretched. "*I would like a double room with a bath, please,*" he said with an unrecognisable European inflection which only smeared the top of his Yorkshire accent. A hilarious combination. "This is mind numbing stuff," he said. "I'm absolutely sick of this book."

"Why do it, then?"

"Pays the bills, of course, keeps me in Lycra."

"I wanted to ask you something about that. Do you remember I asked you that time – that time – remember? In my kitchen?"

"What's the question?"

"Why do you never go out unless you are in your cycling gear?"

He put down his pen, sat back on his chair, and pushed his hands in his pockets.

"Do I really have to tell you?" He sounded as though he was putting up some kind of resistance, but not convincingly.

"Rob, aren't we friends now?"

"Yes." He picked up his pen again and resumed his drawing. He looked as though he was doodling.

"Well? Come on, this is me you're talking to."

"My wife. My ex-wife," he said, without looking up.

"What's she called?"

"Judith. She said I only looked anything like…when I was in my cycling gear. She said I looked a nonentity in ordinary clothes. And fat."

"You? Fat?"

"I've lost a lot of weight since then."

"Even so, what a vile thing to–"

"Quite."

"But why do you still think about it? How long have you been divorced?"

"Ten years."

"And anyway, you're *lean*. You're as lean as a whippet that's been on a diet."

"That's what I like to hear."

"But Rob!"

"Look. She destroyed me. I mean it. She destroyed me. When I'm wearing civvies like I am now – this T shirt," he plucked at it, "these jeans," he pulled at them, "I feel like Mr Blobby. I can't help it, I do. When I'm in my jersey and my shorts and I'm on my bike I feel like a racehorse – sleek and fit and dazzling. On my bike's the only time I feel anything approaching attractive. And the cycling gear is half way there." He scratched his head. "So."

He glanced in my direction and then got a new sheet of paper and started drawing again. I wanted to rush over and shake him and tell him how attractive he was. How sweet, how kind, how caring. I wanted to put my arms around him and tell him that I loved his eyes, the colour of the peaty brown river in Wensleydale. I wanted him to know that one of his wry looks could turn me to jelly; that actually he could do with putting on some weight. That I worried about how thin he was.

He broke into my thoughts. "Sad, isn't it?" he said, without looking up.

"Mad is what I call it. Not attractive? The only reason you're not overwhelmed with female attention is because you never go anywhere, and if you do you're never in one place for long enough."

He blushed. "Oh sure." He got down from his chair. "I'm having a coffee. Do you want some? I'm sorry, but I've only got the best." Rob hated fresh coffee and only bought Somerfield Fair Trade Instant. It was a running joke between us, and I'd ended up keeping a jar of the stuff in my cupboard, for when he came round. "Want something cold?" he said.

"Do you know what?"

"What?"

"I want to cook for you tonight. I haven't cooked a big meal since – since-" *since I cooked for Charles,* "Let me cook for you."

"That's very kind. But I'm fully domesticated. I can cook."

"I know. I know. And you know that's not the point."

"What *is* the point?"

"I want to do something nice for you. You've been looking after me. I'd like to do something for you."

"Kind, but not necessary."

"I know it's not necessary."

"So please don't cook for me."

"But-"

"Do something else, if you must. Clean my windows. That'd be great. Go to the post for me. Tidy my garden. Bring in my washing. I know you have a fetish about the smell of clean washing. But please don't cook for me. Any road, enough of this, I'm putting the kettle on. What are you supping?"

✳ ✳ ✳

The season was turning. When I went upstairs one early morning to get something from the attic I looked through the skylight to see the park and it wasn't there – just mist. And when I stepped outside in my pyjamas to pick up the milk bottle from the step, there was a September nip in the air. And the last time Viv had called she'd brought me a bunch of Michaelmas daisies – a present from Albert. She was now a confirmed allotment dweller.

I was working in the wash house, when Rob appeared in the doorway.

"Hi. Want to go for a walk?" he said. We often went for walks together. Sometimes local ones. Sometimes I'd drive us out to the Peak District. I loved the way he was always pointing things out to me when we were out – the way a tree arched over a stile, or a pretty group of rowan trees behind a dry stone wall, all the berries bright. And I liked the way that when we went round the Botanical Gardens I could say "I hate that yellow" and he knew what I was talking about, because unlike Mark, Rob could see five different yellows in a flower bed, and just like me, had opinions about every one of them.

He was standing there waiting for an answer.

"I'm working."

"I can see. Want to go for a walk?"

"How well you know me," I said. I switched off the soldering iron and hung up my apron. "You never know," I said. "It could be the last of the fine days. It would be a sin to miss it."

We walked down Oakbrook Road and then up through Bingham Park, following the valley through Whiteley Woods. The leaves were turning, a few had already dried up and dropped, but it would be another month or so before there'd be sufficient on the ground for scrunching through.

After a while, the footpath up the valley is crossed by Whiteley Wood Road and as we stood, waiting to cross it, a cyclist whizzed past. Rob turned his head to watch the guy cycle up the hill.

"Blimey, did you get a look at his clusters?" he said.

My mind reeled.

"*What?*" I said.

"So tight and highly polished."

"Do I want to know what clusters are?"

"The gears on his bike, of course."

"Of course."

We crossed the road and climbed up the grassy slope to Wire Mill Dam. A man threw a stick over the water for his golden retriever, and the dog went splashing after it.

"I used to come up here with my mates when I was young, and watch the old men with their radio-controlled boats," said Rob.

"Didn't you have one?"

"Nah. Too skint. It was OK just watching, though. They let us have a go sometimes. They'd not be able to do that now, would they? Be accused of being paedophiles."

"Do you think they were?"

"What? Course not. And you see that corner over there? That's where I lost my spud gun. I had a fight with Tom Hewitt and dropped it in the water. I was ten. I never managed to find it. I even borrowed Jackie's – that's my sister's – snorkel one time, but the mud was so thick I couldn't see owt."

He walked off the path, onto the grass, and through the sycamores to the other side of the dam.

"Where are you going?" I said, following him.

"To look for my spud gun, of course" he said. "And if there are two of us, the chances of finding it are even better."

"You're bonkers."

As we walked up the valley, he told me more about his childhood, growing up in Walkley, about his mum and dad and his two sisters. I scavenged for every detail of his childhood and his youth. Every titbit was as appealing as the patches in the quilt I was sewing.

When we got to Forge Dam, we called in at the café for drinks. When I was at Art College I used to go there with friends. We (me and the other two girls I shared a house with) often walked up the valley from Hunter's Bar on a Saturday morning in an effort to clear thick heads from Friday night in *The Lescar* pub. If it was winter we huddled inside the café, making sure we bagged a table by a radiator. In summer we took our mugs outside and sat on a bench overlooking the pond. The café has a couple of small tables outside and an electrical rocking giraffe for toddlers to ride on, but apart from that it's a throwback to the 1950s, with a corrugated metal roof, patterned curtains at the windows and a formica counter, and everyone loves it that way.

Except for Mark. The first time I took him there he asked for an espresso and the woman behind the counter gave him a blank look and said "Is that a new kind of chocolate bar, love?'

He turned to me with his eyebrows raised, and a look in his eyes that was a mixture of disbelief and disgust and it cracked me up.

"I like this place," said Rob. "I used to come with my mam and dad on Sundays sometimes. After my dad got back from his Sunday ride with his club."

"Are *you* in a cycling club?" I asked.

"Not these days. I have a couple of friends I go out with every few weeks, though. Look-" he pointed to the notices stuck above the shelves behind the counter, "they've been got at. Two different price lists for the coffee – that one just says *Coffee* and another up there says *Posh coffee.*"

I laughed. "It's the thin end of the wedge," I said. "Next time we come, milky coffee will be a thing of the past and I'll have to order café latte. Just like Starbucks."

The bloke behind the counter heard us. "Credit us with a bit of gumption. We know what the locals like." And he gave me a wink to show there were no hard feelings.

Rob had his usual black instant, and I had tea and a bacon butty because I'd had no breakfast.

We sat on a bench by the water. I was wearing boots and needlecords and my fair isle jacket, but there was a chilly breeze blowing down the valley and I shivered. Rob zipped up his fleece. He had taken to going out in civvies when he was with me. The sun was low in the sky. It shone in my eyes, and bounced off the pond where the ducks disturbed the water as they dove for food, and it made bright shining ripples around them. When they swam the length of the pond they left V shaped trails in their wake, and the bright spots of water were spotlights trailing them across the dam.

I offered Rob my bacon butty. "Do you want a bite?"

"No, ta."

"I thought you liked bacon – that's why I got it."

"I don't eat till later. I mean, I'm not hungry thanks."

"You don't eat till later? It sounds like a policy."

Rob didn't answer.

A young woman with a toddler started to throw bread to the ducks, and a host of them flew and scooted and swam in a hungry crowd towards her, leaving behind them a mass of criss cross trails in the water.

"What do you mean?" I said.

"I try not to eat too much. Did you know that if you reduce your calorie intake, it makes you live longer?"

"Really?"

"I'm hoping to live to 130."

"What for?"

"Don't you like being alive?" he said.

"What do you think? Of course I do. I know I've been miserable lately about Pa, but-"

"Rats on a restricted calorie intake have been shown to age more slowly," he said. "They live up to 50% longer than rats who eat what they like."

"But what's the point of living longer if you're not enjoying yourself? I wouldn't want to live to be 130 if it meant I had to give up all my small pleasures. Imagine never being able to have another bacon butty."

"Living longer will be the best revenge."

What was he talking about? "Revenge on who, Rob? And it's living *well* is the best revenge."

"Each to his own." He got up from the bench and went over to the water, standing with his hands in his pockets. After a few minutes he came back. "Can you remind me when we go past the chemists on the way home – I need to get a new toothbrush to clean the gears on my bike."

"OK," I said, swallowing the last of my butty. "But can't you use an old one you're throwing away?"

"The toothbrush has to be new."

"Surely what's good enough to put in your mouth is good enough for your bike?"

"Corinne. I don't mean the bike I rescued from the skip. I'm talking about my *best* bike. The Condor."

I rolled my eyes. "Oh, well, why didn't you say?"

"Give over," he said, punching me on the arm. "Are you ready for off?"

We walked back down the cobbled slope to the café, and found Elspeth sitting at one of the tables. Minnie-May was riding on the mechanical giraffe.

"Corinne says you're looking for a shop," said Rob. "Have you seen that one with the *For Let* sign at Nether Green, opposite the school?"

"Is that the greengrocers shop that has just closed down?"

"Yep."

"Thank you for the suggestion, but I think Broomhill would be better, if I can afford the rent. I would catch the hordes of passing students, there."

"Do students knit?"

"It is very fashionable. Judging from the – Minnie-May, come off there now and let the little boy have a turn – judging from the numbers of students who bring their knitting into my lectures."

"Really?"

"You would be surprised. If a hand goes up in a lecture these days, it is as likely to be someone who has dropped a stitch, or someone who cannot understand a knitting pattern abbreviation as it is to be someone with a question on the topic of my lecture. It has become quite a challenge to leap from the language of Crabbe to the niceties of buttonholing. *What does psso mean?* was a query I had last week in Combined Arts 2a. They do not teach young people anything these days."

"Are you talking about manners or concentration?"

"I mean that I knew what *psso* meant when I was seven."

"Well?"

"Pardon?"

"What does it mean?"

"Pass slipped stitch over, of course."

Minnie-May had stopped watching the boy on the giraffe and was tugging on Elspeth's sleeve.

I squatted down to be the same height as her. "How is your lip?" I asked. "Is it better, now?"

"Nearly. Do you want to see it?" She tightened her lips and thrust out her chin for me to examine it.

It was barely visible. "Where is it?" I said.

"Here," she said, pointing at the wound.

"Oh yes," I said. "I can only just make it out. It hardly shows. Would you like an ice cream?" I said. I turned to Elspeth, "Or has she already had one?"

"No, lovely."

Minnie-May took my hand and we went into the café, leaving Rob and Elspeth talking. Minnie-May dithered over her choice of flavour – should she have a strawberry mivvi or a chocolate lolly? I glanced through the open door at Rob and Elspeth who were deep in conversation. Rob was sitting next to her and leaning in as if he was speaking confidentially.

When we came out again he leant back in his chair and stopped talking, and they both tried to look as though they had been discussing the weather. Rob said "Quick, look at that squirrel, Minnie-May." He pointed to the stone steps that went down to the sunken lawn.

On the way back, Rob asked me for suggestions for a birthday present for his daughter Bella. She'd just bought her first house with her partner, and Rob had given her a cheque to fund a trip to IKEA, but he wanted to give her the birthday equivalent of a stocking filler. Something small but immaculately chosen.

"I was wondering about a piece of stained glass," he said. "Just a small one."

"Like a suncatcher to hang in the window?"

"She likes butterflies. Could I do her a couple of butterflies? Will you teach me?"

"Yes, I'll, hey - can you see that bloke over there?" I said. There was a man on the other side of the stream, crouching down beside a tree, stuffing something into a rucksack. He kept glancing round, as if he was nervous about someone seeing what he was doing. "What's he up to?"

Rob said, "Come behind here." He grabbed my arm and dipped behind a shrub, and I staggered and lurched into him. When we had righted ourselves, we peeked through the leaves like a couple of kids, and watched the man. He was wearing very short shorts and a tracksuit top and he had thick blond hair, cut short. It was Tim!

"I know him from the allotment," I said to Rob. I walked back onto the path again. "Hi, Tim!" I shouted.

Tim jumped and tensed up, but when he looked round and saw it was me who was shouting, he relaxed a bit. "Corinne." He jinked between the trees and down to the stream, found a firm spot on the bank and then he leapt over in a single bound. He climbed up the little slope to the path where we were standing and I introduced him to Rob.

"If I didn't know you," I said, laughing, "I'd have thought you'd just buried a body over there."

He blushed. "Well, actually, I was…" he trailed off, slung the rucksack onto his back and shoved his hands in his pockets. Then he started rocking back and forth on the balls of his feet. "I was…"

"Yes?"

"This is rather delicate, Corinne. Especially as you've just lost your father."

What on earth was he talking about? "Yes?" I said.

"I understand why people do it, of course, but it isn't right. It's litter. Pollution."

"What is?"

"All these people who come out and leave bouquets of shop-bought flowers, wrapped up in cellophane. Some of them even nail them to the trees. *In loving memory*. Oh dear. I wish it hadn't been you."

"Please explain, Tim. And don't worry. I hate it when

people leave bunches of flowers in plastic wrappers around the place, so I'm not offended. I agree – the aesthetics of it…well…oh, God."

"But some people don't have a grave to put their flowers on," said Rob. "Aren't you being a bit harsh?"

"There are surely other ways," said Tim. "Every time I walk up through Whiteley Woods – and in the Peak District too – I am assaulted by flowers wrapped in plastic, decaying…*for Grandpa, who loved this spot.* I feel like stuffing every last one of them into the nearest litter bin."

"What?" Rob and I said together.

"I don't. All I do is take the plastic and cellophane away and leave the flowers to rot. I've found five bouquets between here and Hunter's Bar so far today. It really is too bad."

✳ ✳ ✳

When I got back I looked for a butterfly pattern for Rob, to save me the trouble of drawing one. In amongst the papers was an envelope of photographs. There was a small passport photo of Pa, looking old, but not ill. Last time I saw the photo I hated it because he did not look his handsome self in it. He looked jowly and with over-big glasses from the eighties, and I had shoved it away.

This time I could look at the photo and remember what he was like before he was ill. He'd become so deaf it was hard to talk to him. To see the photograph reminded me of the reality of who had died: not an ideal, handsome, James Stewart kind of father, but a grouchy and impatient and deaf old man, who nevertheless I loved. When he died I didn't lose the father of my childhood. He'd already translated into another father, maybe a version who was easier to lose. I realised I'd been grieving about my family and my childhood as much as my father.

In the evening I rang Elspeth.

"So what were you and Rob talking about?" I said.

There was a miniscule pause and then she said, "This and that. He asked me if I had a business plan, I believe."

"Elspeth, what were you *really* talking about?"

"You, of course. I said that you had found his friendship a great support, a significant comfort in your bereavement."

"What did he say?"

"He said he had not done anything special."

"Is that all?"

"He said he was hoping to persuade you to buy a bicycle."

"He's never mentioned it to me. Anything else?"

"He said that you were a great shape for–"

"He said I was a great shape? Wow!"

"Let me finish. He said you were a great shape for cycling. That being slim and having long legs you had a superb, no, let me get it right, a *champion* power to weight ratio."

CHAPTER 16

"This is it, Corinne," said Albert. "There's nothing to beat sweet peas. I'm fair pleased you asked me."

I hadn't been up to the allotment for ages, but Viv – who was coming with me to Wensleydale - suggested I ask Albert for some flowers. I found him sitting in his deck chair outside his shed, drinking from his mid-morning flask of tea.

"Do you want to just step inside my shed and fetch me the scissors? They're on the shelf at the back. Mind you get the sharp ones – they've got orange handles."

"Come on, then," he said when I came out. He hauled himself out of his chair. "Come with me and tell me which colours you'd like."

"Any you can spare, Albert." I touched his arm and he turned to look at me. "And thanks. I wanted to take some sweet peas to put on Pa's grave, to make up for the fact that I couldn't get any in May - you know – at his burial."

We walked along between two rows of sweet peas that were tall and rangy now at the end of the season, the foliage lower down gone pale and dry.

"I always plant them later than anyone else. But that means they hang around well into September – if I water them, that is. Have you seen that son of mine lately? It was his mam's birthday yesterday and he never sent her a card, or rang, or owt."

"I haven't seen him for a bit."

"I thought you two were an item – that's what they call it these days, isn't it?"

"No. I mean yes. Yes, it's what they call it. But I'm not sure you'd say we were one - an item."

I'd been out with Charles a couple of times in August, but when he wanted to come back to my place afterwards, I didn't feel like it and fobbed him off.

One time he spent ten minutes trying to persuade me to go to the sailing club with him. He wanted me to spend the day with him on a friend's boat and then stay for the barbecue in the evening, but he asked me on a bad day, when the thought of seeing anyone that I didn't know and having to make social chitchat was all too much.

He said "Corinne, let's have a break for a while. I can see you have your mind on other things. Call me when you're feeling better."

Albert was still cutting sweet peas. "Well," he said, "all I can say is the lad's as daft as a brush." He turned to me and held up a generous bunch of flowers – carmine, deep cobalt blue, white, violet, and the palest powder blue. "Is that sufficient?"

I kissed him on the cheek. "Thanks, Albert. You're a love."

"Gormless, he is. A ninny." I assumed he was referring to Charles. "This is it – he talks all stuck up, but he's as daft as a brush."

※ ※ ※

Viv and I drove up to Wensleydale that afternoon. We stopped at the burial ground on the way. It was odd, because when I walked up the path of stone flags to the grave, I didn't feel as though Pa was there, and I wondered why I was leaving him flowers. Should I take the sweet peas to Ma instead? Or should I split the bunch in two, and take half to Ma and leave the others on the grave? In the end I left them all for Pa, thinking it might be the last time I took him flowers.

Viv was expecting me to get upset at the cottage, but I didn't.

When I went inside, it didn't seem strange that the dining table was over by the window, or that Ma had moved a small armchair into the porch so she could enjoy the sunshine away from draughts. And the sitting room was different – the telly was on a low table, and the bookshelves were to the right of the bureau, rather than in the alcove behind the telly. It looked much better and seemed to make the small cottage room look deeper and more spacious.

That night Viv was in the spare room, and I slept in Pa's, and it felt comfortable.

Pa was gone from the cottage, and that's why I wasn't upset. He didn't seem *missing* this time, though maybe another time he would. I asked Viv if it felt different from the last time she went. She said it felt more relaxed.

He was gone. He was far away. When I thought about him, I felt dull and sad, not tearful and heartbroken. It's dreadful – it very soon becomes as though they aren't here. And that's why it's important to do something that lasts.

Of course Pa lives on in me and the sibs – through his

genes – and he lives on in the effect he had on us – for good and bad.

Later in the week when I was back in Sheffield, I collected a print from the picture framer, and I missed him again. I'd just got back to Ferndean Row, and was taking the picture out of its brown paper wrapper, when Rob called in.

"*The Snail* – I wondered where that had disappeared to. Great! You ditched the clip-frame. Though I'm not sure that the colour of this one's…what's this wood?" he said.

"Maple?" I said. I folded up the paper and put it in a drawer. Then I started to wind up the string.

He held up the picture to the window so he could see the frame better. "Yes. I think it's bird's eye maple."

Bird's eye maple. Pa used to read us the Stanley Holloway monologue about Noah building his ark and asking Sam Oglethwaite, a joiner, for bird's eye maple, to panel the side of his bunk. My eyes filled with tears.

Rob said in an attempt at a Lancashire accent, *"Now Maple were Sam's Mon-o-po-ly ; That means it were all 'is to cut, And nobody else 'adn't got none; So 'e asked Noah three ha'pence a foot."*

"You know it!" I laughed and wiped my tears on my sleeve.

"Of course I know it. Doesn't everyone?"

The following day Steve was on the phone, talking about how he and Martine had been to call on Ma and then walked up the Thornton Rust road to see where Ma wanted to plant the tree for Pa, and I cried. I didn't want to plant a tree for Pa. I wanted Pa alive so I could talk to him, so he could tell me about his grandfather's cow, *The Bride of Windsor*, being roasted whole for the poor of Chelsea. I missed him. I wanted him back. Could I not have him back just for half an hour to talk to him?

Megan emailed me the next day:

Hi Corinne,
I had a nice surprise this morning while looking for a postcard
to send to someone. I unearthed a very nice one from Pa in 1991
telling me about a weekend away in the Lake District with Ma. Pa
always chose very nice cards to send - I like it when people take the
trouble to choose a picture carefully, a picture they know the receiver
will enjoy. Pa always made an effort. Love Megan x

She was right: Pa did take an effort with cards and similar
things - it showed his sensitivity, which I valued a lot. But
then something else popped into my mind: the time he sent
me a very rude note.

If I ever phoned him and Ma between 6 and 7 in the
evening, he was furious, because that's the time they usually
had their tea. Ma was never cross. Whatever time we rang,
whatever time we ring now, it's the right time for her. She
loves to talk to us. Even in the middle of tea, with Pa in the
background spluttering with irritation over his home made
chicken soup, she'd say "No, of course I don't mind, of course
I want to talk. My soup's too hot anyway. I love it when you
children ring." *You children* she calls us, even though we're
in our forties. But none of us minds. How could we, when
she sees the best in us, loves us unconditionally, makes us
feel special? We are the beloved ones. She wants to hear
everything: to share, to praise, to encourage. Then when
we've told her all our news she'll say "Now what can I tell
you?" as if she's a newsreader who's lost her script. One time
when I forgot about the tea time phone prohibition and rang
them during their tea, Pa was so cross that he sent me a curt
note in the post to tell me off, and he wrote it on a piece of

Izal - hard, utility toilet paper that smelled of disinfectant. What an old sod he could be.

✳ ✳ ✳

One evening in early October, out of the blue, Charles appeared on my doorstep. I must have looked aghast when I opened the door to him. I hadn't seen him since the summer. I hadn't missed him, but when I saw him so tall and so gorgeous and with that seductive smile and the loose way he leaned against the doorway, relaxed and confident, I remembered all the great times we'd had. All the great times we'd had in bed. There – I said it. Being with Rob felt so right, but the unspoken ban on the tiniest sign of affection was wearing me down. Some days I avoided him because the strain of it got on my nerves.

Charles was smiling at me, but I couldn't make out the expression in his eyes. He touched my cheek lightly with the back of his finger and then let his hand drop. He said "You have every right to slam the door on me. I've been a bally selfish blighter. I see that now. You can tell me to go away and boil my head if you like, but-"

"Come in."

"Corinne," he said, taking each of my hands in his, "Corinne, lovely, please forgive me."

"What for?" I said, and you might think I'm a nutcase, but in that moment I held no grudge. I'm a soft touch sometimes, if you hadn't noticed.

"For ditching you, because you were grieving. I see that now. And I-"

"Would you like to come in and sit down? Would you like a drink?"

"Only if that's what you want."

"Of course. I wouldn't have asked you otherwise. So – wine? Coffee?"

"A glass of something would be welcome. It's very sporting of you."

I took a bottle of Pinot Grigio out of the fridge and handed it to him. Come on, then," I said, touching his arm and standing on tiptoe to kiss his cheek "It's nice to see you again. Come on, I'll grab a couple of glasses. Let's go in and sit down."

I watched him pour the wine, and wondered what had caused the change in him.

As if he could read my thoughts he said "Carol gave me a talking to, last week in the shop. We didn't have many customers and she was asking after you."

"Oh?"

"She managed to make me see things from your point of view, and when I thought about how I behaved, I…I… goggled. I was ghastly to you. You would have had every right to send me packing just now." He took a giant swig of his wine.

"Oh, Charles. Life's too short. You understand now."

He looked relieved. He smiled. "And I have a proposition."

"Yes?"

"Would you like to come away for the weekend with me? A nice quiet weekend. Just you and me. No socialising. No demands. I'll follow your lead in everything."

"That sounds… pleasant." I didn't want to commit myself, but a change, a trip somewhere new sounded appealing.

"Lloyd, a friend in Buxton, good man - I met him at the Chamber of Commerce – Lloyd - he has a barge moored on the Cheshire Ring."

"I'd love to go on a barge. But you said it would be just me and you."

"Oh, what a lovely smile. I've missed your pretty teeth."

"My teeth?"

"Yes. But back to the barge. Lloyd has given me the run of it for a few days – a Friday to Monday. Any time in the next four weeks. What do you think?"

✳ ✳ ✳

On the way back from Broomhill the next day I called in to see Mrs Galway. She looked fantastic. She had the heating cranked up and a fire lit and she was wearing a scarlet silk blouse with short sleeves, and a flowery skirt in black, yellow and red, and a fancy leather belt.

"You're all dressed up – you look fab," I said. "And the room smells lovely. Or is it you? Is it lavender?"

"Thank you for the imprimatur, Caroline."

"*Alpha-Omega*?"

"How did you guess?"

"Is it a special day? Blimey, it's hot in here." I took off my jacket and then my cardigan and sat down in the corner, away from the fire.

Mrs Galway picked up a duster from the sideboard and started polishing the brass drawer handles. "I am expecting a gentleman caller," she said. "Someone I know from years ago. I was chatting to the young blood who delivered my computer from Finch Electronics, and–"

"What, Derek Finch? He's the same age as me!"

"Don't interrupt. I was chatting to him while he was fannying around with all the plugs and sockets, and I asked him how his father was. I know his father from years ago.

Years and years. I used to go dancing with his sister. And Derek said his father's wife - second wife as was – she'd died, and his dad was lonely. So I said *You tell your dad that I'm lonely too.* So he-"

"*Are* you lonely?"

"No, but…anyway, he rang me up and I invited him round to tea. And now I'm wishing I hadn't." She moved over to the fireplace and started lifting up ornaments and dusting underneath them.

"But why?" I said.

"I'm perfectly happy as I am. Why would I want a man in my life?"

"For a bit of company?"

"But that's not what he'll be wanting. There'll be a lot more on *his* shopping list, you can be sure."

"Do you mean sex?"

"I was already including that in the company equation."

"What then?"

"He'll want to move in. I can't be doing with that. A fancy man is all very well, but I'm not wanting another husband."

"I thought you and Mr Galway had a happy marriage."

"We did. And there you have it," she said, turning round to face me. "I don't want another man in my life mucking up my memories of him. Muddying the clear water of my happy past. And quite apart from that…I can't be bothered with sharing my house with someone else. I have my friends. And now I'm wired up and on the internet, I'm connected to the world. Why do I want a sad old man in my life?"

"Poor Mr Finch, is all I can say. You've raised his hopes, and now you'll be dashing them again."

There was a knock at the door.

"Oh my God, he's here already."

"Shall I go and answer it for you?"

"Thank you." She hobbled over to the sideboard and shoved the duster in the top drawer.

It was Viv. Between the front door and Mrs G's sitting room I filled her in on what was going on.

"Oh, Vivien. Hello." Mrs G took the duster out again.

"What are you going to do with this man, then?" said Viv.

"I'll show him my computer. I know. I can show him some on-line dating sites. That'll keep him quiet. Talking of sites, did I tell you I found one all about graves? It's this man, and he goes about taking photographs of graves. There's a nice churchyard in Cornwall – right on the cliffs, it is. I'm thinking of being buried there when I die."

"What about your children?" said Viv. "It will be hard for them to visit, if it's all the way down in the West Country."

"They never come home from Australia as it is. When I'm dead, they definitely won't come home, so what's the difference?"

"What about us?" said Viv. "What about me? I thought I was your adopted daughter. Don't you think I'd like to come and visit your grave?"

"Don't be silly," said Mrs G. She was still pottering round the room with her duster, re-arranging ornaments and tweaking anti-macassars.

"I wasn't joking about you being my mum," said Viv. "I told you my childhood was rubbish. No room to play, no space to be boisterous. It was full of old people in various stages of gangrenous decay."

"Viv!" I said, shocked, but unable to stop myself from laughing.

"A constant stream of ancient relatives came to stay and

then died – Auntie Edith, Auntie Kitty, Great Grandma, Auntie Jessie," she said. "They weren't like you, Mrs G – hale and hearty. If a relative arrived at the door with a suitcase, you knew that death was just round the corner. If an auntie came and just brought a sponge cake, you had a fighting chance she might leave again. Auntie Kathleen always brought a cake, and she always got out safely. Sometimes she brought a salad in a green plastic box."

"Stop telling us stories, Vivien. Here, just straighten that curtain, will you? It's caught on the radiator."

Viv smoothed the folds of the curtain. "But it's true," she said. "It was like a stacking system for the crematorium. Great Grandma used to whittle on about what would happen at the resurrection. She had several missing digits and a wooden leg. She was worried about how she would manage."

"I take it she hadn't read her Bible," said Mrs Galway. "At the resurrection we're all going to get a new body. Personally, I'd like a new nose."

"Oh she knew about the new body thing, but she saw it as a straight trade rather than new for old."

Mrs Galway seemed to have the room to her liking, now. She was sitting in an arm chair next to the fire. "Talking of trade-ins," she said, "to keep costs down for my funeral, I searched for second-hand coffins on the internet - but I couldn't find any."

"Did you Google for them – sorry – you know – use a search engine to–"

"Don't be so patronising, Caroline – I know perfectly well what Googling is. Yes, I Googled for them, but they're as rare as… I don't know what. The only place you can get second-hand ones is in Muslim countries, and that's because they use the coffins just to carry the body to the grave. Then they take it out to bury it. So the second-hand idea is out of the window. But then I had another idea. If I pay for my funeral now, and I do it with the *Co-op*, I'll be able to collect the divi on it and spend it before I go. How about *that*?"

✳ ✳ ✳

Rob came racing round the next day and came straight in the wash house without knocking or calling "Hello."

"The postman brought this for you yesterday, and I forgot all about it." He held out a large thick jiffy bag.

"Oh, thanks. It'll be a book of glass patterns from Kansacraft. Could you put it over there on the shelf for me? I'll look at it later. I'm trying to get this finished before I go away." I carried on sprinkling plaster of Paris onto the piece of glass I'd just finished. I do this to absorb the residue from the putty and solder, before I polish the glass.

Rob wedged the envelope on the shelf behind me and then leaned against the wall, watching me work. "Are you off to Wensleydale?" he said.

"No, on a barge on the Cheshire Ring. With Charles."

"Him?" he said, with huge disdain.

"You can keep your views to yourself, matey."

"I didn't say anything."

"Your tone said it all."

"He's a tosser. You're way too good for him," he said. He was leaning forwards on the work bench with his head bent round, trying to catch my eye.

I wouldn't look at him. "But not good enough for you, apparently." I picked up a duster and wiped my hands. "Would you mind moving back a bit?"

"That's not how it is, and you know it."

I looked at him directly then. "No?"

"Corinne!"

"OK, OK. I don't want to fight. But I must get on with this. So can you…?"

"I'm going, so don't get your knickers in a twist."

"Chance would be a fine thing when you're in the room."

But he'd gone.

CHAPTER 17

It was dusk when Charles and I arrived. There was a line of barges moored by the towpath, all dark and apparently unoccupied, but the lights from the *Lock-Keeper's Arms* bounced off the water. I was lugging a holdall and a basket with a loaf, butter, cheese, milk and wine. Charles had brought a sleek flight case and a carrier bag full of Waitrose ready meals. The grass on the towpath was thick and wet, and the hems at the bottom of my jeans were sopping, sticking to my ankles.

Charles shone his torch on the sides of the barges as we walked along, reading the painted names. "Here we are - *The Old Pearl*," he said when we got to the fifth one. He walked to the back of the barge and climbed aboard, putting down his bags and reaching out his hand to help me over the gap. As soon as I'd stepped across, he put his arms round me and gave me a gentle kiss.

"Happy sailing," he said.

"That's sweet, Charles. I hope you enjoy the weekend, too."

"I fully intend to," he said. He took a bunch of keys from his Barbour pocket and unlocked the door while I held the torch. He pushed the low double doors open and when he slid back the hatch, it sounded like a brick scraping on sandpaper, outrageously loud in the quiet evening. He carefully descended the steps into the kitchen and switched on a light, and I went down to join him.

"It's surprisingly warm in here, " I said.

"Jolly good show, too. I asked Lloyd to have someone switch on the heating for us." He filled up a little whistling kettle and lit the gas under it. Then we loaded our provisions into the fridge. "Now, let's have a squiz round, shall we?"

The barge was cosy, but not fancy. There was match-boarding from the floor to the bottom of the windows, and above that the wood-panelled walls were painted cream. The red and white gingham curtains were on those stretchy wired elastic cords with a hook at each end. The seats were upholstered in a dark red tweedy material. I loved it all.

The bench on two sides of the table opened out into a double bed, there were two bunk beds at the back, and in between was the bathroom with a tiny shower, and the loo. "Would you like the double bed and I'll have a bunk?" he said.

"Do I have B.O.?" I said.

"I was trying to be sensitive," he said, with a hurt expression. "I know you're still feeling sad about…your old man."

I put my arms round his neck and kissed him lightly. "Sorry," I said. "That's very genteel of you, but I'm OK. I'd like us to share a bed."

We had a cuppa and unpacked our things and made up the bed. Then we got ready to go to the pub for something to eat.

I pulled my wellies out of the carrier bag in my holdall and put them on. I'd changed my jeans and didn't want to get these ones wet as well.

"Those aren't very safe for barge use, sweetheart," said Charles. "You'll slip. Don't you have deck shoes? I thought I mentioned it."

"This is all I've got," I said, and he shrugged.

We had a great time at the pub. They served a home-made chicken casserole with baked potatoes, and we played darts and pool. It was fun. When we emerged into the dark at the end of the evening to quietness broken only by muted chat from inside the pub, and the crackle of the undergrowth as a small animal scuttled from the towpath, I felt relaxed and hopeful. Maybe – if Charles had changed – I'd be able to rekindle my passion for him and make myself fall out of love with Rob. Maybe Charles had more to offer than I'd given him credit for.

I punched him playfully on the arm and said "Last one back to the barge is a sissy," and raced off ahead. I got to *The Old Pearl* and jumped onto the narrow walkway that runs round the edge of the barge. I judged the distance right, but I slipped and lost my footing. I shrieked and grabbed wildly at the rail on the roof to stop myself from falling into the water between the barge and the bank, and my knees crashed into a window. The sound of shattering glass cut open the quiet night, and Charles shouted "Corinne! Are you all right?"

I hauled myself straight and upright, found the walkway with my feet and edged along it to the back of the barge, clutching the rail all the way, swearing under my breath as I went. I'd just got to the deck by the back door, when Charles strode over the gap and caught me up in his arms.

"Oh God, Charles. I'm sorry. Oh I'm so-o-oh sorry. Can we take the barge somewhere tomorrow and get it fixed? How *awful*. You told me about these boots. Oh God."

"Are you all right?" he said. "Have you hurt yourself?"

Nothing else. No *What the hell have you broken?* No admonitions, no complaints, no *I told you so* about the unsuitability of my wellington boots.

"And that was how the weekend went on," I said to Viv and Elspeth the following Friday night. I was giving them the lowdown on the whole weekend. I'd cooked us a meal, based on produce which Viv had grown on the allotment. Viv was too exhausted to cook it herself, as she'd just been through a school inspection.

"It was a catalogue of disasters – all my fault," I said. "Oh dear, I think I overcooked these suet crusts."

"Some of them look like fossilised turds," said Viv.

"Really!" said Elspeth.

"What do you mean – a *catalogue* of disasters? I know you're accident prone but–"

"The next day we'd been sitting in the sunshine on the front deck, reading, and Charles went in to make us a drink and I somehow knocked his *Jeeves* book in the canal. And it was a first edition! Imagine!"

"Oh for God's sake – who takes a first edition to read on a barge?" said Viv. "What a poser."

"That's hardly the point," I said. I cringed at the memory of Charles coming back on deck and finding me holding the limp, wet book that I'd just retrieved from the water. His face was ashen. But he was calm when he took it from me and went inside to lay it on a towel on the table. All the delicate yellowing pages were sticking together in a sodden wedge. I found the kitchen roll and tore off pieces one by one and Charles, his mouth a straight thin line, silently inserted them between the pages until the kitchen roll was all used up and I said *Sorry*, again, in a pathetic voice. And he looked at me, and said *Did you expect me to play merry hell with you? Poor baby.*

Elspeth put down her plate and stretched. "It is not *so* strange that he took a first edition with him," she said, "Sometimes, the reading experience can be enhanced if one reads something in the original medium. Was it a hardback or an orange Penguin? I like the advertisements in the back of those original Penguins – I have a *Cold Comfort Farm* with an advertisement for Mars Bars in the back. It says *Slice it up and share it with all the family.*"

"I do like Mars Bars," said Viv, "but I've given them up. I've put on weight lately. I hate the feel of the tops of my legs touching in bed when I'm overweight. Eating too much because of stress. Did I tell you the inspectors didn't sit in on one of my philosophy lessons? It didn't fit into their schedule, is what they said."

"After the *Star* did that feature on how successful they were? That is a travesty," said Elspeth.

I scraped up the last of my food with my fork, wiped the plate clean with my finger and licked the garlicky olive oil from that.

"Shall I just shut up about Charles and the barge?" I said.

"No, no. We want to know. It's just that it's a Friday night and I'm tired." She rubbed the back of her neck. "It's hard to concentrate. That's why I went to the hairdressers tonight. I was too exhausted to talk to her, and I knew she'd be too tired to talk to me. Oh God, I'm doing it again. Sorry. Sorry. Tell us about the barge."

Someone's mobile beeped.

"Bother," said Elspeth. "Mine." She took it out of her bag and read the message. "Jessica telling me that there's a sparrow in her room. What does she expect me to do about it? I'm switching this thing off."

"And then," I said, "there was the case of the empty tank."

"What?" said Viv.

"By the time we'd got back from the pub and made up the bed on the Saturday night I was wiped out from the fresh air and all the exercise – you know, cranking open lock gates – and Charles started snoring as soon as he got into bed. He woke me up next morning, stamping up and down the barge, clattering and swearing that there wasn't any water, and I realised I'd forgotten to turn off the blasted water pump when I'd been to the loo in the night."

"What?" said Viv.

"When you went to the loo on this barge, you had to turn on the water pump before you flushed it," I said. "And then after you'd flushed it you had to turn the pump off again. Because I left the pump on, the water tank ran dry and the sewage tank filled up. So, before we could go any further, we had to chug to the nearest service station which was one we'd already passed the day before."

"I am not sure that service station is the correct name for it, Corinne."

"I know, I know, but I can't remember what is. Anyway, whatever it's called, we wasted a whole morning going back, just so we could fill the water tank and empty the sewage."

"And Charles?"

"He did look a bit grim that morning. But by dinner time he was as affectionate as ever."

"Do you think he was high?" said Viv. "God, I'm dying for a fag."

"No," I said. "Of course not." But there *had* been an other-worldly dream-like quality to the whole weekend. I'd felt like a princess in a fairy story, with a handsome pauper trying to win my hand in marriage. He has to pass all these tests, do all these deeds, but in this case the princess keeps testing him by doing annoying things to see if he will lose his rag, and in the end, if he doesn't, he wins her hand in marriage.

"So did you get it together?"

"I tried. I wanted to make it work, but… well…I spent the whole weekend with my head full of Rob, wondering what he was doing, wishing I was back here, where I might stand a chance of seeing him."

"But the goon has given you the flick," said Viv. "And I still don't know why you went with Charles when he was so nasty to you in the summer. You should ditch them both."

"Rob's *not* a goon. And Charles has apologised. And changed."

"Did Charles get his nookies?"

"*He* thought I couldn't because I was sad about Pa, and he was really understanding. But it wasn't that. It was because of…well, I don't think I'm interested in sex for its own sake any longer. I want a relationship that means something or it's not worth…and…I was thinking of Rob. But maybe if I work at it, I'll get over Rob. I've *got* to get over Rob."

"Maybe you should tell him how you feel," said Viv.

"He knows – so what's the point?" I got up, and smoothed the front of my jeans. "Can we go in the hot tub now and wash it all away?"

"It's not a miracle cure," said Viv.

"I had better just check my phone before we do, to make sure no-one has died," said Elspeth. She switched it on and there was a beep. "A message from Jessica again - Why is your phone switched off when I've got a bird trapped in my bedroom? Bah!"

"Come on, then," said Viv.

"I just need to take my vitamin C tablet," said Elspeth. "Now where did I put them?"

"If you have a decent diet you don't need to take extra vitamins," said Viv.

"My diet is veritable ichor. And my vitamin tablets are the Roman legion against the Mongol hordes of germs I meet at work."

✳ ✳ ✳

One day after breakfast, I was ready to go out to the wash house to finish off my latest piece, when someone knocked on the door. I opened it to find a twenty-something woman with untidy brown hair and big dark eyes and a familiar mini-frown - two vertical notches - between her eyebrows. Her trench coat was flapping open, showing a nurse's uniform. It could only be Bella.

"You don't know me," she said. "I'm Rob's daughter, Bella. Are you Corinne?"

"Yes. How nice." I held out my hand and she pulled hers from her pocket and gave mine a brief, light, half-hearted shake and I caught a whiff of *Eternity* perfume. "Come in, I'll put the kettle on."

She looked discomfited, hesitant.

"Thanks. Just for a minute, if you don't mind. But I'm not stopping."

"It's good to meet you."

"I like the stained glass butterflies that Dad gave me – he said he made them. Did he really?"

"Of course. I showed him how."

"Yes, well, they are really cool, but…" She looked embarrassed.

"Is there a problem? Have you broken one? I can fix it without Rob knowing if you want."

"No, no, nothing like that. Actually I…what I want to say…it has nothing to do with glass…"

"Yes?"

She was standing in front of the kitchen table, and she started to pat it with the flat of her hand. That nervous tic must run in the genes.

"Look," she said. "I feel stupid, now. Maybe I shouldn't have come."

"But it's great to meet you. Rob's told me so much about you."

"He never stops talking about *you*," she said, with a tone that sounded like resentment.

My heart took a leap. "Really?" *Really? How mind-blowingly, heart-stoppingly……really?*

She went on. "That's why I've come. Not everybody realises how sensitive he is because of his break–up with my mother. How much she hurt him."

"He told me," I said.

"He did? He probably didn't tell you how deep it went. He appears so strong, so steadfast. He takes on other people's troubles all the time. People don't generally see…" she trailed off.

"Yes?"

"You'd better watch your step," she said.

I was flabbergasted. "Watch my step?" I said.

"I don't want him hurt. I want you to stop. Leave him alone."

"Look, there's nothing between us. I've just got back from a weekend away with someone else."

"That's what I mean – I don't want you messing my Dad around."

"There is *nothing* between us. Your father doesn't want me, I mean... He doesn't want me to be anything other than a friend." I wasn't going to tell her how much I wanted him, and that he'd shunned me.

"I don't believe you. He talks about you all the frigging time."

"He does?" My heart was bouncing on an inner trampoline. I was sweating as if I'd just run a marathon. I was as elated as if I'd just bumped into David Hockney.

"He never wants to come round to our house these days, cos he wants to be at home – to *support* you, is what he says."

"He does?" I tried not to show how ridiculously happy she was making me with everything she said. "But I've told you we're only friends," I said.

"It doesn't wash," she said. "Yesterday he said that his favourite days are ones he spends with you. That he can't settle to his work, that he feels like there's something missing when you're not there. Does that sound like someone talking about a friend?"

I was all smile, inside and out. If this were a scene in a film with fantasy effects, I'd have been floating out of the window in a pink fuzzy bubble.

"Look," she said, "I don't know why you're laughing at this. This is heavy duty stuff. Do you know about this eating-less-to-live-longer crap that he does?"

"Yes. A bit. But I'm not laughing, Bella. I'm really not."
Where was this leading?

"The only reason he's doing it is so he can live longer than
the bloke who my Mum went off with. Dad thinks it's a way
of getting revenge. How sad is that?"

The fuzzy pink bubble burst. Poor Rob. Poor, dear Rob. I
was starting to get an inkling as to why he was so reluctant
to be involved with anyone, with me.

Bella looked at her watch. "I have to go. Just remember
what I said. My Dad is special. He's precious. If you hurt
him, I'll stab your eyes out."

"You don't have to worry. I won't be hurting him," I said.
"Really."

She walked to the door and opened it. I followed her round
the corner and watched her go. Halfway down the passageway
she turned round and looked me in the eyes.

"Think on," she said.

I couldn't sleep that night. I was thinking about all the
time that Rob and I had spent together, how we fitted so well,
how much I yearned for us to be a couple, and wondering if
I waited long enough whether he would trust me enough to
trust *love* again.

✻ ✻ ✻

At the beginning of November, Rob and I went to see
an exhibition of Angus McBean photographs, at the Graves
Art Gallery. We both wanted to see McBean's personalised
Christmas cards, and Rob was interested in his surrealist
work.

I like going to exhibitions with someone else so I can
talk about the pictures. Every year Pa and I would go to the

exhibition of local artists in Wensleydale. I loved that little annual jaunt. We both liked to see the latest offerings from Piers Browne, Judith Bromley, Robert Nicholls, and all the others. Pa loved paintings, and oh how he loved to criticise. The last summer I went with him was the August before he died. He was speaking so loudly because of his deafness that everyone in the place could hear what he was saying, and some of his comments were excoriating, so much so that they made me cringe. It was funny in a black kind of way, but I had to say to him, "Let's go *outside* to discuss the paintings, Pa."

I told Rob about this on the bus journey back. It was the first time I thought about Pa and told a story about him without getting upset. Remembering with fondness, rather than sadness. I had got past the stage of saying "I wish he hadn't died," which means, I suppose, that I must have reached a stage where I accepted his death.

The day after the exhibition, we had a gale. Actually, we had a week of gales. Ferndean Row was much more sheltered than my old house had been at Ranmoor Hilltop, but the wind was whipping the birches at the bottom of my back garden. It was whistling down the passageway, blowing peoples' wheelie bins over and battering Rob's lilac tree against the fence.

Even when I don't have to go out anywhere, strong winds drive me crazy. I've been like that since I was little. When I'm with Ma and it's a windy day, she always imitates me at the age of three, saying "Go 'way wind. I hate you, wind." Nowadays it's the noise that I find oppressive: it puts me in a filthy mood.

I'd had a very bad-tempered day and not achieved much. I'd tried to do glass work but stopped after botching three cuts in a row and consequently running out of the right kind of glass for that piece. I'd prodded my thumb while rag-rugging, and I'd made a fundamental error in the three-colour socks I was knitting as a Christmas present for Steve – through reading the knitting pattern wrong.

Now I was trying to sort out photographs for Christmas cards. I'd taken a beauty the last time Rob and I had been for a walk right to the top of the Mayfield Valley to Porter Clough: a leafless sycamore tree against a winter sunset - blotches of plum and egg-yolk, streaked on a sky of duck-egg-blue. The trouble was that there was a telegraph wire behind it, that I hadn't noticed at the time, and now I was trying to erase it on the computer. But my scratchiness and impatience was making the task impossible.

I couldn't clone the right patch of colour to wipe out the wire, no matter how many times I tried, and Rob being always in my mind – and that was probably adding to my general frustration level - I flung down the mouse and stomped round to his house, knowing he would be patient and helpful and calm me down and show me gently how to achieve the effect that I wanted.

He didn't answer my frantic hammering on his back door but as I turned to leave his yard, I walked straight into his bike wheel held high up in front of him. He was wheeling his bike through the gate on the way back from a ride.

"Watch out!" I shrieked.

"Why are you battering my door down? What's to do? Is there a fire?"

"You'll bloody well knock someone out with that bike wheel one day!"

"Who's rattled your cage?" he said.

"Oh, Rob, I'm sorry. I'm sorry. I came to ask if you could

help me sort out something on my computer. I'm going to break something soon. I'm in a really bad mood."

"You make a trip round to your house sound very appealing."

He propped up his bike in his yard and then followed me back to my house. He shrugged off his cycling jacket and whipped off his hat and his arm warmers and sat down in his sweaty jersey on my chair, in front of the computer. I drew up another one and sat beside him. I took hold of the mouse and leaned in close and said "Look, this is what I was trying to do, get rid of this stupid wire," and started to show him and then snapped, "Just take it! Do it! I am sick of the bloody thing!"

He turned and smiled, and said "Have you got any orange juice? I could really do with a drink." And I went off to get him one.

How could he be so nice to me, so patient with me, such a good friend, spend all this time with me, go for walks, etc, etc, etc, say what he had to Bella, and still hold out to be separate, detached and safe? I loved the man. I wanted the man.

Even my hair was getting on my nerves, and I brushed it back roughly behind my ears, catching an ear-ring which dropped on the floor.

"Bugger!" I said. I got down on my knees and found the clip from the back, but couldn't see the earring anywhere. "Oh sod it, sod it, sod it."

"What's up with you now?" he said. "Blimey, you are in a state."

"My ear-ring! It's gone. It's gone forever. And these are my favourites. Oh fuck!"

He pushed back his chair and came down on the carpet with me on his hands and knees, moving across the carpet like those policemen you see on the telly at the scene of a crime when they're inching across a field, searching for clues.

"Got it!" he said. "Look – over in the corner." He sat down and reached and I wasn't looking at the earring, I was looking at his nice smooth, muscly thighs encased in his Lycra cycling tights, and the curve of his bum, and I stroked his leg down towards his knee, and then up again, right up, and he turned and pulled my head towards him and kissed me as if he was as desperate as me, and we couldn't stop, we didn't stop and we did it, right there under the table – him still sweaty from his ride, me with my skirt pulled up round my waist, him with his Lycra tights pulled off, still hanging round one of his ankles. The carpet was scratchy and my head was banging against the skirting board and…and… and …and making love to Rob was as fabfabfab as I always thought it would be…and afterwards, we lay together and he tenderly swept my hair off my face and pulled down my skirt and cradled my cheek and said "Let's go up to bed and be comfortable."

It wasn't just the sex, it was feeling close to him, one with him, wanted in every way by him. Afterwards, we lay under my new patchwork quilt and he said "This fabric with the cabbage roses looks familiar. Have I seen it before?" and I said, "Wasn't I right to want to rescue it? And all the others?" and he said "Aren't you right about everything?"

CHAPTER 18

Two years before Pa died, I drove Ma and Pa to the Lake District for a weekend away. Pa had deep vein thrombosis, and when he drove the car he had to stop every twenty minutes to rest his leg, with his foot up on the dashboard. Ma found their long drawn-out trips a trial, with the stops for the leg rests. I'm sure that Pa found it a drag as well, though he didn't complain about his leg. He just did the drive and took the rests.

He complained about a lot of things. He complained when his egg was not done as he liked it, or when his beef was undercooked, or that the room was too cold or when someone left the door open and there was a draught. He complained when his tummy played him up, or when he was constipated, or when he hadn't had a good night's sleep because something he had eaten had disagreed with him, but he didn't complain so much about his leg.

We planned that trip so that I could do the driving and they could both have a rest. Pa wanted to sit in front so that he could navigate (though not always accurately), so that he could see where we were going and warn me of driving hazards, and so that he could be near the heater, and also have the better view. He was selfish; I might as well say it because it is true.

Ma, therefore, had to sit in the back. There was some compensation: she could have more fresh air. I could open the roof and she would get a nice breeze, or I could open my window and she'd get some air, and neither would usually bother Pa. There were times, even so, when they would argue about the air and the cold and the draughts, even though Pa had a rug for extra warmth.

They also argued about which was the right way to go, which was the best place to park, where we should drive to next.

All in all, though, I think they enjoyed their weekend away. (I came back exhausted.) They enjoyed the hotel. They liked the food. Pa liked to have a choice of food, and to have people wait on him. Ma liked to dress up for dinner and to have someone else think about the cooking, and to know that if there was something wrong with it, it wasn't her fault.

Pa liked certain foods above all others – raspberries, kippers, Stilton cheese – and their provenance was important. The Stilton had to come from the right dairy, for example. He asked the waiter if the hotel Stilton came from Long Clawson or Hartington.

"Oh," said the waiter, "we get it from *Pricerite* in Kendal."

The day after Rob and I made love under the table, Megan and I were due to take Ma to the Lakes for a weekend away. Megan was going to drive, my mother was paying, I was tagging along for the company and to make up the party to three; it was a treat from my mother to us. We stayed at the hotel that Pa had picked out for their next weekend away.

Megan was driving up from Bristol and collecting me on the way.

I decided to phone Charles before she arrived. I rang him at the shop, but I had to hang on for ages for him to answer the phone, and by the time he did, I was tense, my heart was beating fast.

"Corinne! I've been missing you dreadfully. Did you pick up my calls from your voicemail? Why haven't you got back to me? Have you been down in the dumps? That weekend on the barge was wonderful. I can't wait to do it again."

"Oh Charles — wonderful? With all the stupid boobs I made?"

"But we were *together*. That's what mattered." His voice was so loving, so tender, I felt so mean. This was going to be harder than I'd imagined.

"I need to talk to you," I said. My face was burning. I was feeling really edgy. I wrapped the cord of the telephone round and round my finger.

"Go on, then, sweetheart," he said. "Spill the beans. I'm in the office. Carol is looking after the shop."

I'd planned to begin by telling him how much I'd enjoyed spending time with him, telling him kind, friendly things to soften the news, but I'd got so jittery, that I blurted it all out straight.

"I'm sorry, Charles. I'm in love with someone else."

There was no reply.

"Charles?"

Still no reply.

"Charles? Are you there?"

"Did I hear you right?" he said. "There's somebody else? That was bloody quick. Or were you…when you came on the barge, were you…who the devil is it?"

"I'm so sorry, Charles."

"Who the hell is it? You didn't tell me you'd been seeing someone else. What a…" he trailed off. I could hear a woman in the background saying something. It would be Carol. She'd be leaning round the door between the shop and the office.

"Charles? Are you there?" I said.

"Who is it?" he said.

"It doesn't matter who it is. But Charles, I am *so* sorry."

"I demand to know."

I took a deep breath. "It's Rob. Next door."

"Walker? That loser? That no-hoper who's glued to his bloody push bike? Doesn't even own a car? You'll make a fine pair. You giving up a profession to piss about with bloody craft, and him a cartooning recluse. May you sink into oblivion together."

He slammed down the phone. And that was it.

✳ ✳ ✳

When Megan and I first arrived at the cottage, I didn't expect to find Pa there, and because of that, I felt that I'd reached a new stage. The new order had established itself. Ma had made changes to the spare bedroom and it was lovely – she'd chucked out the old carpets in green and brown with the leaf patterns, and she'd replaced them with a plain carpet in a soft sage green. It went well with the wall paper of pink dog roses and green leaves on a white background. The room was so much clearer, cleaner and lighter. I slept well in there. And I didn't feel sad about Pa, though I didn't like going into his room and being reminded that he was no longer there.

The stone for his gravestone had arrived the previous

week, and the village stonemason had carved Pa's name, and placed the stone in the burial ground. When Megan saw the gravestone she was upset, because the stone was not the type she was expecting, not the type that she and Ma had ordered. I thought the colour of it too light, and we both hated the fact that the stonemason had painted inside the grooving of the letters with black gloss paint, even though we told him we wanted it plain.

I don't think Ma cared. I don't think she thought of Pa as being in the graveyard. She'd planted a beech tree in remembrance of him on a spot above the village on the Thornton Rust road, on a piece of land that belongs to the parish. Steve had emailed me and Megan a photo of Ma in her wellies with the spade, standing behind the tree. The tree was about three feet high and had dry brown leaves clinging to it. Ma looked old, but very smiley, and I wished I'd been there with them.

She had a photograph on the mantlepiece that was taken from where the tree was planted, looking over the valley. Maybe she liked that better than the graveyard. She said Megan and I should sort out the headstone as we wanted: maybe the easiest solution was to paint the lettering grey.

As Megan drove us up dale on the way to the Lakes, we passed the big copper beech in Bainbridge. When we drove past it with the coffin in May it was in the first rich surge of pink-brown leaves. Now it stood bare.

At the hotel, Megan and I shared a room.

"Which bed do you want?" I said, when we first went in to drop off our cases.

"I don't mind – you choose."

"Go on, Megan. I know you have a thing about being near the window but I can't remember if you like it or hate it."

"For God's sake, stop fussing. I said I don't care."

It wasn't like us to be scratchy with each other. I was irritable because I didn't want to be there: I wanted to be with Rob. I think Megan was overtired from work.

On the Saturday morning, the hotel left us papers when we hadn't ordered any, and I complained to Megan.

She said, "Oh stop making such a fuss. They've only left us a couple of papers. Anyone would think they'd opened the door and chucked in two dead rats. You've said *Oh no* three times, and all because of a simple mistake. It *doesn't matter*, Corinne."

"Have you been counting?" I said, and then let out a yelp as I tripped on the bedside rug.

"And now you're squawking, for God's sake. Pa was just the same. He never stopped huffing and puffing either. Yesterday when you slipped a millimetre on the mud near the lake you shrieked. Can't you be a bit quieter? Button your lip?"

She got on my nerves too. I'd forgotten how much she could talk. She went on and on about this and that and nothing. She gave her opinion on everything. And she snapped at me all weekend.

We took Ma on a visit to Blackwell House, designed by one of the principal architects of the Arts and Crafts movement. We all enjoyed looking at the interior – the stained glass, the carved oak panelling, the stonework and the friezes, with symmetrical stained glass windows on each side of the inglenook fireplaces. Then we went to the café for afternoon tea.

"We didn't see the stained glass design that's on this leaflet," I said. "This one, here, Megan. The one with the pale pink tulips and the blue birds."

"What?" she said.

I held out the information leaflet to show her the picture.
"This one."

"Why are you asking me?" she lashed out. "Why do you
expect me to know everything? Why don't you ask the
woman on reception?"

Pa was irritable, and so am I. I had never pegged Megan
as irritable too.

In the evening when we were sitting in the lounge
choosing what to have for dinner, Megan spoke in a loud
voice and criticised the menu – "Gressingham Ducks are
bred for their flavour – why do they want to obscure it with
all these ridiculous sauces?" Just like Pa.

It's a good job he wasn't there because the food was
poor. They piled ingredient upon ingredient in an unhappy
assembly of wildly conflicting flavours, as if it was somehow
sophisticated and clever to have lamb carved on prunes sitting
on turnips and marinated in lime overnight. Not really. But
that's the sense if it, the pretentiousness of it.

I didn't want to eat late – just like Pa. On the first night we
ate at 7.30: too early for Megan and too late for me. All night
I lay with my stomach like a stone, feeling miserable, missing
Rob, hoping we'd reached a new place in our relationship, but
not convinced that he wouldn't chicken out again. It had felt
so painful to drag myself away from him.

Fed up with not sleeping, I lifted my bedside light down
onto the floor so it wouldn't wake Megan and switched it
on and read a book Elspeth had lent me, a poetry book she
thought I might like: William Carlos Williams' *Collected
Poems*.

I was entranced by the poems, even though I didn't
understand their subtleties and sometimes even their
meanings - I just enjoyed the word pictures they painted.

They were like Scottish Colourist paintings, so vivid, with such strong and lovely colours. I wished I could show them to Pa and discuss them with him. Once he wrote a poem for my homework - when I had to write a ballad and couldn't do it. And when I was sixteen he wrote a poem for me when I was so cut up over a boy I liked who didn't like me. I could talk to Pa about affairs of the heart and he understood.

I switched off the light, but an hour later – at half past two in the morning, I was still lying there wide awake, missing Pa and missing Rob, and wrestling with the outsize hotel counterpane, and Megan reached out her hand across the divide between the twin beds and said "Are you having a horrid night?" in the exact same words and exact same tone that Pa would have used, sympathetic and sensitive.

The next morning at breakfast I couldn't decide what to eat. There were so many nice things, and yet I didn't want to eat too much. But there were kippers, and I rarely cook them for myself. But I only wanted kippers if they were decent kippers – not bright orange salty frozen fillets. So I asked the waiter where the kippers came from. (Craster would be best, Loch Fyne would be acceptable. I had never asked such a question before: I am not a foodie, and making queries about menu items is not what I do.)

The waiter didn't know. He was pompous, and I could see he was cross with himself that he didn't know. I asked if they were whole kippers or fillets. He said they were fillets. I said that in that case I would forget it and just have toast. I was holding the fort for Pa.

We got back to Hollycroft on Sunday night. On Monday morning Megan and I said goodbye to Ma and drove back down south, calling at the burial ground on the way.

We stood by the grave, so close to each other that our sides touched. We were quiet. The grass on the grave still showed the shape of the coffin. How long would that go on?

"Does it seem like a long time ago?" Megan said.

"I don't know. It seems like I've reached the next stage." Quiet.

"What are you thinking?" she said.

"I was thinking about his hands."

"I shall always remember his hands," she said. "He had lovely hands. They were always nice."

"They went dark and blotchy."

"Yes, but he had big strong hands right to the end. The fingers didn't go thin and nobbly. His hands were beautiful."

We walked back down the path and she put her arm around my waist, and then let it drop. We got into the car and I put my arm round her shoulders and kissed her cheek.

"Thank you," she said.

After that, all the impatience and irritability between us melted away and we drove southwards chatting non-stop in our usual fashion, and listening to James Taylor and Carole King on the CD player.

When we got back to Sheffield, Megan came in for a coffee and a piece of cake to break her journey. She wanted to look at all the glass I was making, all the handicrafts, and the cards, and normally I would have loved showing them to her. I would have wanted her to stay all afternoon, but that day I was jittery and couldn't wait for her to leave so I could go and see Rob.

Finally she said she ought to be leaving, and I walked with her to her car. I stood and waved as she drove down the lane, and as soon as her car had disappeared round the corner onto Fulwood Road, I rushed back down the passageway and through Rob's gate, rapped on his door and went in.

"Rob! I'm back!"

I heard him coming downstairs and went to meet him. I put my arms around him and kissed him. He kissed me back half-heartedly and then pulled away.

"Let's go and put the kettle on," he said, shepherding me back into his kitchen.

"Rob?" I said. "What's the matter?" His face looked blank, like a cartoon of a dead person's face.

He filled the kettle and switched it on and turned round and leaned against the sink.

"We need to stop thinking of each other as friends," he said.

"Yes," I said, going up close to him, taking his hands and searching his face, his eyes, for clues. His cheek muscles twitched. His hands remained limp in mine. He glanced into my eyes and then looked away, over my shoulder. "We're not just friends, we're lovers, as well," I said. "Lovers and friends."

"No. We need to stop it all. Stop seeing each other. It doesn't work."

Oh God! Not this again! I couldn't bear it! I dropped his hands and grabbed his shoulders. I put my hand on his cheek and turned his face so he had to look at me.

"What the hell do you mean, it doesn't work? It works very well."

"It can't work." He broke free and walked over and sat on one of the stools at his breakfast bar. The width of the room was between us. He folded his arms. Then he unfolded them and started to pick at something stuck on the granite worktop. "I don't want to try. I told you all this before."

"What's happened to you while I've been away? What about last Thursday?"

"I'm so sorry, Corinne. It was a mistake. I'm so sorry, but I can't."

"Don't be such a wuss," I shouted. "It works. I love you. Don't you love me? I thought you did." The words from a Buffy St Marie song went through my head. *Take my hand for awhile, explain it to be once again, Just for the sake of my broken heart, Look into my eyes and maybe I will understand, How love I counted on was never there.* "Rob – do you love me?"

"Of course, but that's not the-"

"Get out!" I yelled at him. "Sod off! Go on – get the hell out of here. I hate you and your namby-pamby hesitation, your wussy-pussy sensitivity. Go on – go on and be miserable and shut up and lonely and don't ever come in here again. Don't even speak to me again."

"Corinne," he said in a small voice.

"What?" I shouted.

"This is my house."

I stalked out and slammed the door so hard I shattered the glass in it. I turned to see the door window falling in fragments, inside and out, and Rob behind it, in pieces, too.

CHAPTER 19

Oh dear…Rob.

I avoided him.

I told Elspeth and Viv what had happened and no-one else.

I couldn't get on with my work. I sat and watched telly all day. I have no idea now what I watched. My *Due South* videos were in the bin.

Situations like this, emotional upheavals, make it hard to work when you're self-employed, with all demands and deadlines being self-imposed. I wished I had some decorating jobs booked in so there'd be something to get me up and out of the house in the mornings. I slobbed around for days in my pyjamas.

I was a mess, as pathetic and odd and ugly as a balloon that you find behind the sofa, weeks after a party, when it's deflated slowly and gone all wrinkly and dusty and disgusting. I lived on porridge, with golden syrup trickled on the top, like I used to have as a child. And I was addicted to liquorice.

I woke every morning at 3 a.m. and couldn't get back to sleep again, which meant that by nine in the evening I was completely knocked out and slunk off to bed, only to wake again at 3.

I hobbled along, mostly managing, but with occasional bleak and terrible mornings when I got up for a mug of tea and a stick of liquorice and then went back under the quilt. When Viv or Elspeth rang to see if I was OK, and to ask "Is there anything I can do?" I asked them to bring more liquorice. One day I opened the back door and leaned down to pick up that day's bottle of milk and found a brown paper bag full of Giant Flyers - liquorice tubes filled with sherbet - and stapled to it, a compliments slip from Walkerstone Community Primary School signed "Get these stuffed down you, love Viv."

One early morning I went into the kitchen to make some porridge and found the empty jar and remembered I'd finished it the day before and forgotten to go to the shop. And I'd run out of all the basics - bread and butter and eggs. Even the Earl Grey jar was down to just two torn and leaking tea bags. Pathetic. I made a shopping list, and looked at my watch - a quarter to eight — and thought I could get to Somerfield at Broomhill for when they opened at eight, and beat the traffic as well. I pulled on my dungarees and my fleece, grabbed my purse and the list and went.

It was all right until I got to the tea and coffee section. I took a big box of Earl Grey tea bags, but then found myself reaching up for a jar of Fair Trade instant coffee for Rob, and then I was leaning against a nearby pillar, clutching the coffee, with tears running down my face.

"Corinne?"

I turned and saw Viv.

"What's up, babe?"

I didn't say anything, but seeing her friendly face and hearing the concern in her voice, I cried even harder.

"Do you want this?" she said, pointing to the coffee.

I shook my head and she took the jar from me.

"OK, then. Let's put it back on the shelf. Here," she handed me a tissue and I wiped my eyes. "My God! You've still got your pyjamas on, under your dungarees. Did you know?"

I shook my head.

"Come on. You're coming to school with me."

"What?"

She guided me to the checkout and paid for her small basketful and waited while I paid for mine. "Are you parked on the roof?"

I nodded.

"OK, come and get into my car. I'm taking you home to get some clothes on and then you can come to school and sit in my office and I'll give you something to do. OK?"

Relief swept over me at the thought of having my day arranged for me, at the thought of spending it with someone other than myself.

"But what about my van?" I said.

"Give me the keys."

I fished them out of my pocket and handed them over.

"Right. Let's go."

"But I can't leave it here all day."

"I'll sort that out." And she bundled me upstairs and into her car and drove me back to Ferndean Row. "Now you go and get dressed - the dungarees are fine, we just don't want pyjamas."

I got out of her car and so did she, and I thought she was following me, but she didn't, and when I came out of the house five minutes later she was coming out of Rob's back yard.

"Viv?" I said, aghast. "Why have you been to see Rob? What have you been saying to him?"

"I told him that this was his mess, so he could at least be a little bit helpful and go and fetch your van for you."

"What?"

"He said 'right enough.'"

"Really?"

"Come on, I should be at school by now."

When we got into her office, we were greeted by a mountain of packages piled in one corner of the room, the armchair completely submerged, and Viv said "OK, that's what you can do to keep yourself occupied. Sort out my school uniform order."

"But you don't have a school uniform, do you? You've always said you'd die rather than have a school uniform."

"Sadly, the governors think differently. And I don't want to touch the stuff, besides which I have a mountain of important things to do, things that actually matter, so you'll be doing me a favour if you go through the order and sort it out. Here's the list of who's ordered what. Can you sort it by class and by child. Here – you can use these post-its."

So that's how I spent the morning. And in the afternoon she gave me a pile of winter paintings to display in the foyer, and sent along two seven year old girls to help me. "You used to be an art teacher – make yourself useful."

I managed to persuade Grace and Sophia (the girls) that we shouldn't have pink backing paper, and then we discussed which of the three strongest paintings we should place at the centre of the display. My afternoon with them was engrossing and fun, and when the bell rang for the end of school I realised that I hadn't thought about Rob since dinner time. Maybe I'd go into school again to help. I could do craft with the children – teach them to knit and to make rag rugs.

When Viv had eventually finished her work, she took me back to her house, and fed me pizza and salad. We watched a succession of soaps on the telly, went in the hot tub, and then she drove me back to Ferndean Row. It worked. I slept till six the next morning, and woke up feeling stronger. Miserable still, but slightly more robust, like the first day you're up and about after being ill in bed for a week.

❋ ❋ ❋

One hopeful thing that happened in someone else's life, but was cheering, even so, was Elspeth giving in her notice at the University, and taking a lease on a tiny shop at Broomhill, next door to Record Collector. She couldn't leave her job completely until Easter, but she was winding down her commitments, and shuffling off her current research onto junior members in her department.

One afternoon a couple of weeks before Christmas, she rang and invited me to see the shop and to offer suggestions on décor and shopfittings. She planned to have shelves on every wall but she wanted my suggestions as to colour of paint and where to site the till, the coffee machine and the sofa.

I took some goodies and a flask of hot chocolate with me and arrived to find Minnie-May saying "Please, Gran, please can we go to the cake shop and buy a doughnut?"

"I've got some chocolate brownies," I said. "Would you like one?"

"Please can I look at them?"

I opened the tin and showed her the brownies – a vintage set – gooey and rich and thick.

"Have you got anything else?" said Minnie-May.

"Mince pies? Would you like a mince pie?"

"Yes, please."

Elspeth pushed two old boxes together to make Minnie-May a mock up of a table and chair, and I gave her the lid of the cake tin as a plate and she and her cuddly rabbit sat and had afternoon tea together.

"I love the way children are so direct," I whispered to Elspeth. "When you go to someone's house and they offer you a biscuit with your tea, wouldn't it be great to say *Can I look at them first?* and then if it's just a boring old Rich Tea that's not worth the calories, you can say *No thanks.*"

❋ ❋ ❋

"I have to come down to Derbyshire to check out some in-calf heifers I'm thinking of buying," said Steve on the phone. "On Thursday – will you be home?"

"Yes – absolutely – can I come to the farm with you?"

"It won't be very exciting."

"I don't care. I need to get out somewhere and if I come with you, I'll see you for the maximum possible time. I don't suppose you'll be staying overnight, will you?"

He left home straight after morning milking. When he arrived he said "God, you're looking peaky. Have you had a bug, or something?"

"No, no. It's just my winter colouring – pale and interesting." I wasn't going to tell him about Rob. It felt too painful to talk about.

"You look pale and puffy like uncooked pastry."

"Thanks, Steve," I said. Trust a brother to be blunt. "Don't you remember? I'm the pale one of the family. Don't you remember that Ma and Pa were always worried about how pale I was when I was little?"

"I seem to remember Pa always giving you the first spoonful of meat juices when he was carving the Sunday joint – what did he call it? Carver's perks. Jammy bloody devil."

"I want to show you something," I said.

I took him into the dining room and showed him the table. It was time to admit to myself that it was too late now to have a family. I asked Steve if he and Martine would like to have the table for the farmhouse. He looked pleased and said he'd consult with Martine.

Then we set off to see the heifers. It was fun to be driving in his smelly old Land Rover out of Sheffield. I shut my eyes and inhaled the scent of straw and faint diesel fumes and it took me straight back to being little when life was easy and happy and full of people I loved.

The day was clear and blue and frosty. The farm was a pedigree dairy farm near Ashover, a village south west of Chesterfield. It was at the end of a long muddy track, the mud hard frozen, and the Land Rover was crunching along bumpily, with Steve and me bouncing up and down on our seats, and a litter of empty cardboard boxes – Steve's old bullet boxes – rattling around in the back.

The farmer gave us a mug of coffee in his kitchen, and then took us out to see the heifers, which were due to calve in the spring. But the shed was too dark to get a proper look at the animals, so he let them out into a paddock and Steve examined them while I stood there in my duffle coat and my old wellies with the split in them and wished my life was as simple as it had been when I was young. To distract myself, I asked Steve what he was looking for.

"Deep-bodied sort of thing, a good shape for easy calving, straight legs, sound feet, neat udder, four teats well spaced and pointing in the right direction."

He was impressed with the heifers, said he'd have four of them, and agreed the price. He'd ring later to arrange transport and delivery.

He'd finished the business by half past eleven, and the day was still bright and beautiful, so I suggested we drive back on a roundabout route, through Chatsworth Park, calling in at the farm shop for something for lunch.

"Do you mean dinner?" said Steve. "You're turning into a southerner."

I gave him a playful thump and said "OK. Shall we go to the farm shop? Viv's always going on about how good the meat is."

I don't eat much meat myself, but Steve is like Pa – he's a man who likes his meat. Pa could be outrageous about it. When Megan and Ed went to stay at the cottage, Pa, knowing full well that Ed was a vegetarian, would always offer Ed a portion of meat. And once, when Megan's children were small and staying with Ma and Pa on their own, Pa took a photograph of three year old Jonathan chewing on a beef bone, and sent the photo to Ed.

We drove to Chatsworth over Beeley Moor, where the heavy frost coated the broken bracken, and the dry stone walls looked as though they'd been sprayed with Christmas glitter.

Once inside the farm shop, Steve made straight for the meat counter, just as I expected. He cast his discriminating eye over the cuts of meat. When Pa went into a strange butcher's shop he would come out with a series of questions. That joint there – what breed was the beast? How many teeth did it have? How long had the meat been hung? Not just the answers, but the sure and easy knowledge of the butcher was crucial to Pa sticking his hand in his pocket.

Steve was in his element. "Look at that fine piece of beef. Those pork chops look grand. Look at those rib eye steaks. Look at the marbling on them!"

I turned round from eyeing up the ice cream in the freezer, wondering what on earth a rib eye steak was, and trying to dredge from my family memory the significance of marbling in beef.

"Shall we get some?" said Steve. "I'll pay for them. With that marbling. They'll be really tender."

"It's my treat."

"I'll cook them, then," said Steve.

"Fine."

"Can I help, you, sir?" a member of staff said to Steve.

"Those rib eye steaks – what breed was the beast?"

"Limousin. I think," said the girl.

"Cross or pure?" said Steve.

The girl went to check with a man wielding a chopper at a block in the back of the shop.

She came back. "Pure, sir," she said.

"And how long was it hung for?"

"Two weeks, sir."

"I'll take those two on the top."

Steve was abuzz with appetite. He searched the shop for beer to go with his steak. And at the till, he found some watercress. His joy was complete.

"Good job I don't live near here," he said, as we walked to the car. "I'd be bloody bankrupt."

Back at Ferndean Row, he scrubbed a couple of baking potatoes and shoved them in the microwave, while I made a salad with carrot, red cabbage and watercress. When the potatoes were almost done and the grill was hot, Steve put the steaks in the pan and slid them under. Soon they were ready - medium rare - and the salad, the potatoes and the beer were all on the table. We sat down to eat. Steve cut into his steak.

"Look at how tender it is!" he said. "I can't believe how easy it is to cut. It's like a knife going through butter. But it's not like cutting butter. There's some resistance. It's more like cutting a cooked courgette." He took a mouthful. "Mmm."

I felt I was intruding on an intimate moment. I was enjoying my dinner for the first time since Rob and I had… but across the table, Steve was in ecstasies.

"It's a shame Pa can't taste this," he said. "He would do his nodding dog act and say, *It's as good a steak as I've tasted in years.* We should drink a toast to him." He held up his beer glass and I held up my water. "To Pa," we said. Our plates were empty. Steve sat back in his chair and sipped his beer, eating cheese and looking happy.

When he'd driven away, I felt strangely cheered and at last felt I had the heart to write some Christmas cards. When I rootled through my box of Christmas stuff, looking for my Christmas card list, I came across the card that Pa had sent me the year before. It was a fine card – a print of a painting by Herring – a horse being shod and a snow scene outside the forge. I stood it on the dining table next to my computer. I would keep it forever and get it out every year. It meant so much more to me now than it did when he sent it.

Megan and I spent a long time discussing Christmas on the phone – Ma's first Christmas without Pa – and the plan evolved for me to drive up to the cottage and then Ma and I would travel down to Bristol on the train, to spend Christmas at Megan's house.

I was feeling gloomy when I drove away from Ferndean Row. Rob had pushed a cartoon Christmas card – which wasn't funny - through my letterbox. Inside it said *Season's Greetings* – an epithet I loathe for some reason – why can't *cards say Merry Christmas* or *Happy Christmas?* – that's what they mean, don't they? Anyway, underneath the *Season's Greetings* he'd just written *Rob*.

Rob. That was it. Is that all he had to say to me??

I spent a sad night at the cottage, the night I arrived. Ma went to bed early at 6 o'clock because she was tired and felt unwell. And I felt the weight of sadness at Pa being gone and Ma being old. She had aged five years in six months. Maybe not surprising, but marked even so. Life must seem such a struggle for her in the cold dark days of winter. It was a struggle for me. How must it feel when you are 84 and your husband of 60 years has gone, and you can't see well and you feel oh so weary, right down to your toe nails? How did she carry on?

She seemed to have withdrawn into herself. I'd not seen her like that before. She had never been a person who spoke about her feelings, but sometimes I wished that she could - even if it was just to say "I don't feel like doing anything today. I don't even feel like talking. Can we just sit together and be quiet?" Or even – "Will you go away and leave me alone?" It's not that I wanted her to open her heart to me, I just wished she would tell me where she was, sometimes, as if grief were a map and she could give me a grid reference.

Oh how miserable I was, thinking about Rob. His stingy card had set me off.

And I missed Pa. I missed him sitting in the corner. I missed him lying on the couch. I missed him sitting by the dining room window in the morning, in his tasteless black leather reclining chair, reading the paper. He was a fine man. So handsome. So clever. I wished he were still alive.

It felt very sad at the cottage. Maybe it was because Ma was so tired. I don't know. When she went to bed at six, it felt as though both she and Pa had died. I could remember how I felt when I was young and she went to bed ill, which admittedly was rare. How I hated it. How I felt bereft, as if the world was cold and bare and had no comfort. It was all too easy to imagine what it would be like when Ma died, being at the cottage without her.

I woke up the next morning early and sat in bed in my jumper, and with a mug of tea. I sat there thinking about Pa and how I didn't want him to be dead. The winter up there is very cold. There was a low heater in the bedroom and still the air felt icy. I was worrying about Ma and how if I felt miserable, how on earth did she feel?

In amongst the Christmas cards on her dresser downstairs, there was a photo that a cousin had sent, of last Christmas dinner at the cottage, and there was one of Pa carving the turkey, and Ma looked at it sadly and said "Oh - look at that." I wished he were there. I wished he were still alive, being grumpy and selfish and annoying. I loved him so.

Despite all this, Christmas at Megan's was fine. She's a wonderful hostess and a really good cook and their house is large enough for everyone to have their own room. She has a big kitchen with an Aga, a sofa in the corner, and visitors hang out in there all the time because it feels so homely.

When Ma and I got back to the cottage on New Year's Eve, I think we both felt better. I slept well in a cosy bed in Pa's old room.

I'd been searching for a pair of new wellies since the autumn, because mine leaked in wet weather. I was looking for some tall, soft black ones, like Pa used to wear when I was little. On my way back to Sheffield I stopped in Leyburn and found just the wellies I wanted at an agricultural suppliers. When I put them on I felt a burst of happiness.

I arrived back at Ferndean Row in a shower of sleet. I grabbed my bag from the van and rushed up the passageway with my key all ready to shove in the door, but smack in the middle of the doorstep was a bright red cyclamen in an earthenware pot. Who was giving me flowers? There was a black plastic spike sticking in the soil and an envelope attached to it. I was shivering with cold, so instead of reading the card straightaway, I stuffed the envelope in my pocket and lifted the pot off the step and carried it into the back yard. The leaves were pretty - the shape of them and the colouring - and I made a mental note to use them in a stained glass design.

As soon as I got inside the house I put the kettle on and sat down, still in my coat. The kitchen was freezing. I got up and turned the heating on and the thermostat up high. Then I took the envelope from my pocket and looked at the card. It said: *I'm sorry. Rob. Happy New Year.*

I ripped it in half and chucked it across the kitchen. He could shove his happy new year. What did he want? To be friends again? I wasn't going to fall into that.

There was a knock on the door and I went to open it, hoping and dreading that it would be him.

"Happy New Year?" he said, the cadence of the sentence rising at the end.

I looked at his face. I'd missed his face. I'd missed his deep dark eyes, his – *Stop it!* I said to myself. I dragged my eyes away from his face and concentrated on my hand, resting on the door jamb.

"Thanks for the plant," I said in a flat and toneless voice. "It's nice," I said, dull and muted. I looked at his face again for a millisecond and then over his shoulder at the silver birches at the end of my back garden. Their leafless twigs were quivering in the chilly breeze. "I'm busy," I said, "so I won't ask you in." And I pushed the door to, but it jammed. I looked down and saw his foot in it. He was wearing his dark red Guat boots that I'd helped him to choose in the summer. There was a knot in one of the leather laces, where it had broken.

"Please, Corinne. Can I talk to you for a minute?"

"What about?" I said, sharp and brusque. I stepped back and folded my arms.

"Please. It's important." He pushed the door open and came inside.

"Shut the bloody door, then. It's parky, and I'm trying to warm up the house."

He closed the door, stood on the door mat, and patted the side of the dresser with the flat of his hand. He looked at me steadily. "I-"

"OK," I snapped. "You've got two minutes." I bent my arm and pulled up my coat sleeve and looked at my watch, using over-dramatic, exaggerated movements done just to make a point.

"I've missed you," he said tenderly.

"And?" I couldn't keep a slight break out of my voice.

"Please look at me, Corinne."

I looked at my feet.

"I've been talking to Bella…and she said…."

"So?" I managed to make my tone tougher and harder this

time. "It's not unusual for fathers to talk to their daughters, is it?"

"I miss you. I want to go back to how things were before," he said in a choked voice.

"I'm not interested in being your friend any more." I looked again at my watch as if I'd really been timing him. "You have thirty seconds left."

"I mean…go back to being lovers." He reached out and touched me on the shoulder. I shrugged off his hand and stepped backwards.

"What?" I said, looking at his face now. Looking at his hair, the silver bits at his temples. Oh, how I loved him.

"I love you," he said, and moved towards me.

I took another step back. "Is that it? And I'm supposed to trust you that you won't throw in the towel again?" He reached out his hand to touch my hair. I brushed his hand away. "Don't touch me. Leave me alone. You've got no idea. You go on and on about how hurt *you've* been and then you hurt me…OK, not the same thing, not the same way that you were hurt, maybe, not as…" My eyes welled up and a tear spilled out and rolled down my cheek.

"Corinne," he said, stepping forwards again. "Corinne."

"Bugger off," I said. "You stand by me when I need someone, you make me depend on you, love you, you make yourself bloody indispensable and just when we're intertwined in a way that is wonderful and comforting and makes me feel so…so…I don't know – whole - then you push me away and pull up the drawbridge. I just can't…" I slumped in my carver chair and cried, noisily to start with, my head in my hands. Then I wiped my eyes and sat quiet, my hands in my lap, just the odd stray tear slipping down my face and dripping off the end of my chin.

He pulled the chair out from the other side of the table and sat down near to me, at right angles, facing my side. He took my hands from my lap and chafed them.

"Your hands are freezing."

"As if that matters." I left my hands in his, and turned to look at him.

"Corinne. I know I've been a cloth head. Namby pamby – that's what you called me."

"Did I?"

"You were right. *Please* give me one more chance."

I looked him in the eyes. "Are you sure this time?" I said.

He nodded.

"Can I rely on you?"

"Yes." He wiped the last tear from my cheek with the cuff of his sleeve. "Absolutely."

"OK," I said.

CHAPTER 20

The leaves are out on the copper beech in Bingham Park, new and pink and tender, and the sweet cicely is frothing up in Whiteley Woods. It's May, and I've been thinking about Pa.

This time last year he was in hospital and I was visiting him. He missed May, the loveliest month of all - the fresh bright green of the spring - because he was stuck in hospital. And I missed it last year because although I noticed it on the day he was buried, the rest of the month leading up to that was lost in thinking about him, visiting him, watching him disappear.

It has all come back to me with the beauty of the season and the birds singing at half past five in the morning. I have been feeling sad again. But this time, although I am missing Pa, I no longer have the questions swilling round my head about the rest of my life and about how I want to spend it.

Rob and I discussed it and agreed that it was more appropriate for me to go up to Wensleydale without him for Pa's anniversary.

I managed to order some sweet peas from the flower shop in Broomhill for Pa's grave. When I couldn't get any last year for his burial, I was upset and somehow getting some this year seemed like a completion. Last week when I rang the shop the man thought they would be £1 a stem and I dithered. He knew that was expensive and he said "It just depends how extravagant you want to be." As it turned out, they were half the price he quoted.

On the way up the dale from the A1 I called in at the burial ground. I walked up to the grave, and the stone was still stark and new and horrid. And the black paint in the lettering was nasty. The bunch of sweet peas felt small. The grass was long, and there was still a long coffin-shaped mark in it.

I didn't stand there and talk to Pa. Partly, it's the off-putting thought of the people who live in the old Meeting House behind, and partly it's because I don't think he is still around. He isn't there. He isn't anywhere. I don't believe in life after death, in spirits hanging around waiting to be talked to. The only life after death is in what the person has left in memories. And then there's his deeds, his creations, his influence on his children and his genetic heritage. I see both of the latter in traits and physical characteristics in Megan and Steve, and I expect they see it in me. That is where the comfort is. There's no comfort in going to the grave.

I didn't know what Ma wanted to do for Pa's anniversary. She never mentioned Pa, she was quiet all day. We did a bit of paperwork in the morning when I got there – sorting out her bills. She had an annual electricity statement which was impenetrable, so we took her off direct debit and put her back on quarterly payments.

I asked her if there were any consolations in being old.

"Having you children come and look after me," she said.

But that was all she could think of.

Megan and Ed arrived after lunch. I was pleased to see them. After drinking a cuppa and munching through a bowl of cherries that Megan had bought on Bristol market, we walked up to see Pa's tree. It was showery and there was a cold wind.

In the evening Steve and Martine came over and we had roast beef and raspberry trifle. Ma had ordered a big piece of beef. She told me she had asked the butcher to her house especially to give him her order, and not just rung up the shop.

Pa was not mentioned, apart from when Megan opened a bottle of pink champagne in the kitchen while she was cooking, and poured us all a glass, and I said "To Pa."

Megan and Ed and Steve and Martine said "Yes, to Pa."

Ma nodded, and said "Yes," and took a sip.

Steve sharpened the carving knife and prepared to carve the joint.

"I'd better get this right or I'll be in trouble."

"Don't worry," I said. "Now Pa's not here, no-one's going to complain about how you carve."

Steve looked meaningfully at Megan's back as she drained the potatoes at the sink.

She turned round and laughed and said "He lives on!"

After dinner she and I walked up to the gate on the Thoralby road, the one we walked up to on the same night last year, on the day he died. Then we walked down to the hotel, and back across the fields. I don't think Pa was mentioned.

At the cottage there is a tiny red stapler which lives in the two inch square box it came in, and on it Pa had written STAPLER in his fine strong capitals. Since he died, every time I've used the stapler, I have found it a comfort to see his writing. This time I was up at Hollycroft I went to get the stapler and Ma had scrawled *Stapler* over his writing in inky rollerball, completely obscuring that winning remnant of Pa - his writing. It was a trivial sentimental thing, but I showed it to Megan, and she understood.

I drove all the way up the Thornton Rust road to the nursing home to see the sweet cicely and the cow parsley along the roadside and to see if any lambs were playing on the road as they were last year.

There were no lambs. And the verges had less sweet cicely than the country lanes down here in the Mayfield Valley. On the way back I stopped at Pa's tree. Then I drove to say goodbye to the Falls. I slowed the car down on Church Bank and wound down the van window and smelled the wild garlic in the woods. I could see the river without getting out of the car – it was a lovely colour – dark peaty brown with a creamy head of foam. Pa always commented on the colour of the river, and if there'd been a lot of rain he'd say, "It's running a full pot."

When I got home, I talked to Rob about Pa, and the gravestone, and about the fact that Ma didn't mention Pa the entire time I was there, and yet she seemed so pleased that Megan and I went up. She mentioned it so many times. She wanted to mark the day, yet didn't talk about Pa, or about anything that wasn't mundane. If Megan had not been there no-one would have mentioned Pa, and I would have found that hard.

Megan just rang me to tell me that there's a jar on the top shelf in the cloakroom at Hollycroft with a label on, written by Pa - SALTPETRE. He bought it when he was planning to cure his own bacon. She said she had hidden the jar at the back of the shelf so that it wouldn't catch Ma's eye.

I'm sitting in the sunshine with Rob, just now, at home. He's drinking black instant coffee, I'm drinking tea, and we're both eating parkin. I remember sitting here last summer on my steamer chair, feeling utterly wretched about Pa. Rob said then that it might be a long time before I felt better.

Now I am happy. And I think that Pa would be pleased.

ACKNOWLEDGEMENTS

I'd like to thank:

Anna Torborg and Emma Barnes of Snowbooks, for being great publishers;

Jane Linfoot, for encouraging and helpful comments, and for the use of her sharp red pen on some of the material I used in this book - before I even thought of writing *Zuzu's Petals;*

Chrissie Poulson, for all kinds of help;

Ruth Carter, Tricia Durdey, Karen Fine, Chris Holbrook, Kathryn Lester, Maria Longwright, Mary Scurfield, for reading earlier drafts, and all the Scarthin Writers for their invaluable comments on excerpts;

Kate Charlesworth and Nigel Sutherland, for generously giving their time to tell me about their work as cartoonists;

and Richard Wetherall, for letting me watch him milk his cows.

Finally, loving thanks to all my family, for being so supportive in so many ways;

and to Dave, for too much to write about here.

ABOUT THE AUTHOR

Sue Hepworth was born in rural Lincolnshire and now lives in the Derbyshire Peak District with her husband and her younger son. She has worked as a research psychologist, a social researcher, a full time mother and various combinations of these. She has been a frequent contributor to *The Times*, and she wrote the comic novel *Plotting for Beginners* with Jane Linfoot. Sue is addicted to sweet peas and romantic comedies, but no longer thinks that everything in life has a happy ending.

Visit www.suehepworth.com for more information.

PLOTTING FOR BEGINNERS
BY SUE HEPWORTH AND JANE LINFOOT

TUESDAY, APRIL 1ST

Gus has gone.

As a mark of tenderness he let me drive the car to the airport.

"Well I suppose you'll be doing it all year when I'm not here so at least I can supervise your last practice."

"Cheeky sod," I said.

As I turned onto the A6 I said "Do you want me to run through everything again?"

"Yes, just to calm me down."

So as I drove I explained again about checking in and talked him through all the procedures and destinations – customs, security, gate numbers, Heathrow, Denver.

When we reached the security barrier we gave each other the biggest hug of our lives.

"Just make sure you come back in one piece," I said. "I don't want to get an email from Dan telling me you've been savaged by a bear."

"Will you be OK?" he said. "You know how long I've wanted to try this, don't you?"

"Of course. Go on, you'd better go."

We kissed each other as if it was the last time (hark at me, I sound like Ingrid Bergman in Casablanca). Then he walked off to be searched.

"I love you," I called after him.

"Love you, too."

I watched him go through the arch and collect his bag. He turned round and caught my eye and grimaced. Then he put down his holdall and held out his hands in front of him and made them shake, pretending to be even more nervous than he was. Then he smiled and waved again, picked up his bag and went.

I walked back to the café near the entrance, the one that smelled of apricot and almond cookies. I treated myself to a celebratory pot of earl grey tea because there was no-one to complain about the "extravagance." And it felt like an occasion so I bought a pack of shortbread fingers too. I saw an empty sofa, which felt like a sign – a sofa is just what a newly liberated writer needs. I got out my note book and described the scene...the waitress flirting with the Jon Snow lookalike in crushed corduroy suit and exquisite arty tie, and the business woman who thought no-one could see her flicking her nose-pickings under the table.

On the way home I played my Fred Astaire tape. I sang along to all the songs and joined in the taps on the steering wheel, and there was no-one to moan about the choice of music, or the taps. And when I got home I watched Neighbours and no-one moaned.

What fun! I have a whole year of this ahead.

The above is what I was expecting to write here tonight.

This is what I am writing…

I wanted to go to the airport starting on the A623 via Chapel-en-le-Frith, but Gus preferred the "far superior route" via Buxton. There was no third way. Balls to compromise. Compromise just means that at least one person is unhappy. Sometimes it's both.

Once I got there I was dying for a cuppa but Gus said Thoreau would have waited for a drink till he got back to Walden, and I should do the same.

We had a long-married, businesslike hug at the barrier.

"Just make sure you come back in one piece," I said. "I don't want to get an email from Dan telling me you've been savaged by a bear."

"Will you be OK?" he said.

"Of course. Go on, you'd better go."

"Well," said Gus. "Just think. The next time you drop me off here I'll be on my way to Australia."

"What?" I said.

"If the Rockies goes well, I'm planning on doing the same in Western Australia."

"What?"

"It's another type of wilderness, and I thought-"

"If you're planning on going to the bloody Rockies for a year and coming back and then going to Australia for another year we might as well be separated."

"But isn't this year a kind of separation?"

"What?"

"You were so adamant you weren't coming with me. I did wonder if a trial separation was what you were wanting."

"You wondered what? Are you mad?"

"I just thought-"

"OK. Why don't we? If you're planning on doing your Thoreau crap in every wilderness in the world for the next ten years, why don't we treat this year as a trial separation?"

"I only said Australia, I didn't say-"

"They're calling your flight number. Go on, piss off. See you next March."

He strode off without looking back. I stood there with my arms crossed and watched him go.

I had been planning to listen to my Fred Astaire tape on the drive home, singing along and doing all the taps with my hands on the steering wheel but I didn't feel like it. I scrabbled around on the passenger shelf, looking for something to suit my mood. I ended up putting on a Loudon Wainwright tape of Sam's that was lurking in there. The first track was 'I'm All Right Without You.' I joined in very loudly.

I've just rung up to cancel The Times and order The Recorder. There'll be no more monthly flipping between the two. And I'm having something really smelly for tea – maybe a kipper. Tonight I shall read in bed till midnight and no-one will carp about the light. (Do I detect a fish motif? Is this what Bodmyn Corner means by subtext?)

It's wonderfully quiet here.

Now it's make or break.

Double or drop.

WEDNESDAY, APRIL 2ND

When I woke up this morning to silence and the blissful freedom of an empty house, and I thought of my computer sitting waiting for me to go and start writing, a holiday mood swept over me.

And then I remembered what happened at the airport.

I still can't believe I said it. I still can't believe I said that about the trial separation. Where did it come from? I love the man, goddammit. Well, I'm fond of him. How could I not be? But we have always wanted different things, and now that the children are gone our differences have come out in starker relief.

I can't believe I said it.

But what I really can't believe is that he didn't try to argue me out of it.

I've always wondered how people our age who have been married forever, how they agree to separate – when there's no-one else involved. It has crossed my mind maybe once a year that as Gus and I are so incompatible we'd be better off apart, but I've always thought that once you actually voice the idea of divorce as a possible option, the marriage has lost its innocence and even if you don't split up, the idea would always be hanging in the air, tainting everything. Well now I know how people do it, how they take that first awful step of mentioning it, though the hordes of fifty-somethings who are splitting up can't all be having rows at airports.

It's typical, isn't it? My very first untrammelled day as a writer has been taken over with inescapable, swirling thoughts about all of this. Well, I've decided. He's going to be away for a year anyway, so it's a good opportunity to see how I manage. I'm going to go for it. There'll be no retracting from me.

from: daniel howe
to: sally howe
subject: dad

The eagle has landed and is asleep in my spare bed. I am going to drive him up to the cabin tomorrow when he has got everything on his huge long list of supplies. Don't worry, Ma - I'll sort him out and get him installed and teach him all about bears, and spend a night with him before I head back to Denver. Love Dan.

When Dan got the job in Denver I was gutted. Not that I told him that: I was exceptionally well behaved. I said "Wow!" and "How exciting!" and "What a great opportunity!" and "So near to the Rockies – you'll be able to drive up for the day and go snowboarding." But when Gus and I left him at the airport that dreary January day, I snivelled all the way home. What's the point of having children if they live a ten hour flight away?

THURSDAY, APRIL 3RD

When I was down in the village today, Mrs Mountain – busybody suprema - asked me if I would miss Gus while he's away.

I wanted to say "It would be a lot easier to miss him if he hadn't gone and left me with blocked drains."

But I didn't. I said what a respectable, middle aged, middle class woman should say when her husband of thirty-one years has just flown off to spend a year on the other side of the world without her, and when she's decided not to tell people that it's a trial separation.

"Yes, Mrs Mountain."

Nor did I tell her that I'm glad Gus has gone away because it means I can get on with writing my novel, undisturbed. Trying to write with a houseful of newly retired husband is impossible.

There you are, relishing your empty nest after waving the last fledgling goodbye as he flies off into the world. There you are, eager to embark on all the projects you have been saving up until there's sufficient personal space to be able to think, about to launch into becoming the new creative you - and then what happens? The bloody bald eagle decides he's had enough of hunting for prey and plumps back down in the nest wanting all your attention.

Early retirement. Hmmph. Women reach fifty and think they're on the verge of liberation and excitement, and their broken down men just want to stay home and fart. Or in my case go and live in a cabin in the Rockies and fart.

FRIDAY, APRIL 4TH

If I were writing a book about my year without Gus then today would contain what Bodmyn Corner – creative writing maestro buonissimo - calls the inciting incident (*Write Your Way to Fame and Fortune,* page 43.)

It was about eleven in the morning and I'd done really well - 986 words in two hours - when I got to the bit where Pam tells Maurice she lied about the job, and I got stuck and found myself staring out of the window at two giant hares in the field beyond the back wall. I got up to tell Gus to get out his binoculars and have a look. I was opening my study door, mouth open to shout his name, when I remembered where he was and got this sharp 'oh bugger' stab, (though why I should think this I have no idea – it must be just habit.) Anyway, I sat down again and checked my email as a distraction and got this little beauty from *The Observer* (a broadsheet no less, not some poxy local paper):

from: kelly trounce
to: sally howe
subject: re: my true confession

If we wanted to use your true confession at some
time, would that still be ok with you? And would
you want us to use your real name? I think I've
had it for more than a year, but it reads very
nicely.

I couldn't believe it. Bodmyn Corner (*Write Your Way to Fame and Fortune,* page 56) says beginners should be patient and not pester editors, but it's so long since I sent this off I'd forgotten I'd sent it.

I jumped around my study shrieking "Yes ! Yes ! It reads very nicely," and twisted my arthritic knee, so I sat down again and wrote a reply.

Do I want her to use my real name? Is she kidding? How can I be a famous writer with a pseudonym? I emailed her back saying yes to everything, and how much would they pay ?

Then I went down to the kitchen and rang (best friend) Wendy and she was suitably impressed and sounded as excited as me, bless her. Chomsky was sitting on the windowsill miaowing and giving me his when-you-have-time-perhaps-you'd-be-good-enough-to-let-me-in look, so I did, and I told him about *The Observer* email as well. I'll be delivering two hour monologues to Chomsky before I know it.

SATURDAY, APRIL 5TH

It's only 7.30 a.m. and I'm sitting at my desk and raring to go because I slept so well on my own.

Not one night sweat. I lay dozing for a while this morning and it was only when I stretched out my left arm onto Gus's side that I remembered he was 4,000 miles away and it would be this time next year – if then – that he would be back beside me, listening to the World Service and snoring.

SUNDAY, APRIL 6TH

The drains, the drains.

Damn the drains. Damn Gus. What on earth is the point of having a husband with a shed full of DeWalt boys toys, if he doesn't use them. He knew the drains were squiffy two days before he left and yet he still didn't sort them out. I shall have to get a man in. I've tried putting bleach down, and I've tried poking about with one of Gus's crow bars, but it's no better. There was I thinking one of the joys of having the house to myself would be baths with no interruptions and now I can't even have a bath because the front path gets flooded. Yesterday I found Badedas bubbles on the aubretia. I had a bath an inch deep this morning because of the drains. I can't even have a long hot shower, because the shower has been on the blink since Christmas.

I bought *The Observer* today to see if my article was in. It wasn't. In the True Confessions slot it was a professor of English Literature writing about how he hates Shakespeare. Maybe they'll have mine in next week.

I was listening to *Open Book* on Radio 4 this afternoon. They were just about to launch into a studio discussion with literary agents about what they look for in a submission from a new author, when the phone rang, and instead of letting the machine get it I picked it up, dammit. It was brother Richard.

"I'm overwhelmed with disappointment," he said. "Paul's just rung and told me VSO have accepted him."

"Disappointed? You should be proud."

"Of course I am. But it means that now I'm completely bereft of family. You know I was planning on going to live near him."

Personally I think it's rather sad for a fifty-seven year old to want to move to live near his son. Not that Richard's had any interest from potential buyers. His house has been on the market for 18 months and he's had no offers, and Izzy is hassling him to lower the price just so she can have her share and buy somewhere new and get on with her life (another early retirement divorce.)

"It's hard for you, I know," I said.

"Yes, well, let's change the subject. Did Gus get off all right?"

"He got off. I'm not sure all right is the phrase I'd use. It depends on your point of view."

"You're being most abstruse."

"We've decided to have a trial separation." I couldn't help blurting it out. I hadn't been going to tell anyone, but it's a poor do if you can't tell your brother something so huge.

"Not you as well, Sally. I always thought you and Gus were different. I know you've had your troubles, but no, not you. You and Gus are an institution."

"So are the Post office and the NHS and look what a mess they're in."

"But still intact."

"Yes, well, it's possible that Gus and I will be when he

gets back. Though I doubt it. I'm already enjoying my empty house." I smacked my hand over my mouth. What was I saying? Poor Richard was beside himself when Izzy walked out. And he's been utterly miserable in his empty house.

"You just wait," he said. "And it's just a trial in your case: it's not the same. Whose idea was it?"

"I'm not sure whose idea it was. It just kind of sprang out of nowhere. But it makes a lot of sense. The kids have gone – though Sam being at Uni and only twenty is still technically a dependent, I suppose. Anyway, it's obvious we want different things. I want to write. I want to see the kids and my friends. I want to do what normal empty nesters do and go away for weekends to see all the places I've never seen. Gus wants to be a cross between Henry Thoreau and a hermit."

"What do you mean?"

"Oh come on, Richard. You know he's always had a thing about Walden. You know he's always wanted to try to do what Thoreau did – subsistence living in a cabin in the woods. If he hadn't been married to me he would have done it years ago on a permanent basis. Now he's retired he wants to try it before he's too old. I would have done it with him, just for a year, if he hadn't also insisted on doing it in a wilderness."

"But surely you can write anywhere."

"Yes but I would go absolutely nuts living miles from anywhere and seeing no-one but Gus. Aren't the fifties the time when we're supposed to do what we want?"

"But a trial separation? Haven't you and Gus ever heard the word compromise?"

"It's not as though we're all going to die at sixty, Richard. There might be another forty years ahead – that's a hell of a lot of compromise."